"Conan! Where are the pendants?" The heavily muscled man wore a spiked helmet, and chain mail descended to his knees. In one hand he gripped a great double-bladed ax, in the other a round buckler.

With no more warning the ax leaped toward Conan, who danced back, broadsword flickering in snakelike thrusts. The mighty barbarian swung, felt his blade bite through bone, and ax and severed hand fell together. Blood pumped from the stump in regular spurts. The man hurled his round shield at Conan's head. Conan ducked; even as he recovered, his opponant was coming to his feet with the battle-ax in his left hand.

"Conan!" he screamed. "You will die!"

Conan's blade leaped forward once more, and the helmeted head rolled in the dust.

"Not yet," the Cimmerian said grimly.

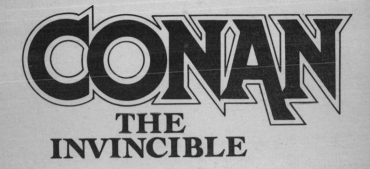

CONAN
THE
INVINCIBLE

BY ROBERT JORDAN

TOR

A TOM DOHERTY ASSOCIATES BOOK

CONAN THE INVINCIBLE

Copyright © 1982 by Conan Properties, Inc.

A Tor Book

Published by Tom Doherty Associates, 8-10 W. 36th St., New
York City, N.Y. 10018

First printing, June, 1982
Second printing, July 1982
ISBN: 0-523-48050-4

Printed in the United States of America

Distributed by Pinnacle Books, 1430 Broadway, New Yor
N.Y. 10018

To William Popham McDougal
a minor demon

WESTERN SEA

VANAHEIM

ASGARD

CIMMERIA

PICTISH WILDERNESS

BORDER KINGDOM

MARCHES

GUNDERLAND

NEMEDIA

Velitrium

Galparan

Numalia

Tanasul

Belverus

Tarantia

Shamar

OPHIR

Ianthe

Khorshemish

KO

Kordava

ZINGARA

Eruk

ARGOS

SHEM

BARACHA ISLES

Asgalun

River Styx

Khemi

Luxur

STYGIA

SIPTAH'S ISLE

Sukhmet

KUSH

DARFAR

Xuthal

BLACK

Zarkheba R.

Xuchotl

CHAZAUD

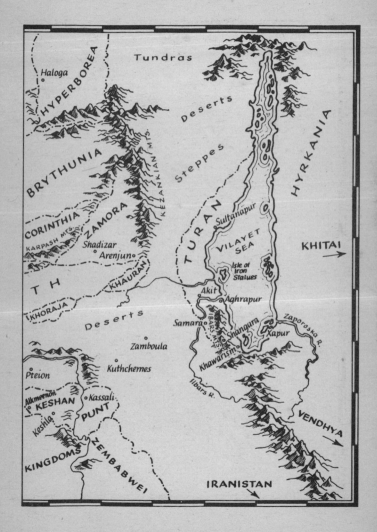

I

The icy wind whipping through the brown, sheer- walled chasms of the Kezankian Mountains seemed colder still around the bleak stone fortress that grew from the granite flank of a nameless mountain in the heart of the range. Fierce hillmen who feared nothing rode miles out of their way to go around that dark bastion, and made the sign of the horns to ward off evil at its mention.

Amanar the Necromancer made his way down a dim corridor that violated the very heartstone of the mountain, followed by those no longer human. He was slender, this thaumaturge, and darkly handsome, his black beard cropped close; but a vaguely serpentlike streak of white meandered through his short hair, and the red flecks that danced in his eyes drew the gaze, and the will, of anyone foolish enough to look deeply. His henchmen looked like ordinary men, at first glance and from a distance, but their faces were vaguely pointed, their eyes glinted red beneath ridged

9

helmets, and their skins bore reptilian scales. The fingers of the elongated hands that held their spears ended not in nails, but in claws. A curved tulwar swung at the hip of every one except for him who marched close behind Amanar. Sitha, Warden of the S'tarra, Amanar's Saurian henchman, bore a great double-edged ax. They came to tall doors set in the stone, both doors and stone carved with serpents in endless arabesques.

"Sitha," Amanar said, and passed through the doors without pausing.

The reptiloid warden followed close behind, closing the massive doors after his master, but Amanar barely noticed. He spared not a glance for the naked captives, a man and a woman, bound hand and foot, who lay gagged at one side of the column-circled room. The mosaicked floor bore the likeness of a golden serpent, surrounded by what might have been the rays of the sun. The mage's black robe was wound about with a pair of entwined golden serpents, their heads finally coming over his shoulders to rest on his chest. The eyes of the embroidered serpents glittered with what would not possibly be life. He spoke.

"The man, Sitha."

The prisoners writhed in a frenzy to break their bonds, but the scaled henchman, muscles bulging like a blacksmith's, handled the man easily. In minutes the captive was spreadeagled atop a block of red-streaked black marble. A trough around the rim of the dark altar led to a spout above a large golden bowl. Sitha ripped the gag away and stepped back.

The bound man, a pale-skinned Ophirian, worked his mouth and spat. "Whoever you are, you'll get naught from me, spawn of the outer dark! I'll not beg! Do you hear? No plea will crack my teeth, dog! I will not . . . ."

Amanar heard nothing. He felt beneath his robe for the amulet, a golden serpent in the clutches of a silver hawk. That protected him, that and other things he had done, yet each time there was the realization of the power he faced. And controlled.

Those fools of Stygia, those who called themselves mages of the Black Ring, had so condescendingly allowed him to study at their feet, confident of his worshipful admiration. Until it was too late, none of them knew the contempt that festered in his heart. They prated of their power in the service of Set, Lord of the Dark, yet no man of them dared so much as lay a finger on the dread Book of Typhon. But he had dared.

He began to chant, and behind the altar a mist formed, red and golden, as a mist of flames. Beyond the mist blackness stretched into infinity. The Ophirian's tongue was stilled, and his teeth chattered in their place.

It was said that no human mind could comprehend the terrible knowledge contained in the book, or hold a single word of it without madness and death. Yet Amanar had learned. But a single page, it was true, before the numinous powers of it, wrenching at his mind, turning his bones to jelly, sent him grievously wounded and howling like a dog out of the city of Khemi into the desert. And in his madness, in that waterless waste beneath a burning sun, he had remembered that page still. Death could not come near him.

In the mists, from the mists, a shape coalesced. The Ophirian's eyes bulged in silence-stricken terror. The woman screamed into her gag. The golden head that reared above them in the swirling vapors—neither quite serpent nor lizard—was surrounded by a halo of a dozen tentacles longer than a man. The serpentine, golden-scaled body stretched back into the darkness, on beyond the reach of eye to see or mind to know. A bifurcate tongue flickered between fangs, and eyes holding the flames of all the furnaces that ever were regarded Amanar. Greedily, the mage thought, and fingered his amulet once more.

Across the sands he had stumbled, burning, drying, thirsting, remembering that page and unable to die. At last he came on Pteion the Accursed, fear-haunted ruins abandoned in the days of dark Acheron, before Stygia was aught but a stretch of sand. In the nameless, forgotten cavern beneath that city he had found Morath-Aminee, bound there for rebellion against Set when those who now called themselves men walked on all fours and rooted beneath stones for grubs. With his memories of that page—would they never stop burning at him?—he found the means to release the god-demon, the means to keep it in rein, however tenuously, and the means of his own protection. He had found power.

"Morath-Aminee," he half-chanted, half-hissed. "O Eater of Souls, whose third name is death to hear, death to say, death to know, thy servant Amanar brings these offerings to thy sacrifice."

He held out his hand. Sitha placed a golden-hilted knife, its blade gilded, in his grasp. The

Ophirian opened his mouth to scream, and gurgled horribly as Amanar slit his throat. At that instant the golden tenacles of the god-demon struck at the man on the altar, clutched him where he lay amid the spreading pool of his own blood. The tentacles avoided the proximity of Amanar.

"Eat, O Morath-Aminee," the mage chanted. He stared into the eyes of the sacrifice, waiting the proper moment.

Horror grew on the Ophirian's face as he realized he was dying. And yet he did not die. His heart pumped; his life blood poured from his ruined throat, the rubiate liquor flowing over ebon marble, channeled to the golden vessel at the foot of the altar for later necromancies. But he was not allowed to die.

Amanar heard in his mind the satisfied sibilation of the god-demon feeding. The Ophirian's pale eyes filled with desolation as the man realized what was being taken from his besides his life. The mage watched those eyes become lifeless though yet alive, empty windows on a soulless depth. With care he made a precise slit in the twitching chest. His hand poised above it, and he met the Ophirian's despairing gaze.

"Thank me for the release of death," he said.

The Ophirian's lips labored to form the words, but no sound emerged. Only horrendous bubbles in the diminishing flow of blood from the chasm that had been his throat.

Amanar smiled. His hand thrust into the slit, caught the pulsing heart, and ripped it free. It beat one last time as he held it before the Ophirian's eyes.

"Die," the mage said. The god-demon released its hold, and the husk on the altar slumped at last in death.

Sitha appeared beside the mage with a golden plate, on which Amanar placed the heart. That, too, had its uses in his magicks. He took the linen cloth the reptilian offered, and wiped his blood-stained hands. Sitha turned away.

"Amanar." The god-demon's susurration rolled against the walls. "Thou useth my sacrifice, soul-less one, for thine own pleasure."

Amanar glanced hurriedly about him before answering. The woman writhed in her bonds on the edge of insanity. She heard nothing beyond the shrieks her gag choked back. Sitha continued out of the sacrificial chamber as if he had not heard. The S'tarra had little capacity to think for themselves, but they could obey orders. Sitha would place the heart in a golden bowl prepared beforehand with spells to keep its contents fresh. Only then would he be able to consider anything else, if his soulless mind were ever capable of considering anything.

The mage dropped his head on his chest and bowed in his most humble fashion. "O, great Morath-Aminee, I am but thy humble servant. Thy servant who freed thee from the bonds set upon thee by the Dark One." Gods and demons could not forget, not as men forget, but oft did they prefer not to remember debts in their dealings with men. The reminder could not be amiss.

A golden-scaled tentacle reached toward Amanar —it was all he could do not to flinch away—then jerked back as if from a great heat. "Thou wearest the amulet still."

"O Most High among the Powers and Dominions, this one is so insignificant beside thee that thou mightest destroy him without noticing such a speck in thy path. I wear this merely that thou mayst be aware of me, and spare me to thy service and greater glory."

"Serve me well, and in that day when Set is bound where I was bound, in that day when I rule the Outer Dark, I will give thee dominion over my herds, over those who call themselves men, and thou shalt bring the multitudes to my feeding."

"As thy word is, so shall it be, great Morath-Aminee." Amanar became aware that Sitha had returned with two other S'tarra. The necromancer flicked his hand in a summoning gesture, and the two scurried toward the bloodstained altar, dropping to all fours as they came near the black marble slab. Their eyes did not rise to the god-demon towering over them as, half-groveling, they unfastened the sacrifice and bore it away.

A different tap jerked Amanar around to stare at the tall cavern doors. No one dared disturb these ceremonies. The tap came again. He twitched as the voice of the god-demon hissed in his mind.

"Go, Amanar. This concerneth thee most vitally."

He glanced back at the great golden serpent-shape, rearing motionless above the black altar. The flame-filled eyes watched him with—what?—amusement? "Prepare the next sacrifice, Sitha."

The bound woman spasmed in ever greater frenzy as scaly hands lifted her from the tiled floor. Amanar hurried from the chamber.

A Turanian with a pointed beard stood eying the S'tarra nervously, his slight plumpness and loose yellow robes contrasting sharply with the empty red eyes and ring mail of the guards. The man craned to look beyond the mage into the sacrifical chamber, and Amanar closed the door firmly. He had few human servants who could be trusted beyond the Keep; it was not yet time for them to learn what they served.

"Why have you left Aghrapur, Tewfik?" he snapped.

The plump man put on a fawning smile and washed his hands in front of his chest. "It was not my fault, master. I beg you to understand that."

"What do you babble about, man?"

"That which you set me to watch, master. It is no longer in the strongrooms of King Yildiz."

Amanar blanched. Tewfik, taking it for rage, cringed, and the S'tarra guardsmen stirred uneasily, but the thaumaturge was quaking inside. He gripped the Turanian's robes with iron fingers, pulling the man erect. "Where is it now? Speak, man, for your life!"

"Shadizar, master! I swear!"

Amanar glared at him and through him. Morath-Aminee had known the import of this message. The god-demon must know of what was now in Shadizar. A new hiding place must be found, but first he must secure within his power that which was gone. That which must be kept from Morath-Aminee at all costs. And to do that, he must risk bringing it within the very grasp of the god-demon. The risk! The risk!

He was not aware that he still carried the sacrificial knife until he slid it into the Turanian's ribs. He looked into the face that now stared open hate at him, and felt regret. Human servants were useful in so many ways that S'tarra could not be. Too useful to be thrown away casually.

The mage felt something thump against his chest and looked down. Jutting from his black robe was a knife hilt from which Tewfik's hand fell away. Contemptuously Amanar hurled the dying man from him. He plucked the knife free, held up its bloodless blade before the man on the stone floor, whose mouth was filling with his own blood.

"Fool," Amanar said. "You must kill my soul before mortal weapon can harm me."

He turned away. The guards' desire for fresh meat would dispose of what remained of Tewfik. If Amanar were to have the time he needed, Morath-Aminee must be kept satiated. More prisoners must be brought. More sacrifices for the Eater of Souls. He reentered the sacrificial chamber to attend to the first of these.

II

The purple-domed and many-spired city of Shadizar was known as 'the Wicked,' but the debauches of its high-chinned nobles, of their cruel-eyed wives and pearl-draped daughters, paled beside the everyday life of that part of the city known as the Desert. In those narrow, twisting streets and garbage-strewn alleys, haven of thief, kidnapper, murderer and worse, the price of a body was silver, the price of a life copper, the price of a soul not worth speaking of.

The big youth lounging on the bed upstairs in the tavern of Abuletes, in the heart of the Desert, had no thought of those who might be coughing out their lives in the fetid squalor outside. His eyes, sapphire blue beneath a square-cut black mane, were on the olive-skinned woman across the small room, who was adjusting the gilded brass breast-plates that displayed rather than concealed her swelling bilobate chest. The rest of her attire consisted of transparent pantaloons, slashed from

waist to ankle, and a gilded girdle of no more than
two fingers' breadth, slung low on her rounded
hips. She wore four rings, green peridot and red
almandine on her left hand, pale blue topaz and
red-green alexandrite on her right.

"Do not say it, Conan," she said without looking at him.

"Say what?" he growled. If his unlined face pro-
claimed that he had seen fewer than twenty winters, his eyes at that moment said they had been
winters of iron and blood. He tossed aside his fur
covering with one massive hand and rose to dress,
as always first seeing that his weapons were close to
hand, the ancient broadsword in its worn shagreen
sheath, the black-bladed Karpashian dagger that he
strapped to his left forearm.

"I give to you freely what I sell to others. Can
you not be satisfied with that?"

"There is no need for you to follow your profes-
sion, Semiramis. I am the best thief in Shadizar, in
all Zamora." At her laugh, his knuckles whitened
on his leather-wrapped sword hilt. He had more
reason for his pride than she knew. Had he not
slain wizards, destroyed liches, saved one throne
and toppled another? What other of his years
could say half so much? But he had never spoken
of these things even to Semiramis, for fame was the
beginning of the end for a thief.

"And for all your thievery," she chided, "what
do you have? Every copper you steal drips from
your fingers like water."

"Crom! Is that why you will not be mine alone?
The money?"

"You're a fool!" she spat. Before he could say

more, she flounced out of the room.

For a time he sat frowning at the bare wooden walls. Semiramis did not know half of his troubles in Shadizar. He was indeed the most successful thief in the city, and now his successes were beginning to rebound on him. The fat merchants and perfumed nobles whose dwellings he robbed were making up a reward to put an end to his depredations. Some of those self-same men had hired him upon occasion to retrieve an incriminating letter or a gift given indiscreetly to the wrong woman. What he knew of their secrets was likely as big a reason for the reward as his thefts. That, and their hot-eyed daughters, who found it delightfully wicked to dally with a muscular young barbarian.

With a grunt he got to his feet and slung a black Khauranian cloak edged in cloth-of-gold around his broad shoulders. These ruminations were gaining him nothing. He was a thief. He should be about it.

As he made his way down the rickety stair into the crowded common room, he ground his teeth. In the center of the room Semiramis sat on the lap of a mustachioed Kothian kidnapper in a striped cloak of many colors. Gold armlets encircled his biceps, and a gold hoop hung from one dark ear. The oily man's right hand gripped Semiramis' breasts; his left arm flexed as the other hand worked beneath the table. She wriggled seductively, and giggled as he whispered in her ear. Conan ignored the pair as he strode to the bar.

"Wine," he ordered, and dug into the leather purse at his belt for the necessary coppers. There were few enough remaining.

Fat Abuletes made the coins disappear, replacing them with a leathern jack of sour-smelling wine. His neck rose in grimy folds above the collar of a faded yellow tunic. His dark eyes, sunk in the suet of his face, could weigh a man's purse to the last copper at twenty paces. Instead of moving away, he remained, studying Conan from behind the fat, flat mask of his face.

The smells of the thin wine and half-burned meat from the kitchens warred with the effluvia wafted in from the streets whenever the door opened to let another patron in or out. It yet lacked three full glasses of night-fall, but the tables were filled with cutpurses, panderers and footpads. A busty courtesan in brass-belled ankle bracelets and two narrow strips of yellow silk hawked her wares with lascivious smiles.

Conan marked the locations of those who looked dangerous. A turbanned Kezankian hillman licked his thin lips as he studied the prostitute, and two swarthy Iranistanis in loose, flowing red pantaloons and leather vests ogled her, as well. Blood might well be shed there. A Turanian coiner sat hunched over his mug, pointed beard waggling as he muttered to himself. It was known in the Desert that he had been badly bested by a mark, and he was ready to assuage his humiliation with the three-foot Ibarri sword-knife at his hip. A third Iranistani, dressed like the first two but with a silver chain dangling on his bare chest, attended a fortuneteller turn-ing her cards at a table against the far wall.

"What hold you, Conan," Abuletes said abruptly, "on the coming troubles?"

"What troubles?" Conan replied. His mind was not on the tavernkeeper's words. The soothsayer was no wrinkled hag, as such women were wont to be. Silken auburn hair showed at the edges of her voluminous brown cloak's hood, framing a heart-shaped face. Her emerald eyes had a slight tilt above high cheekbones. The cloak and the robe beneath were of rough wool, but her slender fingers on the K'far cards were delicate.

"Do you listen to nothing not connected to your thievery?" Abuletes grumbled. "These six months past no fewer than seven caravans bound for Turan, or coming from there, have disappeared without a trace. Tiridates has the army out after the Red Hawk, but they've never gotten a glimpse of that she-devil. Why should this time be any different? And when the soldiers return empty-handed, the merchants screaming for something to be done will force the king to crack down on us in the Desert."

"He has cracked down before," Conan laughed, "and nothing changes." The Iranistanis said something with a smirk. The soothsayer's green eyes looked daggers at him, but she continued to tell her cards. Conan thought the Iranistani had the same idea he did. If Semiramis wanted to flaunt her trade before him . . . . "What proof is there," he said, without taking his eyes from the pair across the room, "that the Red Hawk is responsible? Seven caravans would be a large bite for a bandit to chew."

Abuletes snorted. "Who else could it be? Kezankian hillmen never raid far from the mountains. That leaves the Red Hawk. And who knows how many men she has? Who knows anything of her, even what she looks like? I've heard she has five hundred rogues who obey her like hounds the huntsman."

Conan opened his mouth for an acid retort, and at that moment the situation at the fortuneteller's table flared. The Iranistani laid a hand on her arm. She shook it off. He clutched at her cloak, whispering urgent words, hefting a clinking purse in his other hand.

"Find a boy!" she spat. Her backhand blow to his face cracked like a whip.

The Iranistani rocked back, his face livid. "Slut!" he howled, and a broad-bladed Turanian dagger appeared in his fist.

Conan crossed the room in two pantherish strides. His big hand clamped the bicep of the Iranistani's knife arm and lifted the man straight up out of his chair. The Iranistani's snarl changed to open-mouthed shock as he tried to slash at the big youth and his knife dropped from suddenly nerveless fingers. Conan's iron grip had shut off the blood to the man's arm.

With contemptuous ease, Conan hurled the man sprawling on the floor between the tables. "She doesn't want your attentions," he said.

"Whoreson dog!" the Iranistani howled. Left-handed, he snatched the Turanian coiner's Ibarri sword-knife and lunged at Conan.

Hooking his foot around the Iranistani's toppled chair, Conan swung it into the man's path. The Iranistani tumbled, springing up again even as he fell, but Conan's booted toe took him under the chin before he could rise above a crouch. He flipped backward to collapse at the feet of the coiner, who retrieved the sword-knife with a covetous glance at the Iranistani's purse.

Conan turned back to the pretty fortuneteller. He thought he saw a dagger disappearing beneath her capacious cloak. "As I saved you an unpleasantness," he said, "perhaps you will let me buy you some wine."

Her lip curled. "I needed no help from a barbar boy." Her eye flickered to his left, and he dove to his right. The scimitar wielded by one of the other Iranistanis bit into the table instead of his neck.

He tucked his shoulder under as he dove, rolling to his feet and whipping his broadsword free of its shagreen sheath in the same motion. The two Iranistanis who had been sitting alone faced him with scimitars in hand, well apart, knees slightly bent in the stance of experienced fighters. The tables around the three had emptied, but otherwise the denizens of the tavern took no notice. It was a rare day that at least one man did not give his death rattle on that sawdust-covered floor.

"Whelp whose mother never knew his father's name!" one of the longnosed men snarled. "Think you to strike Hafim so and walk away? You will drink your own blood, spawn of a toad! You will—"

Conan saw no reason to listen to the man's rantings. Shouting a wild Cimmerian battle cry, he whirled his broadsword aloft and attacked. A contemptuous smile appeared on the dark visage of the nearer man, and he lunged to spit the muscular youth before the awkward-seeming overhand slash could land. Conan had no intention of making an attack that left him so open, though. Even as the Iranistani moved, Conan dropped to the right, crouching with his left leg straight out to the side. He could read death-knowledge in the man's dark bulging eyes. As the gleaming blue blade of the scimitar passed over his left shoulder his broadsword was pivoting, slashing through the leather jerkin, burying itself deep in the Iranistani's ribs.

Conan felt the blade bite bone; beyond the man choking on his own blood he saw the second Iranistani, teeth bared in a rictus, rushing at him with scimitar extended. He threw his shoulder into the pit of the dying man's stomach, straightening to lift the Iranistani and hurl him at his companion. The sword tearing free of the body held it up enough that it fell sprawling at the other man's racing feet. The second Iranistani leaped over his friend, curved blade swinging. Conan's slash beat the scimitar aside, and his backhand return ripped out the man's throat. Blood spilling down his dirty chest, the Iranistani tottered back with disbelieving eyes, pulling an empty table over when he fell.

Conan caught sight of Semiramis heading up the stair, one of the Kothian's big hands caressing a nearly bare buttock possessively as he followed. With a grimace, he wiped his blade clean on the baggy pantaloons of one of the dead men. Be damned to her, if her eyes had not shown her she already had a better man. He turned back to the table of the red-haired woman. It was empty. He cursed again, under his breath.

"This one's dead, too," Abuletes muttered. The fat tavern keeper knelt beside the first man Conan had confronted, his hands like plump spiders as they slipped the silver chain from about the dead man's neck. "You broke his neck. Hanuman's stones, Conan. That's three free-spenders you've done me out of. I've half a mind to tell you to take your custom elsewhere."

"Now you have it all," Conan said sourly, "and you don't have to give them any of your watered wine. But you can bring me a pitcher of your best. Kyroian. On them."

He settled at a table against the wall, thinking rough thoughts about women. At least the red-haired wench could have shown a little gratitude. He had saved her from a mauling, if nothing worse. And Semiramis . . . . Abuletes plonked down a rough earthenware pitcher in front of him and stretched out a grubby hand. Conan looked significantly at the last of the dead Iranistanis being hauled away by the two scruffy men who earned coppers fetching and carrying around the tavern. He had seen all three of the dead men's purses disappear beneath Abuletes' filthy apron. After a moment the tavern keeper shuffled his feet, wiped his fat hands on his apron, and left. Conan settled down to serious drinking.

III

The tables that had emptied during the fight re-filled quickly. No one had given more than a passing glance to the dead men as they were removed; the level of shouted laughter and raucous talk had never decreased. The half-naked courtesan briefly considered the breadth of Conan's shoulder with lust-filled eyes, then passed on from his grim face.

His troubles, Conan decided by the time he had emptied four wooden tankards of the sweet wine, would not be settled by the amounts he normally stole. Had he been a man of means the auburn-haired baggage would not have gone. Semiramis would not have thought it so important to ply her trade. But golden goblets lifted from the halls of fat merchants, pearl necklaces spirited from the very bedsides of sleek noblewomen, brought less than a tenth their value from the fences in the Desert. And the art of saving was not in him. Gambling and drinking took what remained from wenching. The only way to sufficient gain was one grand theft. But what? And from where?

There was the palace, of course. King Tiridates had treasures beyond counting. The king was a drunkard—he had been so since the days when the evil mage Yara was the true power in Zamora—but in justice he should willingly part with some portion of his wealth for the man who had brought Yara and the Elephant Tower down. If he knew that man's deeds, and if he were of a mind to part with anything to a barbarian thief. But the debt was owed, to Conan's mind, and collecting on it—albeit without Tiridates' knowledge or consent —would not be theft at all.

Then there was Larsha, the ancient, accursed ruins not far from Shadizar. The origin of those toppled towers and time-eroded walls was shrouded in the depths of time, but everyone agreed there was treasure there. And a curse. A decade before, when Tiridates was still a vigorous king, he had sent a company of the King's Own inside those walls in the full light of day. Not one had returned, and the screams of their dying had so panicked the king's retinue and bodyguard that they had abandoned him. Tiridates had been forced to flee with them. If any had tried to penetrate that doom-filled city since, none had ever returned to speak of it.

Conan did not fear curses—had he not already proven himself a bane of mages?—as he did not fear to enter the very palace of the king. But which? To remove sufficient wealth from the palace would be as difficult as removing it from the accursed ruins. Which would give him the most for his labors?

He became aware of eyes on him and looked up.

A dark, hook-nosed man wearing a purple head-cloth held by a golden fillet stood regarding him. A purple silk robe hung from the watcher's bony shoulders. He leaned on a shoulder-high staff of plain, polished wood, and, though he bore no other weapon and was plainly not of the Desert, there was no fear of robbery—or anything else—in his black eyes.

"You are Conan the Cimmerian," he said. It was not a question. "It is said you are the best thief in Shadizar."

"And who are you," Conan said warily, "to accuse an honest citizen of thievery? I am a body-guard."

The man took a seat across from him without asking. He held his staff with one hand; Conan saw that he regarded it as a weapon. "I am Ankar, a merchant dealing in very special merchandise. I have need of the best thief in Shadizar."

With a confident smile Conan sipped his wine. He was on familiar ground, now. "And what special merchandise do you wish to acquire?"

"First know that the price I will pay is ten thousand pieces of gold."

Conan set his mug down before he slopped wine over his wrist. With ten thousand . . . by the Lord of the Mound, he would be no longer a thief, but a man with a need to guard against thieves. "What is it you wish stolen?" he said eagerly.

A tiny smile touched Ankar's thin lips. "So you are Conan the Thief. At least that is settled. Know you that Yildiz of Turan and Tiridates have concluded a treaty to stop the depredations against trade along their common border?"

"I may have heard, but there's no loot in treaties."

"Think you so? Then know that gifts were exchanged between the kings in token of this pact, which is to last for five years. To Tiridates Yildiz sent five dancing girls bearing a golden casket, on the lid of which are set five stones of amethyst, five of sapphire and five of topaz. Within the casket are five pendants, each containing a stone the like of which no man has ever seen."

Conan was tiring of the strange man's supercilious air. Ankar took him for a rude, untutored barbarian, and perhaps he was, but he was not a fool. "You wish me to steal the pendants, not the casket," he said, and was pleased to see Ankar's eyes widen.

The self-named merchant took his staff with both hands. "Why do you say that, Cimmerian?" His voice was low and dark.

"The casket you describe could be duplicated for far less than what you offer. That leaves the pendants." He measured the other's age and added with a laugh, "Unless it's the dancing girls you want."

Ankar did not join in, continuing to watch Conan with hooded eyes. "You are not stupid—" He stopped abruptly.

Conan angrily shut off his laughter. Not stupid—for a barbarian. He would show this man a thing or three of barbarians. "Where are these pendants?" he growled. "If they're in the treasure room, I will need time for planning and—"

"Tiridates basks in the reflected glory of a more powerful monarch. The casket shows that Yildiz has concluded a treaty with him. It is displayed in the antechamber before his throne room, so that all who approach him may see."

"I will still need time," Conan said. "Ten days for preparations."

"Impossible! Make fewer preparations. Three days."

"Fewer preparations and you'll never see those pendants. And my head will decorate a pike above the West Gate. Eight days."

Ankar touched the tip of his tongue to thin lips. For the first time he appeared uncertain. His eyes clouded as if he had lost himself in his thoughts. "Fi . . . four days. Not a moment more."

"Five days," Conan insisted. "A moment less, and Tiridates will keep his pendants."

Ankar's eyes dimmed again. "Five days," he said finally.

"Done." Conan suppressed a grin. He meant to have those pendants in his hand that very night, but had he told this Ankar that, when he put the pendants in the man's hands, Ankar would think it nothing out of the ordinary. By negotiating for ten days and settling for five as the absolute minimum, he would be thought a miracle worker when he produced the pendants on the next morn. He had seen each reaction from men before. "There was mention of ten thousand gold pieces, Ankar."

The swarthy man produced a purse from beneath his robe and slid it halfway across the table. "Twenty now. A hundred more when you tell me your plan. The balance when you hand me the pendants."

"A small part beforehand for a payment of ten

thousand," Conan grumbled, but inside he was not displeased at all. The twenty alone equalled his largest commission before this, and the rest would be in hand on the morrow.

He reached for the purse. Of a sudden Ankar's hand darted to cover his atop the gold-filled pouch, and he started. The man's hand was as cold as a corpse's.

"Hear me, Conan of Cimmeria," the dark man hissed. "If you betray me in this, you will pray long your head did in truth adorn a pike."

Conan tore his hand free from the other's bony grip. He had to restrain himself from working the hand, for those icy fingers had seemed to drain the warmth from his own. "I have agreed to do this thing," he said hotly. "I am not so civilized as to break the honor of my word."

For a moment he thought the hook-nosed man was going to sneer, and knew that if he did he would rip the man's throat out. Ankar contented himself with a sniff and a nod, though. "See that you remember your honor, Cimmerian." He rose and glided away before Conan could loose a retort.

Long after the dark man was gone the muscular youth sat scowling. It would serve the fool right if he kept the pendants, once they were in hand. But he had given his word. Still, the decision as to where to gain his wealth had been settled. He upended the pouch, spilling thick, milled-edge roundels of gold, stamped with Tiridates' head, into his palm, and his black mood was whisked away.

"Abuletes!" he roared. "Wine for everyone!"

There would be time enough for frugality when he had the ten thousand.

The man who called himself Ankar strode out of the Desert, trailed to the very end of the twisting, odoriforous streets by human jackals. They, sensing something of the true nature of the man, never screwed their courage tight enough to come near him. He, in turn, spared them not a glance, for he could bend men's minds with his eye, drain the life from them with a touch of his hand. His true name was Imhep-Aton, and many who knew him shuddered when they said it.

At the house he had rented in Hafira, one of the better sections of Shadizar, the door was opened by a heavily muscled Shemite, as large as Conan, with a sword on his hip. A trader in rare gems—for as such he was known among the nobles of the city —needed a bodyguard. The Shemite cowered away from the bony necromancer, hastening to close and bolt the door behind him.

Imhep-Aton hurried into the house, then down, into the basement and the chambers beneath. He had chosen the house for those deep buried rooms. Some works were best done in the bowels of the earth, where no ray of sun ever found its way.

In the anteroom to his private chamber two lush young girls of sixteen summers fell on their knees at his entrance. They were naked but for golden chains at wrist and ankle, waist and neck, and their big, round eyes shone with lust and worshipful adoration. His will was theirs, the fulfillment of his slightest whim the greatest desire of their miserable lives. The spells that kept them so killed in a year or two, and that he found a pity, for it necessitated the constant acquisition of new subjects.

The girls groveled on their faces; he paused before passing into his inner chamber to lay his staff before the door. Instantly the wooden rod transmuted into a hooded viper that coiled and watched with cold, semi-intelligent eyes. Imhep-Aton had no fear of human intruders while his faithful myrmidion watched.

The inner room was barren for a mage's work-chamber—no piles of human bones to stoke unholy fires, no dessicated husks of mummies to be ground into noxious powders—but what little there was permeated the chamber with bone-chilling horror. At either end of a long table, thin, greasy plumes of smoke arose from two black candles, the tallow rendered from the body of a virgin strangled with her mother's hair and made woman after death by her father. Between them lay a book bound in human skin, a grimoire filled with secrets darker than any outside of Stygia itself and a glass, fluid-filled simulation of a human womb, within which floated the misshapen form of one unborn.

Before the table Imhep-Aton made arcane gestures, muttered incantations known to but a handful human. The homunculus twitched within the pellucid womb. Agony twisted its deformed face as the pitiful jaws creaked painfully open.

"Who calls?"

Despite the gurgling distortion of that hollow cry, there was an imperiousness to it that told Imhep-Aton who spoke across the countless miles from ancient Khemi, in Stygia, through another such monstrosity. Thoth-Amon, master mage of the Black Ring.

"It is I, Imhep-Aton. All is in readiness. Soon Amanar will be cast into the outer dark."

"Then Amanar still lives. And the One Whose Name May Not Be Spoken yet profanes the honor of Set. Remember your part, and your blame, and your fate, should you fail."

Sweat dampened Imhep-Aton's forehead. It had been he who brought Amanar into the Black Ring. He remembered once seeing a renegade priest given to Set in a dark chamber far beneath Khemi, and swallowed bile.

"I will not fail," he muttered, then forced strength into his words so the homunculus could hear and transmit. "I will not fail. That which I came to secure will be in my hands in five days. Amanar and the One Whose Name May Not Be Spoken will be delivered into the power of Set."

"That you are given this chance of redemption is not of my will. If you fail . . . ."

"There will be no failure. An ignorant barbarian thief who knows no more of reality than a gold coin will—"

The horrible, hollow voice from the twisted shape in the glass vessel cut him off. "I care naught for your methods. Set cares naught. Succeed, or pay."

The grotesque mouth snapped shut, and the homunculus curled tighter into a fetal ball. The communication was ended.

Imhep-Aton scrubbed damp palms down the front of his purple robe. Some measure of what had been sucked out of him these minutes past, he could regain at the expense of the two girls awaiting his desires. But they knew their place in the scheme of things, if not the brevity of that place. There was little to be gained from such. Not so the thief. The Cimmerian thought himself Imhep-Aton's equal, if not, from some strange barbarian perspective, his superior. The mere fact that he was alive would remind the mage of this time when he stank with fear-sweat. Once the pendants were safely in hand this Conan would find not gold, but death, as his payment.

IV

The alabaster walls of Tiridates' palace stood
five times the height of a man, and atop them
guardsmen of the King's Own marched sentry
rounds in gilded half-armor and horsehair-crested
helms. Within, when the sun was high, peacocks
strutted among flowers from lands beyond the ken
of man, the hours were struck on silver gongs, and
silken maids danced for the pleasure of the drunkard king. Now, in the purple night, ivory towers
with corbeled arches and golden-finialed domes
pierced the sky in silent stillness.

Conan watched from the shadows around the
plaza that surrounded the palace, counting the
steps of guards as they moved toward each other,
then away. His boots and cloak were in the sack
slung at his side, muffling any clank of the tools of
his trade. His sword was strapped across his back,
the hilt rising above his right shoulder, and the
Karpashian dagger was sheathed on his left forearm. He held a rope of black-dyed raw silk, on the

end of which dangled a padded graponel.

As the guards before him met once more and turned to move apart, he broke from the shadows. His bare feet made almost no sound on the gray paving stones of the plaza. He began to swing the graponel as he ran. There would be little time before the guards reached the ends of their rounds and turned back. He reached the foot of the pale wall, and a heave of his massive arm sent the graponel skyward into the night. It caught with a muted click. Tugging once at the rope to test it, he swarmed up the wall as another man might climb a stair.

Wriggling flat onto the top of the wall, he stared at the graponel and heaved a sigh of relief. One point had barely caught the lip of the wall, and a scrape on the stone showed how it had slipped. A finger's breadth more . . . . But he had no time for these reflections. Hurriedly he pulled the sable rope up, and dropped into the garden below. He hit rolling, to absorb the fall, and came up in rustling bushes against the wall.

Above, the guards came closer, their footsteps thudding on the stone. Conan held his breath. If they noticed the scrape, an alarm would surely be raised. The guards came together, muttered words were exchanged, and they began to move apart. He waited until the sounds of their going had faded, then he was off, massive muscles working, in a loping stride past ferns that towered above his head and pale-flowered vines that rustled where there was no breeze.

Across the garden a peacock called, like the plaintive cry of a woman. Conan cursed whoever had wandered out to wake the bird from its roosting. Such noises were likely to draw the guards' attentions. He redoubled his pace. There was need to be inside before anyone came to check.

Experience had taught him that the higher he was above a ground-level entrance, the more likely anyone who saw him was to think he had a right there. If he were moving from a lower level to a higher, he might be challenged, but from a higher to a lower, never. An observer thought him servant or bodyguard returning from his master to his quarters below, and thought no more on it. It was thus his practice to enter any building at as high a level as he could. Now, as he ran, his eyes searched the carven white marble wall of the palace ahead, seeking those balconies that showed no light. Near the very roof of the palace, a hundred feet and more above the garden, he found the darkened balcony he sought.

The pale marble of the palace wall had been worked in the form of leafy vines, providing a hundred grips for fingers and toes. For one who had played on the cliffs of Cimmeria as a boy, it was as good as a path. As he swung his leg over the marble balustrade of the balcony, the peacock cried again, and this time its cry was cut off abruptly. Conan peered down to where the guardsmen made their rounds. Still they seemed to notice nothing amiss. But it would be well to get the pendants in hand and be away as quickly as possible. Whatever fool was wandering about —and perhaps silencing peacocks—must surely rouse the sentries given time.

He pushed quickly through the heavy damask

curtains that screened the balcony and halfway
across the darkened room before he realized his
mistake. He was not alone. Breath caught in a
canopied, gauze-hung bed, and someone stirred in
the sheets.

The Karpashian dagger appeared in his fist as he
gathered himself and sprang for the bed. Silken
gauze as fine as spun cobwebs ripped away before
him, and he grappled with the bed's occupant, his
wild charge carrying them both onto the marble
mosaic floor. Abruptly he became aware that the
flesh he wrestled with, though firm, was yielding
beneath his iron grip, and there was a sweet scent
of flowery perfume. He tore away the silk sheets to
see more clearly who it was that struggled so futilely against him.

First bared were long, shapely legs, kicking wildly, then rounded hips, a tiny waist, and finally a
pretty face filled with dark, round eyes that stared
at him fearfully above the fingers he locked
instantly over her mouth. She wore a silver-
mounted black stone that dangled between her
small, shapely breasts, and beyond that was concealed only by dark, waist-long hair.

"Who are you, girl?" He loosened his grip to let
her speak, but kept his hand poised in case she
took it into her head to scream.

She swallowed, and a small, pink tongue licked
her ripe lips. "I am called Velita, noble sir. I'm
only a slave girl. Please do not hurt me."

"I won't hurt you." He cast a quick eye around
the tapestry-draped bedchamber for something
convenient to bind her with. She could not be left
free to raise an alarm. It came to him that these

were not the sleeping quarters of a slave girl. "What are you doing here, Velita? Are you meeting someone? The truth, now."

"No one, I swear." Her voice faltered, and her head dropped. "The king chose me out, but in the end he preferred a youth from Corinthia. I could not return to the zenana. I wish I were back in Aghrapur."

"Aghrapur! Are you one of the dancing girls sent by Yildiz?"

Her small head tossed angrily. "I was the best dancer at the court of Yildiz. He had no call to give me away." Suddenly she gasped. "You do not belong here! Are you a thief? Please! I will be yours if you free me from this catamite king."

Conan smiled. The idea had amusement value, this stealing of a dancing girl from the king's palace. Slight as she was, she would be no inconsiderable burden to carry over the palace wall, but he had pride of his youth and strength.

"I'll take you with me, Velita, but I have no desire to own slaves. I'll set you free to go where you will, and with a hundred pieces of gold, as well. This I swear by Crom, and by Bel, god of thieves." A generous gesture, he reflected, but he could well afford it. It would still leave nine thousand nine hundred for himself, after all.

Velita's lower lip trembled. "You aren't making sport of me, are you? Oh, to be free." Her slender arms snaked around him tightly. "I will serve you, I swear, and dance for you, and—"

For a moment he enjoyed the pleasant pressure of her firm breasts against his chest, then drew himself back to the matter at hand.

"Enough, girl. Help me obtain what I came for, and you need do no more. You know the pendants that came with you to Tiridates?"

"Surely. See, here is one." She pulled the silver chain from around her neck and thrust it into his hands.

He turned it over curiously. His time as a thief had given him some knowledge in the value of such things. The silver mounting and chain were of good workmanship, but plain. As for the stone . . . . An ebon oval as long as the top joint of his forefinger, it had the smooth feel of a pearl, but was not. Red flecks seemed to appear near the surface and dart into great depths. Abruptly he tore his gaze from the pendant.

"What are you doing with this, Velita? I was told they were displayed in a golden casket in the antechamber of the throne room."

"The casket is there, but Tiridates likes us to dance for him wearing them. We wear them this night."

Conan sat back on his heels, replacing his dagger in its sheath. "Can you fetch the other girls here, Velita?"

She shook her head. "Yasmeen and Susa are with officers of the guard, Consela with a steward, and Aramit with a counselor. As the king has little interest in women, the others take their pleasure. Does . . . does this mean you will not take me with you?"

"I said I would," he snapped. He hefted the pendant on his palm. Ankar would likely not pay any part of the ten thousand for one pendant, but to gather the other four from women scattered throughout the palace, each in the company of a man, was clearly impossible. Reluctantly he replaced the silver chain about her neck. "I will take you away, but I fear you must remain another night yet."

"Another night? If I must, I will. But why?"

"Tomorrow night at this hour I will come again to this room. You must gather the pendants here, with the other girls or without. I cannot carry more than one of you over the wall, but I'll not harm them, I promise."

Velita worried her lower lip with small, white teeth. "They care not, so long as their cage be gold," she muttered. "There's risk in what you ask."

"There is. If you cannot do it, say so. I'll take you away tonight, and get what I can for the single piece."

For a moment longer she knelt frowning among the tangled sheets. "You risk your life, I but a whipping. I will do it. What—"

He planted a hand over her mouth as the door of the darkened room opened. A mailed man entered, the red-dyed crest of a captain on his helm, blinking in the dimness. He was even taller than Conan, though perhaps a finger less broad of shoulder.

"Where are you, wench?" the captain chuckled, moving deeper into the room. Conan waited, letting him come closer. "I know you're here, you hot-bodied little vixen. A chamberlain saw you flee red-faced hence from our good king's chambers. You need a true man to assuage your—What!"

Conan launched himself at the large man as the other jumped back, clawing for his sword. One of the Cimmerian's big hands clutched the captain's sword wrist, the other seized his throat beneath a bearded chin. He could afford no outcry, not even such as the man might make after a dagger was lodged twixt his ribs.

Chest to chest the two big men stood, feet working for leverage on the mosaic arabesques of the floor. The guardsman's free hand clubbed against the back of Conan's neck, and again. The Cimmerian released his grip on the man's throat, throwing that arm around the Zamoran to hold him close. At the same instant he let go the sword wrist, snaked his hand under that arm and behind the other's shoulder to grab the bearded chin. His arms corded with the strain of forcing the helmeted head back. The tall soldier abandoned his attempt to reach his sword and suddenly grasped Conan's head with both his hands, twisting with all his might.

Conan's breath rasped in his throat, and the blood pounded in his ears. He could smell his own sweat, and that of the Zamoran. A growl built deep in his throat. He forced the man's head back. Back. Abruptly there was an audible snap, and the guardsman was a dead weight sagging on his chest.

Panting, Conan let the man fall. The helmeted head was at an impossible angle.

"You've killed him," Velita breathed. "You've . . . I recognize him. That's Mariates, a captain of the guard. When he's found here . . . ."

"He won't be," Conan answered.

Quickly he dragged the body out onto the balcony and dug his rope out of the sack at his side. It would stretch but halfway to the ground. Hooking the graponel over the stone balustrade at the side of the balcony, he let the dark rope fall.

"When I whistle, Velita, unloose this."

He bound the dead guardsman's wrists with the man's own swordbelt, and thrust his head and right arm through the loop they formed. When he straightened, the man dangled down his back like a sack. A heavy sack. He reminded himself of the ten thousand pieces of gold.

"What are you doing?" she asked. "And what's your name? I don't even know that."

"I'm making sure the body isn't found in this room." He stepped over the rail and checked the graponel again. It wouldn't do to have it slip here. Clad in naught but the pendant, Velita stood watching him, her big dark eyes tremulous. "I am Conan of Cimmeria," he said proudly, and let himself down the rope hand over hand.

Almost immediately he felt the strain in his massive arms and shoulders. He was strong, but the Zamoran was no feather, and a dead weight besides. His bound wrists dug into Conan's throat, but there was no way to shift the burden while dangling half a hundred feet in the night air.

With a mountaineer's practiced eye he studied distances and angles, and stopped his descent in a stretch of the carven wall free of balconies. Thrusting with his powerful legs he pushed himself sideways, walking two steps along the wall, then swinging back beyond the point where he began. Then back the other way again. He stepped up the pace until he was running along the wall, swinging in an ever greater arc. At first the dead Zamoran slowed him, but then the extra weight added to his momentum, taking him closer to his goal, another balcony below and to the right of the first.

He was ten paces from the niveous stone rail. Then five. Three. And he realized he was increasing his arc too little on each swing now. He could not climb back up the rope—the guardsman's wrists were half-strangling him—nor could he continue to inch his way closer.

He swung back to his left and began his sideways run toward the balcony. It was the last time, he knew as he watched his goal materialize out of the dark. He must make it this time, or fall. Ten paces. Five. Three. Two. He was going to fall short. Desperately he thrust against the enchased marble wall, loosed one hand from the rope, stretched for the rail. His fingers caught precariously. And held. Straining, he hung between the rope and his tenuous grasp on the stone. The dangling body choked his burning breath in his throat. Shoulder joints cracking, he pulled himself nearer. And then he had a foot between the balusters. Still clutching the rope he pulled himself over the rail and collapsed on the cool marble, sucking at the night air.

It was an illusory haven, though. Quickly he freed himself from the Zamoran and bent back over the rail to whistle. The rope swung as the graponel fell free. He drew it up with grateful thanks that Velita had not been too terrified to remember, and stowed it in his sack. There was still Mariates to deal with.

Mariates' sword belt went back about the officer's waist. There was naught Conan could do about the abrasions on the man's wrists. On the side away from Velita's balcony, he rolled the dead man over the rail. From below came the crashing of broken branches. But no alarm.

Smiling, Conan used the carven marble foliage to make his way to the ground. Evidence of Mariates' fall was plain in shattered boughs. The captain himself lay spreadeagled across an exotic shrub, the loss of which Conan thought the dilettante king might regret more than the loss of a soldier. And best of all, of the several balconies from which the man could have fallen, Velita's was not one.

Swiftly Conan made his way back through the garden. Once more the guards' paces were counted, and once more he went over the wall easily. As he reached the safety of the shadows around the plaza, he thought he heard a shout from behind, but he was not sure, and he did not linger to find out. Boots and cloak were on in moments, sword slung at his hip.

As he strode through pitchy streets at once broader and less odoriferous than those of the Desert, he thought that this might be almost his last return to that squalid district. After tomorrow night he would be beyond such places. From the direction of the palace, a gong sounded in the night.

V

Conan woke early the morning after his foray into the palace. He found the common room empty except for Abuletes, counting his night's take at the bar, and two skinny sweepers in rags. The fat tavernkeeper eyed Conan warily and put a protective arm about the stacked coins.

"Wine," Conan said, fishing out the necessary coppers. For all his celebration the night before there were still six of the dark man's gold coins in his purse. "I don't steal from friends," he added, when Abuletes drew the money down the bar after him in the crook of his arm.

"Friends! What friends? In the Desert, a brother in blood is no friend." Abuletes filled a rough earthenware mug from a tap in a keg and shoved it in front of Conan. "But perhaps you think to buy friends with the gold you were throwing about last night. Where did that come from, anyway? Had you aught to do with what happened at the palace in the night? No, that couldn't be. You were spending like Yildiz himself before ever it happened. You'd better watch that, showing your gold so free in the Desert.''

The tavernkeeper would have gone on, but Conan cut him short. ''Something happened at the palace?'' He was careful to drink deep of the thin wine for punctuation, as if the question were casual.

''And you call a king's counselor dead something, plus others to the king's household and a dozen guardsmen besides, then it did.''

''A dozen!''

''So I said, and so it was. Dead guardsmen at every hand, Yildiz's gifts to Tiridates taken, and never a one who saw a hair of those who did it. Never a one in all the palace.'' Abuletes rubbed his chins with a pudgy hand. ''Though there's a tale about that a pair of the sentries saw a man running from the palace. A big man. Mayhap as big as you.''

''Of course it was me,'' Conan snorted. ''I leaped over the wall, then leaped back again with all that on my back. You did say all the gifts were taken, didn't you?'' He emptied his mug and thumped it down before the stout man. ''Again.''

''Five gemstones, five dancing girls and a golden casket.'' Abuletes twisted the tap shut and replaced the mug on the bar. ''Unless there's more than that, they took all. I'll admit you couldn't have done it. I admit it. But why are you so interested now? Answer me that.''

''I'm a thief. Someone else has done the hard part on this. All I have to do is relieve him of his ill-gotten goods.'' Relieve whom, he wondered.

Ankar had had no other plan beyond himself. Of
that he was certain. That left guardsmen gone
wrong, stolen away with the treasure and the slave
girls after slaying their comrades, or slain themselves after letting someone else into the palace to
do the theft.

Abuletes hawked and spat on a varicolored rag,
and began to scrub the bartop. "Was me," he said
absently, "I'd have naught to do with this. Those
who did this thing aren't of the Desert. Those who
rob kings aren't to be crossed. Necromancers, for
all you know. There was no one seen, remember.
Not a glimpse of a hair."

It could have been a mage, Conan thought,
though why a mage, or anyone else, would go
through the danger of stealing five dancing girls
from the palace, he could not imagine. Too,
magicians were not so thick on the ground as most
men believed, and he was one who should know.

"You begin to sound worried for me, Abuletes. I
thought you said there were no friends in the
Desert."

"You spend freely," the tavernkeeper said
sourly. "That's all there is. Don't think there's
more. You stay out of this, whatever it is.
Whoever's behind this is too big for the likes of
you. You'll end with your throat cut, and I'll be
out a customer."

"Perhaps you're right. Bel! I'm for a breath of
air. This sitting around talking of other men's
thefts gives me a pain in the belly."

He left the fat tapster muttering darkly to himself and found his way to the street. The air in the
Desert was anything but fresh. The stench of

rotting offal blended with the effluvia of human excrement and vomit. The paving stones where they had not been ripped up to leave mudholes, were slick with slime. From the dim depths of an alley, barely wide enough for a man to enter, the victim of a robbery moaned for help. Or the bait for a robbery. Either was equally likely.

Conan strode the crooked streets of that thieves' district purposefully, though he was not himself sure of what that purpose was. A swindler with tarnished silver embroidery on his vest waved a greeting as he passed, and a whore, naked but for gilded brass bells and resting her feet in a doorway, smiled at the broadshouldered youth as she suddenly felt not so tired after all. Conan did not even notice them, nor the "blind" beggar in black rags, tapping his way down the street with a broken stick, who eased his dagger back under his soiled robes after a glance at the grim set of Conan's jaw, or the three who followed him through the winding streets, the edges of their headcloths drawn across their faces, white-knuckled hands gripping cudgels beneath their dingy cloaks, before the size of his arms and the length of his sword made them take another turning.

He tried telling himself that the pendants were beyond his reach now. He had naught beyond glimmers of suspicion who had taken them, no idea at all where they were. Still, ten thousand pieces of gold was not a thing a man gave up on easily. And there was Velita. A slave girl. She would be happy with any master who was kind to her. But he had promised, sworn, to free her. By Bel and by Crom he had sworn it. His oath, and ten thousand pieces of gold.

Suddenly he realized he was out of the Desert, near the Sign of the Bull Dancer, on the Street of the Silver Fish. A tree-lined sward of grass ran down the center of the broad avenue. Slave-borne sedan chairs vied in number with pedestrians, and there was not a beggar in sight. This place was far from the Desert, yet he had friends—or at least acquaintances—here. The tavern hoarding, a slender youth in a leathern girdle, vaulting between the needle horns of a great black bull, creaked in the breeze as he went in.

Taverns, Conan reflected as he searched for a certain face, were much alike, in the Desert or out. Rather than footpads and cutpurses, plump merchants in purple silk and green brocade occupied the tables, but only the methods of stealing were different. In place of a coiner was a slender man holding a pomander before his prominent nose. He did not make the money he passed, rather buying it through the back door of the king's mint. The panderers dressed like noblemen, in scarlet robes, with emeralds at their ears, and some of them were indeed noblemen, but they were panderers no less. The prostitutes wore gold instead of gilt, rubies instead of spessartine, but they were just as naked, and they sold the same wares.

Conan spotted the man he wanted, Ampartes, a merchant who cared little if the king's duties had been paid on the goods he bought, alone at a table against the wall. Whatever happened in Shadizar, Ampartes soon knew of it. The chair across the table from the plump merchant groaned in protest as Conan's bulk dropped into it, a sound not far from that which rose in Ampartes' throat. His oily cheek twitched as his dark eyes rolled to see who had noted the Cimmerian's arrival. He tugged at his short, pointed beard with a beringed hand.

"What are you doing here, Conan?" he hissed, and blanched as if in fear the name might have been overheard. "I have no need of . . . of your particular wares."

"But I have need of yours. Tell me of what happened in the city last night."

Ampartes' voice rose to a squeak.

"You . . . you mean the palace?"

"No," Conan said, and hid a smile at the relief on the merchant's face. He grabbed a pewter goblet from the tray of a passing serving girl, a hand's breadth strip of crimson silk low on her hips her only garb, and filled it from Ampartes' blue-glazed flagon. The girl gave him a coy smile, then tossed her blonde head with a snort and hurried on sulkily when he did not give her a second glance. "But anything else unusual. Anything at all."

For the next two hours the merchant babbled in his relief that Conan was not involving him in the palace theft. Conan learned that on the night before in Shadizar a dealer in rare wines had strangled his mistress on discovering her with his son, and a gem merchant's wife had put a dagger in her husband's ribs for no reason that anyone knew. A nobleman's niece had been taken by kidnappers, but those who knew said her ransom, to come from her inheritance, would pay her uncle's debts. Thieves had entered the homes of five merchants and two nobles. One noble had had even his sedan chair and the robes from his back taken on the High Vorlusian Way, and a slave dealer's weasand had been slit outside his own auction house, some said for the keys to his strongbox, others for not checking the source of his merchandise, thus selling an abducted noblewoman into Koth. A merchant of Akif, visiting a most specialized brothel called The House of the Lambs of Hebra, had . . . .

"Enough!" Conan's hand cracked on the tabletop. Ampartes stared at him open-mouthed. "What you've told me so far could happen on any night in Shadizar, and usually does. What occurred out of the ordinary? It doesn't have to do with gold, or theft. Just so it's strange."

"I don't understand what you want," the oily man muttered. "There's the matter of the pilgrims, but there's no profit there. I don't know why I waste my time with you."

"Pilgrims?" Conan said sharply. "What was unusual about these pilgrims?"

"In Mitra's name, why would you want to know about . . . ." Ampartes swallowed as Conan's steel blue eyes locked his. "Oh, very well. They were from Argos, far to the west, making a pilgrimage to a shrine in Vendhya, as far to the east."

"I need no lessons in geography," Conan growled. "I've heard of these lands. What did these pilgrims do that was out of the ordinary?"

"They left the city two full glasses before cock crow, that's what. Something about a vow not to be inside a city's walls at dawn, I understand. Now where's your profit in that?"

"Just you tell me what I want to hear, and let me

worry about profit. What sort of men were these pilgrims?"

Ampartes threw him an exasperated look. "Zandru's Bells, man! Do you expect me to know more about a mere band of pilgrims than that they exist?"

"I expect," Conan said drily, "that on any given day you'll know which nobles lost how much at dice, who slept with whose wife, and how many times the king sneezed. The pilgrims? Rack your brains, Ampartes."

"I don't . . . ." The plump merchant grunted as Conan lay his left arm on the table. The forearm sheath was empty, and the Cimmerian's right hand was below the table's edge. "They were pilgrims. What more is there to say? Hooded men in coarse robes that showed not a hair of them. No better or worse mounted than most pilgrims. The bodies of five of their number who'd died on the way were packed in casks of wine on camels. Seems they'd made another vow, that all who started the pilgrimage would reach the shrine. Mitra, Conan, who can say much of pilgrims?"

Five bodies, Conan thought. Five dancing girls. "There were fighting men with these pilgrims? Armed men?"

Ampartes shook his head. "Not so much as a dagger in evidence, is what I heard. They told the sergeant at the Gate of the Three Swords that the spirit of their god would protect them. He said a good sword would do a better job, and wearing a soldier's boots wasn't enough."

"What about a soldier's boots?"

"For the love of . . . now I'm supposed to know

about boots?'' He spread his hands. ''All right. All I know is one of them was wearing a pair of cavalryman's halfboots. His robe was caught on his stirrup leather so one showed.'' His tone became sarcastic. ''Do you want to know what they looked like? Red, with some sort of serpent worked in the leather. Strange, that, but there it is. And that, Conan, is every last thing I know about those accursed pilgrims. Will you satisfy my curiosity now? What in the name of all the gods does a man like you want with pilgrims?''

''I'm seeking a religious experience,'' Conan replied, sheathing his dagger. He left the merchant laughing till tears ran down his fleshy cheeks.

As Conan hurried across Shadizar to the stable where his horse was kept, he knew he was right. Not only the five bodies in casks told him, but also the Gate of the Three Swords. That gate let out to the northeast, toward the caravan route that ran from Khesron through the Kezankian Mountains to Sultanapur. Vendhya might only be a name to him, but he knew it was reached by leaving through the Gate of the Black Throne and traveling southeast through Turan and beyond the Vilayet Sea. As soon as he could put saddle to horse, he would be off through the Gate of the Three Swords after Velita, the pendants, and his ten thousand pieces of gold.

VI

The man in field armor contrasted sharply with the others in Tiridates' private audience chamber. From greaves over his halfboots to ring mail and gorget, his armor was plain and dark, so as not to reflect light when on campaign. Even the horsehair crest on the helmet beneath his arm was russet rather than scarlet. He was Haranides, a captain of cavalry who had risen without patron or family connections. Now the hawk-nosed captain was wondering if the rise had been worth it.

Of the four others in the ivory-paneled room, only two were worthy of note. Tiridates, King of Zamora, slouched on the Minor Throne—its arms were golden hunting leopards in full bound, the back a peacock feathered in emeralds, rubies, sapphires and pearls—as if it were a tavern stool, a golden goblet dangling from one slack hand. His amethystine robe was rumpled and stained, his eyes but half-focused. With his free hand he idly caressed the arm of a slender blonde girl who knelt

57

beside the throne in naught but perfume and a wide choker of pearls about her swanlike neck. On the other side of the throne a youth, equally blonde and slender and attired the same, sulked for his lack of attention.

The other man worth marking, perhaps more so than the king, stood three paces to the right of the throne. Graying and stooped, but with shrewd intelligence engraved on his wizened face, he wore a crimson robe slashed with gold, and the golden Seal of Zamora on its emeralded chain about his neck. His name was Aharesus, and the seal had fallen to him with the death of Malderes, the previous chief king's counselor, the night before.

"You know why you are summoned, captain?" Aharesus said.

"No, my lord Counselor," Haranides replied stiffly. The counselor watched him expectantly, until at last he went on. "I can suspect, of course. Perhaps it has to do with the events of last night?"

"Very good, captain. And do you have any glimmering why you, instead of some other?"

"No, my lord Counselor." And this time, in truth, he had not a flickering of an idea. He had returned to the city only shortly after dawn that very morning, coming back from duty on the Kothian border. A hard posting, but what could be expected for a man with no preferment?

"You are chosen because you were not in Shadizar this year past." Haranides blinked, and the counselor chuckled, a sound like dry twigs scraping together. "I see your surprise, captain, though you conceal it well. An admirable trait in a military man. As you were not in the city, you

could not be part of any . . . plot, involving those
on duty in the palace last night."

"Plot!" the captain exclaimed. "Pardon, my
lord, but the King's Own has always been loyal to
the throne."

"Loyalty to his fellows is another good trait for
a military man, captain." The counselor's voice
hardened. "Don't carry it too far. Those who had
the duty last night are even now being put to the
question."

Haranides felt sweat trickling down his ribs. He
had no wish to join those men enjoying the
attentions of the king's torturers. "My lord knows
that I've always been a loyal soldier."

"I reviewed your record this morning,"
Aharesus said slowly. "Your return to the city at
this juncture was like a stroke from Mitra. These
are parlous times, captain."

"Their heads," the king barked abruptly. His
head swung in a muddled arc between the captain
and the counselor. Haranides was shocked to realize
that he had forgotten the king was present. "I want
their heads on pikes, Aharesus. Stole my . . . my
tribute from Yildiz. Stole my dancing girls."
Tiridates directed a bleary smile at the slave girl,
then jerked his gaze back to Haranides. "You
bring them back to me, do you hear? The girls, the
pendants, the casket. And the heads. The heads."
With a belch the king sagged back into a sodden
lump. "More wine," he muttered. The blonde
youth darted away and returned with a crystal
vessel and a fawning smile.

The captain's sweating increased. It was no
secret Tiridates was a drunkard, but being witness

to it could do him no good.

"The insult to the honor of the king is, captain, paramount, of course," Aharesus said with a careful glance at the king, who had his face buried in the goblet of wine. "On a wider view, however, what must be considered is that the palace was entered and the Chief King's Counselor murdered."

"My lord counselor thinks that was the reason for it all, and the other just a screen?"

The Counselor gave him a shrewd look. "You've a brain, captain. You may have a future. Yes, it makes no sense otherwise. Some foreign power wished the Counselor dead for some purpose of their own. Perhaps Yildiz himself. He has dreams of an empire, and Malderes often thwarted those plans." Aheresus fingered the golden seal on his chest thoughtfully. "In any case, it's doubtful that Yildiz, or whoever is responsible, would send his own people into the very palace. One of those being questioned screamed the name of the Red Hawk before he died."

"She's just a bandit, my lord Counselor."

"And a man babbles when he's dying. But she's a bandit who will dare much for gold, and we have no other way to search. Until one of those being questioned loosens his tongue." The chill in his tone promised the questioning would continue until many tongues were loosened; Haranides shivered. "You, captain, will take two companies of cavalry and hound this Red Hawk. Run her to ground and bring her here in chains. We'll soon find if she had aught to do with this business."

Haranides took a deep breath. "My lord Counselor, I must have some idea of where to look. This woman brigand ranges the entire countryside." Incongruously, one of the slaves giggled. Tiridates had both fair heads clutched to his chest.

The stooped counselor flickered an eye at the king and pursed his lips briefly. "Before dawn this morning, captain, a party claiming to be pilgrims departed Shadizar by the Gate of the Three Swords. I believe these were the Red Hawk's men."

"I will ride within the hour, my lord Counselor," Haranides said with a bow. He suspected the guards at that gate were among those under the question. "With your permission, my lord Counselor? My King?"

"Find this jade, captain," Aharesus said, "and you will find yourself a patron as well."

He waved a bony hand in dismissal, but as the captain turned to go Tiridates lurched unsteadily to his feet, pushing the two pale-skinned slaves sprawling at his feet.

"Find my pendants!" the drunken King snarled. "Find my casket and my dancing girls! Find my gifts from Yildiz, captain, or I'll decorate a pike with your head! Now, go! Go!"

With a sour taste in his mouth, Haranides bowed once more and backed out of the audience chamber.

The garden of Imhep-Aton's rented dwelling was pleasant, a cool breeze rustling in the trees and stirring the bright-colored flowers, but the mage took no pleasure in it. He had had some idea that Conan could deliver the pendants before the five days he had bargained for—the necromancer had some knowledge of thieves, and the way their minds worked. But never had he expected the Cimmerian to revert to his barbarism and turn the palace into a charnel house. The chief king's counselor, in Set's name!

He cared not what Zamorans died, or how, but the fool had set the city on its ear with these murders. Now Imhep-Aton must worry that the thief would be run to earth before the prize was delievered into his bony hands.

The mage whirled as his muscular Shemite servant came into the garden, his lean face so twisted that the big man quailed.

"I did as you commanded, master. To the word."

"Then where is the Cimmerian?" The thaumaturge's voice was deceptively gentle. If this cretin had bungled as well . . . .

"Gone, master. He has not been seen at the tavern since this morning, early."

"Gone!"

The brawny Shemite half-raised his hands as if to shield himself from the other's anger. "So I was told, master. He sent a message to some wench at the tavern that he would be away some time, that he was riding to the northeast."

Imhep-Aton's scowl deepened. Northeast? There was nothing to the . . . . The caravan route from Khesron to Sultanapur. Could the barbarian be thinking of selling the pendants in the very country from which they came? Obviously he had decided to work for himself. But, Set, why the dancing girls? He shook his vulturine head angrily.

The savage's reasons were of no account.

"Prepare horses and sumpter animals for the two of us at once," he commanded. "We ride to the northeast." The Cimmerian would pay for this betrayal.

VII

The Well of the Kings lay some days to the east and west of Shadizar, surrounded by huge, toppled slabs of black stone, worn by rain and wind. Some said they were the remains of a wall, but none knew when or by whom it could have been built, as none knew what kings had claimed the well.

Conan walked his horse between the slabs and into the stunted trees, to the well of rough stones, and dismounted. On the other side of the well, back under the trees, four swarthy men in dirty keffiyehs squatted, watching him with dark eyes that shifted greedily to his horse. He flipped back the edge of his Khauranian cloak so they could see his sword, and heaved on the hoist pole to lift a bucket of water from the depths. Other than his cloak, he was covered only by a breechclout, for he liked to travel unencumbered.

The four moved closer together, whispering darkly without looking away from him. One, the leader by the deference the others showed, wore rusting ring mail, his followers breastplates of boiled leather. All had ancient scimitars at their hips, the sort a decent weapons dealer sold for scrap. Behind them Conan could see a woman, naked and bound in a package, wrists and elbows secured behind her back, knees under her chin, heels drawn in tight to her buttocks. She raised her head, tossing back a mane of dark red hair, and stared at him in surprise, tilted green eyes above a dirty twist of cloth for a gag. The fortuneteller.

Conan emptied the bucket in a worn stone trough for his horse, and drew up another for himself. The last time he had helped this woman, she had shown not even the gratitude to warn him of the two Iranistanis' attack. Besides, he had Velita to find. He dashed water in his face, though it made little difference in the gritty heat, and upended the rest of the bucket over his head. The four men gabbled on.

So far he had tracked the pilgrims by questioning those passersby who would let an armed man of his size approach them. Enough had glimpsed something to keep him on this path, but in the last day he had seen only an old man who threw rocks and ran to hide in the thorn scrub, and a boy who had seen nothing.

"Have you fellows seen anything of pilgrims?" he said, levering up yet another bucket of water. "Hooded men on horseback, with camels?"

The leader's sharp nose twitched. "An we did, what's for us?"

"A few coppers, if you can tell me where they are." There was no reason to tempt this lot. After a day when he could be traveling away from the men he sought, he had no time to waste killing vultures. He put on a pleasant smile. "If I had silver or gold, I'd not be out chasing pilgrims. I'd be in Shadizar, drinking." He dried his hands on his cloak, just in case.

"What do you want with those pilgrims?" the sharp-nosed man wanted to know.

"That's my affair," Conan replied. "And theirs. Yours is the coppers, if you've seen them."

"Well, as to that, we have," sharp-nose said, dusting off his hands and getting up. He started toward Conan with his hand out. "Let's see the color of your coins."

Conan dug into the leather pouch at his belt with his right hand, and sharp-nose's grin turned nasty. A short dagger with a triangular blade appeared in his fist. Laughing wickedly, the other three pulled their scimitars and rushed forward to join the kill.

Without pausing a beat Conan snatched up the bucket left-handed and smashed it down on the man's head, blood and water flying in all directions. "No time!" he shouted. He plucked the dagger from its forearm sheath, and of a sudden its hilt was sticking from the throat of the foremost attacker. Even as it struck Conan was unlimbering his broadsword. "Bel strike you!" He leaped across the collapsing man, who was clutching the dagger in his throat with blood-covered hands. "I've no time!" A sweeping slash of the broad blade, and the third man's torso sank to the ground where his head was already spinning. "No time, curse you!" The last man had his scimitar raised high when Conan lunged with a two-handed grip and plunged his blade through leather breastplate,

chest and backbone. Black eyes filmed over, and
the man toppled to one side with his hands still
raised above his head.

Conan put a foot on the leather armor and tugged his sword free, wiping it clean on the man's
dingy keffiyeh before he sheathed it. The dagger
was retrieved from its temporary home in a
brigand's throat and cleaned in the same way. The
woman watched him wide-eyed, starting away as
much as her bonds allowed when he came near, but
he only cut the cords and turned away, sheathing
his dagger.

"If you don't have your own horse," he said,
"you can have one of these vermin's. The rest are
mine. You can have the weapons, if you want.
They'll fetch something for your trouble." But not
much, he thought. Still, he owed her nothing, and
the horses, poor as they were likely to be, would be
a help if he had to pursue those accursed pilgrims
far.

The red-haired woman rubbed her wrists as she
walked to the dead men, unashamed of her naked-
ness. She was an ivory-skinned callimastian delight, all curves and long legs and rounded places.
There was a spring to her walk that made him
wonder if she was a dancer. She picked up one
of the scimitars, ran a contemptuous eye along its
rust-pitted blade, and suddenly planted a bare foot
solidly in the ribs of one of the dead men.

"Pig!" she spat.

Conan went about gathering the horses, five of
them, one noticeably better than the rest, while she
kicked and reviled each body in turn. Abruptly she
whirled to face him, feet well apart, fist on

rounded hip, scimitar swinging free. With her tousled hair in an auburn mane about her head, she had the air of a lioness brought to human form.

"They took me unawares," she announced.

"Of course," Conan said. "I suppose the black is yours? Best of the lot." He braided the reins of the other four, hairy plains animals two hands shorter at the shoulder than his own Turanian gray, and fastened them to his high-pommeled saddle. "Best for you would be to go straight back to Shadizar. It's dangerous out here for a woman alone. What possessed you to try it in the first place?"

She took a quick step toward him. "I said they took me unawares! They'd have died on my blade, else!"

"And I said of course. I can't take you back to the city. I seek men who took something that . . . that belongs to me."

A pantherine howl jerked him around, and he tumbled backwards between the horses just in time to avoid decapitation by her curved blade. "Derketo take you!" she howled, thrusting at him under a horse's belly. He rolled aside, and the blade gouged the packed earth where his head had been.

Scrambling on his back, he tried at once to avoid her steel and the hooves of the horses, now dancing excitedly as she moved swiftly around them trying to stab him. The roiling of them brought him suddenly looking out from under a shaggy belly at her as she pulled back her scimitar for yet another thrust. Desperately his legs uncoiled, propelling him out to tackle her around the knees. They went down in a heap together on the hard ground, and he found his arms full of female wildcat, clawing and kicking and trying to jerk her sword arm loose. Her soft curves padded her firm muscle, and she was no easy packet to hold.

"Have you gone mad, woman?" he shouted. For an answer she sank her teeth into his shoulder. "Crom!"

He hurled her away from him. She rolled across the ground and bounded to her feet. Still, he saw wonderingly, gripping the rusty sword.

"I need no man to protect me!" she spat. "I'm not some pampered concubine!"

"Who said you were?" he roared.

Then he had to jerk his sword free of its scabbard as she rushed at him with a howl of pure rage. Her green eyes burned, and her face was twisted with fury. He swung up his sword to block her downward slash. With a sharp snap the rusty scimitar broke, leaving her to stare in disbelief at the bladeless hilt in her hands.

Almost without a pause she hurled the useless hilt at his face and spun to dash for the dead men by the well. Their weapons still lay about them. Conan darted after her, and as she bent to snatch another scimitar, he swung the flat of his blade with all his strength at the tempting target thus offered. She lifted up on her toes with a strangled shriek as the steel paddle cracked against her rounded nates. Arms windmilling, she staggered forward, her foot slipping in a pool of blood, and screaming she plunged headfirst over the crude stone wall of the well.

Conan dived as she went over; his big hand closed on flesh, and he was dragged to his armpits into the well by the weight of her. He discovered he was holding the red-haired wench by one ankle while she dangled over the depths. An interesting view, he thought.

"Derketo take you!" she howled. "Pull me up, you motherless whelp!"

"In Shadizar," he said conversationally, "I saved you a mauling. You called me a barbar boy, let a man near take my head off, and left without a word of thanks."

"Son of a diseased camel! Spawn of a bagnio! Pull me up!"

"Now here," he went on as if she had not spoken, "all I did was save you from rape, certainly, perhaps from being sold on the slave block. Or maybe they'd just have slit your throat once they were done with you." She wriggled violently, and he edged further over the rim to let her drop another foot. Her scream echoed up the stone cylinder. She froze into immobility.

"You had no thought of saving me," she rasped breathlessly. "You'd have ridden off to leave me if those dogs hadn't tried you."

"All the same, if I had ridden on, or if they'd killed me, you'd be wondering what you'd fetch at market."

"And you want a reward," she half wept. "Derketo curse you, you smelly barbar oaf!"

"That's the second time you've called me that," he said grimly. "What I want from you is an oath, by Derketo since you call on the goddess of love and death. An oath that you'll never again let an uncivil word pass your lips toward me, and that you'll never again raise a hand against me."

"Hairy lout! Dung-footed barbar! Do you think you can force me to—"

He cut her off. "My hand is getting sweaty. I wouldn't wait too long. You might slip." Silence answered him. "Or then again, I might grow tired of waiting."

"I will swear." Her voice was suddenly soft and sensuously yielding. "Pull me up, and I'll swear on my knees to anything you command."

"Swear first," he replied. "I'd hate to have to toss you back in. Besides, I like the view." He thought he heard the sound of a small fist smacking the stone wall of the well in frustration, and smiled.

"You untrusting ape," she snarled with all her old ferocity. "Very well. I swear, by Derketo, that I'll speak no uncivil word to you, nor raise a hand against you. I swear it. Are you satisfied?"

He hoisted her straight up out of the well, and let her drop on the hard ground with a thud and a grunt.

"You . . . ." She bit her lip and glared up at him from the ground. "You didn't have to be so rough," she said in a flat tone. Instead of answering he unfastened his swordbelt, propping the scabbard against the well. "What . . . what are you doing?"

"You spoke of a reward." He stepped out of his breechclout. "Since I doubt a word of thanks will ever crack your teeth, I'm collecting my own reward."

"So you're nothing but a ravisher of women after all," she said bitterly.

"That was close to an uncivil word, wench. And

no ravishment. All you need to do is say, 'stop,' and you'll leave this place as chaste as a virgin for all of me.''

He lowered himself onto her, and though she beat at his shoulders with her fists and filled the air with vile curses the word 'stop' never once passed her lips, and soon her cries changed their nature, for she was a woman fully fledged, and he knew something of women.

After, he regained his clothes and his weapons while she rummaged among the dead men's things to cover herself. Her own garments, she said, had been ripped to shreds. He noted that this time she inspected the weapons carefully before selecting one, but he had no worries at turning his back on her even after she had belted it on. When she had been turning the air blue, not one of her curses had been directed at him. If she could keep her oath then, he was sure she would keep it now.

Once he had filled his goatskin waterbags, he swung into his saddle.

"Hold a moment," she called. "What's your name?" She had clothed herself in flowing pantaloons of bright yellow and an emerald tunic that was far too tight across the chest, though loose elsewhere. A braided gold cord held her auburn mane back from her face. He had seen her dig it out from the purse of one of the dead men.

"Conan," he said. "Conan of Cimmeria. And you?"

"My name is Karela," she said proudly, "of whatever land I happen to be standing on. Tell me, these pilgrims you seek, they have something of great value? I don't see you as a holy man, Conan of Cimmeria.''

If he told her about the pendants, she would no doubt want to go with him. From the way she had handled her sword he was sure she could pull her weight, but even so he did not want her along. Let her get a sniff of ten thousand pieces of gold, and he would have to sleep with both eyes open, oath or no. He was sure of that, too.

"Valuable only to a man in Shadizar," he said casually. "A dancing girl who ran away with these pilgrims. Or maybe they stole her. Whatever, the man's besotted with her, and he'll pay five gold pieces to have her back.''

"Not much for a ride in this country. There are harder bandits about than these dog stealers.'' She nodded to the bodies, where Conan had dragged them, well away from the water.

"I seek pilgrims, not bandits," he laughed. "They won't put up much fight. Farewell, Karela.'' He turned to ride away, but her next words made him draw rein.

"Don't you want to know where these pilgrims of yours are?''

He stared at her, and she looked back with green eyes innocently wide. "If you know where they are, why didn't you speak of it before? For that matter, why speak of it now? I can't see you volunteering help to me.''

"Those jackals . . . made a fool of me.'' She grimaced, but the open look returned to her face quickly. "I was mad, Conan. I wanted to take it out on anyone. You saved my life, after all.''

Conan nodded slowly. It was barely possible. And just as possible she would send him off chasing hares. But he had nothing else to go on besides picking a direction out of the air. "Where did you see them?"

"To the north. They were camped beyond some low hills. I'll show you." She vaulted easily into the saddle of her big black. "Well, do you want me to show you, or do you want to sit here all day?"

Short of dangling her down the well again, he could think no way of making her talk. He moved his black cloak to clear the leather-wrapped hilt of his sword, and motioned her to ride past. "You lead," he said.

"I know," she laughed as she dug her heels into her mount's ribs. "You like the view."

He did that, he thought wryly, but he intended to watch Karela with an eye to treachery. Trailing the robbers' horses, he rode after her.

VIII

For the rest of that day they rode north, across rolling countryside sparsely covered with low scrub. When they camped at nightfall, Conan said, "How much farther?"

Karela shrugged; her heavy round breasts shifted beneath the tight green tunic. "We'll reach it some time after dawn, if we break camp early."

She began to pile dry twigs from the scrub for a fire, but he scattered them. "No need to advertise our presence. What makes you think they'll still be there?"

Tucking flint and steel back in her pouch, she gave him an amused smile. "If they've gone, at least you'll be closer than you were. Who is this man in Shadizar who wants his slave girl back?"

"If we're riding early, we'd better turn in," he said, and she smiled again.

He wrapped himself in his cloak but did not sleep. Instead he watched her. She was wrapped in a blanket she had carried on her horse, and had her head pillowed on her high-pommeled saddle of tooled red leather. He would not have put it past her to try sneaking off with the horses in the night, but she seemed to settle right into sleep.

Purple twilight deepened to black night, and scudding clouds crossed stars like diamonds on velvet, but Conan kept his eyes open. A gibbous moon rose, and at its height the Cimmerian thought he felt eyes on him from the surrounding night. Easing his narrow-bladed dagger from its forearm sheath, he loosed the bronze brooch that held his cloak and snaked into the night on his belly. Thrice he circled the camp in silence, always feeling the eyes, but he saw no one, nor any sign that anyone had ever been there. And then, abruptly, the feeling was gone. Once more he crawled all the way around the camp, but there was still nothing. Disgusted with himself, he got up and walked back to his cloak. Karela still slept. Angrily he wrapped himself in the black wool. It was the woman. Waiting for her treachery was making him see and feel what just was not there.

While the sun was but a red rim shining above the horizon Karela woke, and they rode north again. Slowly the land changed, the low rollings becoming true hills. Conan was beginning to wonder what the men he sought would be doing so far to the north of the caravan route, when suddenly Karela kicked her horse into a gallop.

"There it is," she cried. "Just over those next hills."

Hurriedly he galloped after her. "Karela, come back! Karela!" She hurried on, disappearing around a hill. Fool woman, he thought. If the pilgrims were still there, she would have them roused.

As he rounded the hill, he slowed his mount to a walk. She was nowhere in sight, and he could no longer hear the sounds of her horse running.

"Conan!"

Conan's head whipped around at the shout. Karela sat her horse atop a hill to his right. "Crom, woman! What are you—"

"My name is Karela," she shouted. "The Red Hawk!"

She let out a shrill whistle, and suddenly mounted men in a motley collection of bright finery and mismatched armor were boiling through every gap in the hills. In a trice he was the center of a shoulder-to-shoulder ring of brigands. Carefully he folded his hands on the pommel of his saddle. So much as a twitch toward his sword would put iron-tipped quarrels through his body from the four crossbows he could see, and there might be more.

"Karela," he called, "is this the way you keep your oath?"

"I've said no uncivil word to you," she replied mockingly, "And I haven't raised my hand against you. Nor will I. I'm afraid the same can't be said of my men. Hordo!"

A burly, black-bearded man with a rough leather patch over his left eye forced his horse through the circle to confront Conan. A jagged scar ran from under the patch and disappeared in the thatch of his beard. That side of his mouth was drawn up in a permanent sneer. His ring mail had once belonged to a wealthy man—there were still traces of gilt left—and large gold hoops stretched his ears. A well-worn tulwar hung at his side.

"Conan, she called you," the big man said. "Well, I'm Hordo, the Red Hawk's lieutenant. And what I want to know, what we all want to know, is why we shouldn't cut your miserable throat right here."

"Karela was leading me," Conan began, and cut off as Hordo launched a fist the size of a small ham at him. The big man's single eye bulged as Conan caught his fist in mid-swing and stopped it dead.

For a moment the two strained, arm to arm, biceps bulging, then Hordo shouted, "Take him!" The ring of bandits closed in.

Dozens of hands clutched at Conan, tearing away his cloak, ripping loose his sword, pulling him from the saddle. But their very numbers hampered them somewhat, and he did not go easily. His dagger found a new home in ribs clothed in dirty yellow—in the press he never saw the face that went with them—a carelessly reached arm was broken at the elbow, and more than one face erupted in blood and broken teeth from his massive fists. The numbers were too many, though, and rough hands at last managed to bind his wrists behind him and link his ankles with a two-foot hobble of rawhide. Then they threw him to the stony ground, and those who had boots began to apply them to his ribs.

Finally Hordo chased them back with snarled threats, and bent to jerk Conan's head up by a fistful of hair. "We call her the Red Hawk," he spat. "You call her mistress, or my lady. But don't ever sully her name with your filthy mouth again. Not as you live."

"Why should he live at all?" snarled a weasel-faced man in dented half-armor and a guardsman's helmet with the crest gone. "Hepakiah's choking to death on his own blood from this one's dagger right now." He grimaced suddenly and spat out a tooth. "Cut his throat, and be done!"

With a grin Hordo produced a wavy-bladed Vendhyan dagger. "Seems Aberius has a good idea for a change."

Suddenly Karela forced her horse through the pack around Conan, her green cat-eyes glaring down at him. "Can't you think of something more interesting, Hordo?"

"Still keeping your oath?" Conan snarled. "Fine payment for saving you from the slave block, or worse." Hordo's fist smashed his head back into the ground.

"No man ever had to save the Red Hawk," her lieutenant growled. "She's better than any man, with sword or brains. See you remember it."

Karela laughed sweetly. "Of course I am, good Conan. If anything happens to you, it will be at the hands of these good men, not mine. Hordo, let's take him to camp. You can decide what to do with him at leisure."

The scar-faced man shouted orders, and quickly a rope was passed around Conan, under his arms. The bandits scrambled to their saddles, Hordo himself clutching the rope tied to Conan, and they started off at a trot, the horses' hooves spraying dirt and gravel in Conan's face.

Conan gritted his teeth as he was dragged. With his arms behind him, he was forced to skid along on his belly. Sharp rocks gashed his chest, and hardpacked clay scraped off patches of skin as large as his hand.

When the horses skidded to a halt, Conan spat out a mouthful of dirt and sucked in air. He ached in every muscle, and small trickles of blood still oozed from those scrapes that dust had not clotted. He was far from sure that whatever they had planned for him would be better than being dragged to death.

"Hordo," Karela exclaimed in delight, "you have my tent up."

She leaped from the saddle and darted into a red-striped pavilion. It was the only tent in the camp lying in a hollow between two tall, U-shaped hills. Rumpled bedrolls lay scattered around half-a-dozen burned-out fires. Some of the men ran to stir these up, while others dug out stone jars of *kil*, raw distilled wine, and passed them around with raucous laughter.

Conan rolled onto his side as Hordo dismounted beside him. "You're a bandit," the big Cimmerian panted. "How would you like a chance at a king's treasure?"

Hordo did not even look at him. "Get those stakes in," he shouted. "I want him pegged out now."

"Five pendants," Conan said, "and a jewel-encrusted casket. Gifts from Yildiz to Tiridates." He hated letting these men know what he was after—at best he would have a hard time remaining alive to claim a share of what he thought of as his own —but otherwise he might not live to collect even a share.

"Stir your stumps," the bearded outlaw

shouted. "You can drink later."

"Ten thousand pieces of gold," Conan said. "That's what one man is willing to pay for the pendants alone. Someone else might pay more. And then there's the casket."

For the first time since arriving in the hollow Hordo turned to Conan, his one eye glaring. "The Red Hawk wants you dead. She's done good by us, so what she wants is what I want."

A score of bandits, laughing and already half-drunk, came to lift Conan and bear him to a cleared space where they had driven four stakes into the hard ground. Despite his struggles they were too many, and he soon found himself spread-eagled on his back, wet rawhide straps leading from his wrists and ankles to the stakes. The rawhide would shrink in the heat of the sun, stretching his joints to the breaking point.

"Why doesn't Hordo want you to have a chance at ten thousand pieces of gold?" Conan shouted. Every man but Hordo froze where he stood, the laughter dying in their throats.

With a curse the scar-faced brigand jumped forward. Conan tried to jerk his head aside, but lights flared before his eyes as the big man's foot caught him. "Shut your lying mouth!" Hordo snarled.

Aberius lifted his head to stare cold-eyed at the Red Hawk's lieutenant, a ferret confronting a mastiff. "What's he talking about, Hordo?"

Conan shook his head to clear it. "A king's treasure. That's what I'm talking about."

"You shut," Hordo began, but Aberius cut him off.

"Let him talk," the pinch-faced brigand said

dangerously, and other voices echoed him. Hordo glared about him, but said nothing.

Conan allowed himself a brief smile. A bit longer, and these cut-throats would turn him loose and bind Hordo and Karela in his place. But he did not intend to let them actually steal the pendants he had worked so hard for. "Five pendants," he said, "and a golden casket encrusted with gems were stolen from Tiridates' very palace not half a fortnight gone. I'm on the track of those trifles. One man's already offered me ten thousand pieces of gold for the pendants alone, but what one man offers another will top. The casket will bring as much again, or more."

The men encircling him licked their lips greedily, and shuffled closer. "What makes them worth so much?" Aberius asked shrewdly. "I never heard of pendants worth ten thousand gold pieces."

Conan managed a chuckle. "But these were gifts from King Yildiz to King Tiridates, gems that no man has ever seen before. And the same on the casket," he embroidered.

Abruptly Karela burst through the close-packed circle of men, and they edged back from the rage on her face. Gone were the makeshift garments she had acquired at the Well of the Kings. Silver fili-greed breastplates of gold barely contained her ivory breasts, and a girdle of pearls a finger wide hung low on her hips. Red thigh boots covered her legs, and the tulwar at her side had a sapphire the size of a pigeon's egg on the pommel.

"The dog lies," she snarled. The men took another step back, but there was raw greed on their faces. "He seeks no gemstones, but a slave girl. He

told me so himself. He's naught but a muscle-
bound slave catcher for some besotted fool in
Shadizar. Tell them you lie, Conan!"

"I speak the truth." Or some of it, he thought.

She whirled on him, knuckles white on the hilt of
her sword. "Spawn of a maggot! Admit you lie, or
I'll have you flayed alive."

"You've broken half your oath," he said
calmly. "Uncivil words."

"Derketo take you!" With a howl of rage she
planted the toe of one red boot solidly in his ribs.
He could not contain a grunt of pain. "Think of
something lingering, Hordo," she commanded.
"He'll admit his lies soon enough then." Suddenly
she spun on her heel, drawing her sword till a hand-
breadth of razor-sharp blue steel showed above the
worked leather scabbard. "Unless one of you has a
mind to challenge my orders?"

A chorus of protests rose, and to Conan's amazement more than one gnarled and scarred face was
filled with fear. With a satisfied nod Karela
slammed the tulwar back into its sheath and strode
away toward her tent. Men half-fell in their haste
to get out of her way.

"The second part of your oath," Conan shouted
after her. "You struck me. You're foresworn
before Derketo. What vengeance will the goddess
of love and death take on you, and on any who
follow you?"

Her stride faltered for an instant, but she went
on without turning. The doorflap of the red-striped
pavilion was drawn behind her.

"You'll die easier, Conan," Hordo said, "if you
watch your tongue. I've a mind to rip it out of you

now, but some of the lads might want to hear if
you babble more of this supposed treasure."

"You act like whipped curs around her," Conan
said. "Have none of you ever thought for yourselves?"

Hordo shook his shaggy head. "I'll tell you a
tale, and if you make me speak of it again I'll
skewer your liver. From whence she came no one
knows, but we found her wandering naked as a
babe, and little more than one she was, in years,
but with that sword she now wears clutched in her
fist. He that led us then, Constanius by name,
thought to have his sport with her, then sell her. He
was the best of us with a sword, but she killed him
like a fox killing a chicken, and when two who were
close to him tried to take her, she killed them, too,
and just as quick. Since then we've followed her.
The looting she leads us to has always been good,
and no man who did as he was told has ever been
taken. She commands, and we obey, and we're
satisfied."

Hordo went away then, and Conan listened to
the others talking as they drank around the fires.
Amid coarse laughter they discussed what sport
would be had of him. Hot coals were much talked
of, and the uses of burning splinters, and how
much of a man's skin might be removed and yet
leave him living.

The sun blazed higher and hotter. Conan's
tongue swelled in his mouth with thirst, and his lips
cracked and blackened. Sweat dried on his body till
no more came, and the sun scored his flesh. Aberius and another fish-eyed rogue staggered over and
amused themselves by pouring water on the ground

beside his head, betting on how close they could come to his mouth without letting a drop fall where he could reach it. Even when the clear stream was so close he could feel the coolness of it on his cheek, Conan refused to turn his head toward it. He would not give them so much satisfaction.

In time the other man left, and Aberius squatted at Conan's head with the clay waterbottle cradled in his arms. "You'd kill for water, wouldn't you?" the weasel-faced man said softly. He glanced warily over his shoulder at the other bandits, still drinking and shouting of what tortures they would inflict on the big Cimmerian, then went on. "Tell me about this treasure, and I'll give you water."

"Ten—thousand—gold—pieces," Conan croaked. The words scraped like gravel across his dry tongue. Aberius licked his lips eagerly. "More. Where is this treasure? Tell me, and I'll convince the others to set you free."

"Free—first," Conan managed.

"Fool! The only way you'll get free at all is with my help. Now, tell me where to find—" He squawked suddenly as Hordo's big hand snatched him into the air by the scruff of his neck.

The one-eyed brigand shook the rat of a man, Aberius' feet dangling above the ground. "What are you doing?" Hordo demanded. "He's not for talking with."

"Just having a little sport," Aberius laughed weakly. "Just taunting him."

"Taunting," Hordo spat. He threw the smaller man sprawling in the dust. "It's more than taunting we'll do to him. You get on back to the rest." He waited while Alberius scrambled, half-crawling, to where the other brigands watched laughing, then turned back to Conan. "Make peace with your gods, barbar. You'll have no time later."

Conan worked his mouth for enough moisture to get out a few painful words. "Letting her do you out of the gold, Hordo."

"You don't learn, do you, barbar?"

Conan had just time to see the booted foot coming, then the world seemed to explode.

IX

When the Cimmerian regained consciousness, it was black night and the fires were burning low. A few brigands still squatted in muttered conversation, passing their stone jars of *kil*, but most were sprawled in drunken snoring. There was a light in the pavilion—Conan watched Karela's well-curved silhouette on the striped tent wall—but even as he watched it was extinguished.

The rawhide cords had tightened until they dug into his wrists. Feeling was almost gone from his hands. If he remained there much longer he would not be able to fight even were he to get free. His massive arms corded. There was no give to his bonds. Again he pulled, his body knotting down to the rippled-iron muscles of his stomach with the strain. Again. Again. Blood stained his wrists from the cutting rawhide, and wet the ground. Again he pulled. Again. And there was a slackness to the cord at his left wrist. No more than a fingers-breadth, but it was there.

Suddenly he froze. The feeling that had come in the camp with Karela, of eyes on him, was back. And more than back, for his senses told him the watcher was coming closer. Warily he looked around. The men by the low-burning fire had sunk into sodden mounds, making as much noise asleep as they had awake. The camp was still. Yet he could still feel those eyes approaching. His hackles rose, for he was sure the bearer of those watching eyes now stood over him, staring down, but there was nothing there.

Angrily he began to jerk at the rawhide binding his left wrist, harder and harder despite the quickened flow of blood and the burning pain that circled his wrist. If there was something standing above him—and he had seen enough in his life to know that there were many things not visible to the eye—he would not lie for it like a sheep at slaughter.

Rage fueled his muscles, and suddenly the stake tore free of the ground. Immediately he rolled to his right, clutching that cord in both hands and pulling with all his might. Slowly the second stake pulled out of the hard-packed earth.

Conan's bones creaked as he sat up. The lacerated flesh of his wrists had swollen to hide the cords. Diligently he worked to loose them, then freed his ankles. The craving in him for water was enough to send another man for the nearest water-bag, but he forced himself to work some suppleness back into his stiffened muscles before he moved. When he rose, if he was not at full strength he was nonetheless a formidible opponent.

In pantherine silence he moved among the sleep-

ing men. It would have been easy for him to slay
them where they lay, but killing drunken men in
their stupor was not his way. He retrieved his
sword and dagger and fastened them on. His red
Turanian half-boots he found discarded by the
coals of a burned-out fire. Of his cloak there was
no sign, and he had no hope of recovering the coins
from his purse. He would have to search every man
there. Still, he thought as he stamped his feet to
settle his boots, as soon as he could get to their
horses he would be back on the trail of the pendants. He would take the precaution of scattering
the rest of the mounts before he left. There was no
need to leave the brigands able to pursue.

"Conan!" The shout rolled through the hollow
as if launched from a dozen throats, but there was
only one shape approaching the camp.

The Cimmerian cursed as bandits stirred from
their sodden sleep and sat up. He was in their midst
with no way out short of fighting, now. He drew
his broadsword as a light appeared in Karela's
striped tent.

"Conan! Where are the pendants?"

That booming voice stirred something in
Conan's mind. He was sure he had heard it before.
But the heavily muscled man approaching was
unfamiliar. A spiked helmet covered the man's
head, and a chain mail tunic descended to his
knees. In his right hand he gripped a great double-
bladed ax, in the other a round buckler.

"Who are you?" Conan called.

The brigands were all on their feet now, and
Karela was before her pavilion with her jeweled
tulwar in hand.

"I am Crato." The armored man came to a halt an arm's reach from Conan. Beneath his helm his eyes were glassy and unblinking. "I am the servant of Imhep-Aton. Where are the pendants you were to bring him?"

A chill ran down Conan's back. He knew the voice, now. It was the voice of Ankar.

From behind Conan the voice of Aberius rang out. "He was telling the truth. There are pendants."

"I don't have them, Ankar," Conan said. "I'm chasing the men who stole them, and a girl I made a promise to."

"You know too much," the big man muttered in Imhep-Aton's voice. "And you do not have the pendants. Your usefulness is at an end, Cimmerian."

With no more warning the ax leaped toward Conan. The Cimmerian jumped back, the razor steel drawing a fine red line across his chest. The possessed man recovered quickly and moved in, buckler held across his body, ax at the ready well to his side. If a sorcerer controlled the body, the man whose once it had been was an experienced ax fighter.

Conan danced back, broadsword flickering in snakelike thrusts. A slashing attack would leave him open, and that ax could cut a man half in two. Crato continued his slow advance, catching each sword thrust with his buckler. Watching those lifeless eyes was useless, Conan quickly realized. Instead he watched the massive shoulders for the involuntary movements that would foretell the big man's attacks.

The mailed right shoulder dipped fractionally, and Conan dropped to his heels as the ax whistled over his head. His broadsword darted out to stab through the mail at a thigh, then he was rolling away from the return ax-stroke to come once more erect facing his opponent. Blood ran down the ax-man's leg, but he came on.

Conan circled to the other's right, toward the ax. It would be more difficult for Crato to strike at him, thus. The ax slashed out in an awkward backhand blow. Conan swung, felt his blade bite through bone, and ax and severed hand fell together. On the instant Crato hurled his buckler at Conan's head and threw himself in a roll across the ground. Conan ducked, beat the round shield aside with his sword, but even as he recovered Crato was coming to his feet with the battle-ax in his left hand.

Blood pumped from the stump in regular spurts, and the man—or the sorcerer possessing him—seemed to know he was dying. Screaming, he rushed at the Cimmerian, ax slashing wildly. Conan caught the haft on his blade and smashed a knee into the other's midriff. The big Shemite staggered, but his great ax went up for another stroke. Conan's broadsword slashed into the man's shoulder, half-severing the ax arm. Crato sank to his knees, his mouth opening wide.

"Conan!" Imhep-Aton's voice screamed. "You will die!"

Conan's blade leaped forward once more, and the helmeted head rolled in the dust. "Not yet," the Cimmerian said grimly.

When he raised his gaze from the headless body

on the ground Conan found the bandits had
formed a ring around him. Some had swords in
hand, others merely looked. Karela faced him with
the curved blade of her tulwar bare. She glanced at
the dead man, but kept her main attention on the
big Cimmerian. Her gaze was oddly uncertain, her
head tilted to watch him from the corner of her
eye.

"Trying to leave us, Conan?" she said. "Whoever this Crato was, we owe him thanks for stopping you."

"The pendants!" someone called from among
the gathered men. "The pendants are real."

"Who spoke?" Hordo demanded. The Red
Hawk's bearded lieutenant lashed them with his
eye, and some dropped their heads. "Whatever's
real or isn't, the Red Hawk says this man deserves
to die."

"Twenty thousand gold pieces sound very real to
me," Aberius replied. "Too real to be hasty."

Hordo's jaw worked angrily. He started for the
smaller man, and stopped with a surprised look at
Karela as she laid her blade across his chest. She
shook her head without speaking and took the
sword away.

Conan eyed the woman, too, wondering what
was in her head. Her face was unreadable, and she
still did not look directly at him. He had no
intention of sharing the pendants, but if her mind
was changing on the matter he might yet leave that
hollow between the hills without more fighting.

"They're real, all right," he said loudly. "A
king's treasure, maybe worth more than twenty
thousand." He had to pause to work enough

moisture into his throat to speak, but he would not ask for water. The slightest sign of weakness now, and they could well decide to torture what he knew from him. "I can take you to the thieves. And mark you, men who steal from kings are likely to have other trinkets about." He turned slowly to catch each man's gaze in turn. "Rubies. Emeralds. Diamonds and pearls. Sacks bulging with gold coin." Avarice lit their eyes, and greed painted their faces.

"Gold, is it?" Hordo snorted. "And where are we to find all this wealth? In a palace, or a fortress, with stone walls and well-armed guards?"

"With the men I follow," Conan said. "Hooded men claiming to be pilgrims. They took five women when they stole the rest. Dancing girls from the court of Yildiz. One of those is mine, but the other four will no doubt he attracted to brave men with gold in their fists." Lecherous laughter rose, and one or two of the brigands swaggered posingly.

"Hooded men, you say?" Aberius said, frowning. "And five women?"

"Enough!" Hordo roared. "By the Black Throne of Erlik, don't you all see there are sorcerers in this? Did none of you look closely enough at this Crato to see he was possessed? Didn't you see his eyes, or listen to him speak? No mortal man has a voice like that, booming like thunder in the distance."

"He was mortal enough," muttered a thick-set man with a broad scar across his nose. "Conan's steel proved that."

"And what is sought by wizards," Conan said, "is doubly valuable. Did anyone ever hear of a wizard grasping for something that was not worth a king's crown?''

Hordo looked uncertainly at Karela, but she stood listening as if the talk had no connection to her. The one-eyed man muttered under his breath, then went on. ''Where do we seek these hooded men? The country is wide. What direction do we ride? Conan himself has said he has no idea. He followed the Red Hawk thinking she'd lead him to them.''

''I saw them,'' Aberius said, and stared about him defiantly as everyone turned to look at him. ''I, and Hepekiah, and Alvar. Two days gone, riding to the east. A score of hooded men, and five bound women on camels. Speak, Alvar.''

The thickset man with the scarred nose nodded heavily. ''Aye, we saw them.''

''They were too many for the three of us,'' Aberius went on hurriedly, ''and when we came here to the meeting place, the Red Hawk had not yet come, so we didn't speak of it. You never let us make a move without her, Hordo.'' A mutter of angry assent rose.

Hordo glared, but there was satisfaction in his voice when he said, ''Two days gone? They could be in Vendhya for all the good it does us.''

The mutter grew in intensity, and Aberius took a step toward the huge, bearded man. ''Why say you so? All here know I can track a lizard over stone, or a bird through the air. A two days' trail is a beaten path for me.''

''And what of Hepekiah?'' Hordo growled. ''Have you forgotten the Cimmerian's blade in your friend's ribs?''

The weasel-faced man shrugged. "Gold buys new friends."

Hordo threw up his hands and turned to Karela. "You must speak. What are we to do? Does this Conan die, or not?"

The auburn-haired woman looked fully at Conan for the first time, her tilted green eyes cool and expressionless. "He's a good fighting man, and we may have need of such when we overtake these hooded men. Strike camp, and bring his horse."

Shouting excitedly and laughing, the bandits scattered. Hordo glared at the Cimmerian, then shook his head and stalked away. In an instant the camp was a stirred anthill, the pavilion going down, horses being saddled and blankets rolled. Conan stood looking at Karela, for she had not moved an inch, nor taken her eyes from his face.

"Who is this woman?" she said suddenly. Her voice was flat and expressionless. "The one you say is yours."

"A slave girl," he replied, "as I said."

Her face remained calm, but she sheathed her sword as if slamming it into his heart. "You trouble me, Conan of Cimmeria. See you do not come to trouble me too much." Spinning on her heel she marched toward the horses.

Conan sighed and looked to the east, where the red sun was just broaching the horizon. The night's dew had cleared the dust from the air, and it seemed he could see forever.

All he had to do now was find the hooded men, free Velita and take the pendants, all the while watching his back for a knife from some brigand who decided they had no need of him after all, and keeping an eye on Karela's mercurial temper. Then, of course, there was the matter of relieving the bandits of the pendants in turn, not to mention finding a new purchaser, for in Conan's eyes Crato's attack had finished his agreement with Ankar, or Imhep-Aton, or whatever his real name was. It was just his luck the man seemed to be a magician. But he had a tidy enough bundle without adding that worry to it. All he needed now, he thought, was the Zamoran army. He went in search of his cloak. And a water skin.

X

Puffs of dust lifted beneath the hooves of the column of Zamoran cavalry, a company strong, as they crossed rolling hills sparsely covered with low scrub. Their lance points and chain mail were blackened against reflecting the sun. They rode in a double line, round shields hanging ready to hand beside their saddles, with Haranides at their head, hard men, hand-picked by the captain, veterans of campaigning on the borders.

Haranides unconsciously shifted his buttocks on the hard leather of his saddle as he turned his head continually from side to side, watching, hoping, for a flash of light. With naught to go on but a direction, he had had to take a chance. Half his command was scattered in a line abreast on either side of him, and then only when both topped a hill. Every one of them had a metal mirror, and if any sign of a trail was found . . . .

He grimaced as his second in command, Aheranates, galloped up beside him from his place immediately before the column. A slender youth with smooth-shaven fine-featured face and big dark eyes more suited to flirting with a palace wench than looking on death, Aheranates had been foisted on him at the last minute. Ten years younger than Haranides, in two he would outrank him. His father, much in favor with the king, wanted his son to gain a touch of seasoning, and incidentally to share in the glory of bringing the Red Hawk before the king bound in chains.

"What do you want?" Haranides growled. If he succeeded on this mission, he would not need the good opinion of the youth's father. If he failed, the man could not save him from the king's threat.

"I've been wondering why we're not pursuing the Red Hawk," Aheranates said. Haranides looked at him, and he added, "Sir. Those were our orders, were they not? Sir?"

Haranides restrained his temper with no little effort. "And where would you pursue, lieutenant? In what direction? Or is it just that this isn't dashing enough for someone used to the glitter of parades in the capital?"

"Not the way I was taught to handle cavalry. Sir."

"And where in Sheol were you taught . . . ." A flash of light to the east caught his words in his throat. Once. Twice. Thrice. "Signal recall, lieutenant. By mirror," he added as the other pulled his horse around. "No need to let every running dog know we're out. And bring the company around."

"As you command. Sir."

For once Haranides did not notice the sarcasm.

This had to be what he sought. By Mitra, it had to be. He could barely restrain himself from galloping ahead of his troop, but he forced himself to keep the march to a walk. The horses must be conserved if there was a pursuit close at hand, and he prayed there would be.

The men strung out to the east waited once they had passed on the signal, each man falling in behind the column as it reached him. Those beyond the man who first flashed his sighting would be riding west to join them. If this was a false alarm, Haranides thought . . . .

Then they topped another hill, and before them was a small knot of his men. As he rode closer another rider rejoined from the east. Haranides finally allowed himself to kick his mount into a gallop. One of the soldiers rode forward, touching his forehead respectfully.

"Sir, it looks to have been a camp, but there's . . ."

Haranides waved him to silence. He could see what was unusual about this hollow between two hills. Black-winged vultures, their bald heads glistening red from their feeding, stood on the ground warily watching the quartet of jackals that had driven them from their feast.

"Wait here until I signal," Haranides commanded, and walked his horse down into the hollow. He counted the ash piles of ten burnt-out fires.

The jackals backed away from the mounted man, snarling, then snatched bones still bearing shreds of scarlet flesh and loped away. The vultures shifted their beady-eyed gaze from the

jackals to Haranides. A half-eaten skull showed
the thing on the ground had once been a man, but
it could never have been proven by the scattered
bones, cracked by the jackals' powerful jaws.
Haranides looked up as Aheranates galloped down
the hill.

"Mitra! What's that?"

"Proof there were bandits here, lieutenant.
None else would leave a dead man for the
scavengers."

"I'll bring the men down to search for—"

"You'll dismount ten men," Haranides said pa-
tiently, "and bring them down." He could afford
to be patient, now. He was sure of it. "No need to
grind what little we might find under the horses'
hooves. And lieutenant? Tell off two men to bury
that. See to it yourself."

Aheranates had been avoiding looking at the
bloody bones. Now his face abruptly turned green.
"Me? But—"

"Now, lieutenant. The Red Hawk, and your
glory are getting further away all the time."

The lieutenant stared open-mouthed, then
swallowed and jerked his horse around. Haranides
did not watch him go. The captain dismounted and
slowly led his horse through the site of the camp.
Around the remains of the fires was scruffed
ground where men had slept. Perhaps fifty, he
estimated. Well away from the fires were holes
from the pegs and poles of a large tent. Four other
holes, though, spaced in a large square, interested
him more.

A short, bowlegged cavalryman trotted up and
touched his sloping forehead. "Begging your par-

don, sir, but the lieutenant said I was to tell you he found where they had their horses picketed.'' His voice became flatly noncommittal. ''The lieutenant says to tell you there was maybe a hundred horses, sir.''

Haranides looked to where two men were digging a hole in the hillside for the remains of the body. Aheranates apparently had decided he should search rather than oversee their work as ordered. ''You've been twenty years and more in the cavalry, Resaro,'' the captain said. ''How many horses would you say were on that picket line? If the lieutenant hadn't said a hundred, of course,'' he added when the man hesitated.

''Not to contradict the lieutenant, sir, but I'd say fifty-three. They didn't clear away the dung, and they kept the horses apart enough to keep the piles separate. Some would be sumpter animals, of course, sir.''

''Very good, Resaro. Go back to the lieutenant and tell him I want . . . .'' He stopped at the strained look on Resaro's face. ''Is there something else you want to tell me?''

The stumpy man shifted awkwardly. ''Well, sir, the lieutenant said we was mistaken, but Caresus and me, we found the way they went when they left here. They brushed their tracks some, but not enough. They went east, and a little north.''

''You're sure of that?'' Haranides said sharply.

''Yes, sir.''

The captain nodded slowly. Toward the Kezankian Mountains, but not toward the caravan route through the mountains to Sultanapur. ''Tell the lieutenant I want to see him, Resaro.'' The cavalryman touched his forehead and backed away. Haranides climbed the eastern hill to stare toward the Kenzankian Mountains, out of view beyond the horizon.

When Aheranates joined him, the lieutenant was carrying a stone unguent jar. "Found this down where the tent was," he said. "Someone had his leman along, seems."

Haranides took the jar. Empty, it still held the flowery fragrance of the perfume of Ophir. He toss it back to Aheranates. "More like than not, your first souvenir of the Red Hawk."

The lieutenant gaped. "But how can you be certain this was the trull's camp? It could as easily be a . . . a caravan, wandered somewhat from the route. The man could have been left for some errand and been slain by wild animals. He could even have had no connection with those who camped here at all. He could have come after, and—"

"A man was staked out down there," Haranides said coldly. "'Tis my thought was the dead man. Secondly, no camels were here. Have you ever seen a caravan lacking camels, saving a slaver's? And there is no staking ground for a coffle. Thirdly, there was only one tent. A caravan of this size would have had half a score. And lastly, why have you lost your fervor for pursuing the Red Hawk? Can it be your thought that she has a hundred men with her? Fear not. There are fewer than fifty, though I grant you they may seem a hundred if it comes to steel."

"You have no right! Manerxes, my father, is—"

"Sir, lieutenant! Prepare the men to move out.

Along that trail you thought not worth mention-
ing.''

For a moment they stood eye to eye, Haranides
coldly contemptuous, Aheranates quivering with
rage. Abruptly the lieutenant tossed the unguent
jar to the ground. ''Yes, sir!'' he grated, and
turned on his heel to stalk down the hill.

Haranides bent to pick up the smooth stone jar.
The flowery fragrance gave him a dim picture of
the woman, one at odds with the coarse trollop
with a sword he expected. But why was she riding
toward the Kezankian Mountains? The answer to
that could be of vital importance to him. Success,
and Aharesus would smooth his path to the top.
Failure, and the King's Counselor would give him
not a thought as Tiridates had his head put over the
West Gate. Placing the jar in his pouch, he went
down to join his men.

XI

As the bandits climbed higher into the
Kezankian Mountains, Conan stopped at every rise
to look behind. Beyond the rolling foothills, on the
plain they had left a day gone, something moved.
Conan estimated the lead the brigands had, and
wondered if it was enough.

"What are you staring at?" Hordo demanded,
reining in beside the Cimmerian. The outlaws were
straggling up a sparsely treed mountainside toward
a sheer-walled pass in the dark granite. Karela, as
always, rode well in the lead, her gold-lined
emerald cape flowing in the wind.

"Soldiers," Conan replied.

"Soldiers! Where?"

Conan pointed. A black snake of men inched
toward the foothills, seeming to move through
shimmering air rather than on solid ground. Only
soldiers would maintain such discipline marching
through those waterless approaches to the mountains. They were yet distant, but even as the two

men watched the snake appeared to grow larger. On the plain the soldiers moved faster than the bandits in the mountains. The gap would close further.

"No matter," the one-eyed man muttered. "They'll not catch us up here."

"Dividing the loot, are you?" Aberius kicked his horses in the ribs, and the beast scrambled up beside the other two. "Best you wait till it's in our grasp. You might not be one of those left alive to . . . . What's that? Out there. Riders."

Others heard him and turned in their saddles to look. "Hillmen?" a hook-nosed Iranistani named Reza said hesitantly.

"Can't be," a bearded Kothian replied. His name was Talbor, and the tip of his nose had been bitten off. "Hillmen don't raid far from the mountains."

"And not so many together," Aberius agreed. His glower included both Conan and Hordo. "Soldiers, be they not? It's soldiers you've brought on us."

An excited gabble went up from the men gathered around them. "Soldiers!" "The army's on us!" "Our heads on pikes!" "A whole regiment!" "The King's Own!"

"Still your tongues!" Hordo shouted. "There's no more than two hundred, to my eye, and a day behind us, at that."

"'Tis still five to one against," Aberius said. "Or near enough as makes no difference."

"These mountains are not our place," Reza cried. "We be rats in a box."

"Ferrets in a woodpile," Hordo protested. "If

this is not our own ground, still less is it theirs."
The rest paid him no mind.

"We chase mists," Talbor shouted, rising in his
stirrups to address the bandits who were gathering.
"We ride into these accursed mountains after
ghosts. It'll not stop till we find ourselves with our
backs to a rock wall and Zamoran lances at our
throats."

Aberius sawed his reins, and his horse pranced
dangerously on the steeply sloping ground. "Do
you question my tracking, Talbor? The path we
follow is the path taken by those I saw." He laid
hand to his sword hilt.

"You threaten me, Aberius?" the Kothian
growled. His fingers slid from his pommel toward
the tulwar at his hip.

Karela spurred suddenly into their midst, her
naked sword in hand. "I'll kill the first man to bare
an inch of blade," she announced heatedly. Her
cat-like eyes flicked each man in turn; both
hurriedly removed their hands from their weapons.
"Now tell me what has you at each other's throats
like dancing girls in a zenana."

"The soldiers," Aberius began.

"These supposed pendants," Talbor started at
the same instant.

"Soldiers!" Kareia said. She jerked her head
around, and seemed to breathe a sigh of relief
when she spotted the distant line of men on the
plain below. "Fear you soldiers so far away,
Aberius?" she sneered. "What would you fear
closer? An old woman with a stick?"

"I like not being followed by anyone," Aberius
replied sulkily. "Or think you they follow us not?"

"I care not if they follow us or no," she flared. "You are the Red Hawk's men! An you follow me, you'll fear what I tell you to fear and naught else. Now all of you get up ahead. There's level ground there where we'll camp the night."

"There's a half a day yet we could travel," Hordo protested.

She rounded on him, green eyes flashing. "Did you not hear my command? I said we camp! You, Cimmerian, remain here."

Her one-eyed lieutenant grumbled, but turned his horse up the mountain, and the rest followed in sullen silence broken only by the creak of saddle leather and the slick of hooves on stone.

Conan watched the red-haired woman warily. She hefted her sword as if she had half a mind to drive it into him, then sheathed it. "Who is this girl, Conan? What is her name?"

"She's called Velita," he said. He had told her of Velita before, and knew she remembered the dancing girl's name. In time she would come to what she truly wanted to speak of. He twisted around for another look at the column of soldiers. "They gain ground on us, Karela. We should keep moving."

"We move when I say. And stop when I say. Do you think to play some game, Conan?

He turned back to her. Her green eyes were clouded with emotion as she stared at him. What emotion he could not say. "I play no more games than you, Karela."

Her snort was eloquent. "Treasures taken from a king's palace, so you say, not to mention this baggage you claim to have promised her freedom.

Why then do the thieves flee to these mountains, where none live but goats, and savages little better than goats?''

"I don't know,'' he admitted. "But it convinces me all the more they are the men I seek. Honest pilgrims do not journey to Vendhya by way of the heart of the Kezankian Mountains.''

"Perhaps,'' she said, and shifted her gaze to the soldiers, far below. With a laugh she reared her big black to dance on its hind legs. "Fools. They'll not clip the Red Hawk's wings.''

"It seems most likely they seek Tiridates' pendants, as we do,'' he said. "Much more so than that they seek you.''

The red-haired woman glowered at him. "The Zamoran Army seeks me incessantly, Cimmerian. Of course, they'll never catch me. When their hunting becomes too troublesome, my men disperse to become guards on the very caravan routes we raid. The pay is high, for fear of the Red Hawk.'' Her sudden laugh was exultant.

To his amusement he realized she had been offended by his suggestion that the soldiers hunted other than her. "Your pardon, Karela. I should have remembered that taking seven caravans in six months would certainly rival even a theft from Tiridates' palace.''

"I had naught to do with those,'' she said scornfully. "No creature from those caravans, man, horse, or camel, has ever been seen again. When I take a caravan, those too old or ill-favored to fetch a price on the slave block are turned loose with food and water to find their way to the nearest city, albeit poorer than before.''

"If not you, then who?"

"How should I know? The last caravan I took was a full eight months ago, and fat. When we left our celebrating in Arenjun it was to find the countryside too hot to hold us for those vanished caravans. I sent my men to their hiring, and these four months past have I been in Shadizar telling cards beneath the very noses of the King's Own." Her full mouth twisted. "I would be there still, if the risk of calling my band together once more had not seemed less than the odium of being eyed by men who thought to give me a tumble." Her glare seemed to include him and every other man in the world.

"Strange things are happening in the Kezankians," Conan said thoughtfully. "Perhaps those we follow have something to do with the vanished caravans."

"You make flight of fancy," she muttered, and he realized she was eyeing him oddly. "Come to my tent, Cimmerian. I would talk with you." She spurred away up the mountainside before he could speak.

Conan was about to follow when he became aware of being watched from the jagged mountains to the south. His first thought was of Kezankian hillmen, but then, as the hackles stood on the back of his neck, he knew it was the same invisible eyes he had felt that night with Karela, and again before Crato appeared. Imhep-Aton had followed him.

His massive shoulders squared, and he threw back his head. "I do not fear you, sorcerer!" he shouted. A hollow, ringing echo floated back to him. *Fear you, sorcerer!* Scowling, he spurred his horse up the mountain.

Karela's red-striped pavilion had been set up on a level patch of stony ground. Already the motley brigands had cook fires going, and were passing their stone jars of *kil*.

"What was that shouting?" Aberius called as Conan climbed down from his horse.

"Nothing," Conan said.

The weasel-faced man led a knot of ruffians down to face him warily. When he casually laid his hand on the leather-wrapped hilt of his sword, the memory of how he had used that sword against Crato was clear on those bearded, scarred and gnarled faces.

"Some of us have thought on these soldiers," Aberius said.

"You have thought," another muttered, but Aberius ignored him.

"And what have you thought?" Conan asked.

Aberius hesitated, looking to either side as if for support. There was scant to be found, but he went on. "Never before have we come into these mountains, excepting to hide a day. Here there is no room to scatter. We must go where the stone will let us go, not where we will. And this when five times our number of soldiers follow our back-trail."

"If you've lost your enthusiasm," Conan said, "leave. I'd as lief go on alone as not."

"Aye, and take the pendants alone," Aberius barked, "and the rest. You'd like it well for us to leave you."

Conan's sapphire eyes raked them scornfully. Even Aberius flinched under that lashing gaze.

"Make up your minds. Fear the soldiers and run, or follow the pendants. One or the other. You cannot do both."

"And you bring us to where these soldiers can take us," Aberius began, "you'll not live—"

Conan cut him off. "You do as you will. On the morrow I ride after the pendants." He pushed through them. They muttered fretfully as he went.

He found himself wondering if it would be better for him if they stayed or went. They still had no right to the pendants, in his eyes, but now that they were in the mountains he could use Aberius' tracking ability, at least. The man could tell the mark a hoof made on stone from that made by a falling rock. That was always supposing the weasel-faced brigand did not decide to slip a knife between his ribs. The muscular young Cimmerian sighed heavily. What had started out to be a simple, if spectacular, theft, had grown as convoluted as a pit of snakes, and he had the uneasy feeling that he was not yet aware of all the twists and turns.

As he approached Karela's red-striped pavilion, with half its ropes tied to small boulders because the ground was too hard for driving pegs, Hordo suddenly stepped in front of him.

"Where do you think you're going?" the one-eyed bandit demanded.

Conan's temper had been shortened by knowing Imhep-Aton followed him, and by the encounter with Aberius. "Where I want to go," he growled, and pushed the scar-faced man from his path.

The startled brigand stumbled aside as Conan started past, then whirled, his broadsword coming out, at the whisper of steel leaving leather. Hordo's tulwar darted toward him. Conan beat the curved blade aside in the same motion as his draw, and the bearded man danced backward down the slope with surprising agility for one of his bulk. The scar that ran from under his rough leather eye-patch was livid.

"You have muscles, Cimmerian," he grated, "but no brains. You think above yourself."

Conan's laugh was short and mirthless. "Do you think I intend to displace you as lieutenant? I'm a thief, not a raider of caravans. But you do as you think you must." His broadsword was a heavy weapon, but he made it sing in interlocked figure eights about his head and to either side.

"Put up your blades!" came Karela's voice from behind him.

Without taking his gaze totally from Hordo, Conan took two quick steps to his left, turning so he could see both the bearded bandit and the red-haired woman. She stood in the entrance of the pavilion, her emerald cape drawn close to cover her from her neck to the ground. Her green-eyed gaze regarded them imperiously.

"He sought your tent," Hordo muttered.

"As I commanded him," she replied coldly. "You, at least, Hordo, should know I don't allow men of my band to draw weapons on each other. I'd have killed Aberius and Talbor for it. You two are more valuable. Shall I let each of you consider it the night with his hands and feet bound in the small of his back?"

Hordo seemed shaken by her anger. He sheathed his sword. "I was but trying to protect you," he protested.

The muscles along her jaw tightened. "Think you I need protection? Go, Hordo, before I forget the years you've served me well." The one-eyed man hesitated, cast a sharp glance at Conan, then stalked off toward the fires.

"You talk more like a queen than a bandit," Conan said finally, replacing his sword in its worn shagreen scabbard. She stared at him, but he met her gaze firmly.

"Others end at the headsman's block, or on the slave block, but none of mine has ever been taken, Conan. Because I demand discipline. Oh, not the foolishness soldiers call discipline, but any command I give must be obeyed at once. Any command. In this band the Red Hawk's word is law, and those who cannot accept that must leave or die."

"I am no hand at obedience," he said quietly.

"Come inside," she said, and disappeared through the entrance. Conan followed.

The ground inside the striped pavilion had been laid with fine, fringed Turanian carpets. A bed of glossy black furs, with silken pillows and soft, striped woolen blankets, lay against a side of the tent. A low, highly polished table was surrounded by large cushions. Gilded oil lamps illumined all.

"Close the flap," she said. Her mouth worked, and she added with obvious effort, "Please."

Conan unfastened the flap and let it drop across the entrance. He was wary of this strange mood Karela seemed to be in. "You should be more careful with Hordo. He's the only one of this lot who's loyal to you instead of to your success."

"Hordo is more a faithful hound than a man,"

she said.

"The more fool you for thinking so. He's the best man out there."

"He is no man, as I mean a man." Abruptly she threw back the emerald cape, letting it fall to the rugs, and Conan could not stop the gasp that rose in his throat.

Karela stood before him naked, soft auburn hair falling about her shoulders. A single strand of matched pearls hung low around the curve of her hips, glowing against the ivory skin of her sweetly rounded belly. Her heavy, round breasts were rouged, and the musky scent of perfume drifted from her as she stood with one knee slightly bent, shoulders back, hands behind her, in a pose at once offering and defiant.

He took a step toward her, and there was suddenly a dagger in her hand, its needle blade no wider than her finger but long enough and more to reach his heart. Her tilted green eyes never left his face. "You walk among my rogues like a wolf among a pack of dogs, Cimmerian. Even Hordo is but half wolf beside you. No man has ever called me his, for men come to believe the calling. If a woman must be a man's slave, then I'll be no woman. I'll walk behind no man, fawning for his favor and leaping to his command. I am the Red Hawk. I command. I!"

With great care he lifted the dagger from her fingers and tossed it aside. "You are a woman, Karela, whether you admit it or no. Does there have to be one to command between us? I knew the chains of slavery when I was but sixteen, and I have

no desire to wish them on anyone.'' He lowered her
to the furs.

"An you betray me," she whispered, "I'll put
your head before my tent on a spear. I'll . . . ah,
Derketo." For a time she made no sounds that
came not unbidden to her lips.

XII

The private thaumaturgical chambers of Amanar were in the very top of the tallest tower of the keep, as far from the room of sacrifice as they could be and still remain within that dark fortress. He knew that Morath-Aminee was in no way limited to the columned room in the heart of the mountain, but distance yet gave an illusion of safety.

The walls of the circular stone room were lined with books bound in the skins of virgins, and light came from glass balls that hung from sconces glowing from a minor spell. There was no window, nor any opening save a single heavily barred, iron-bound door. The scent of incense hissing with colored flames on the coals of a bronze brazier warred with the odor of a noxious brew bubbling in a stone beaker above a fire stoked with human bones. On the tables, dried mummies waited to be powdered for philters, among carelessly scattered ewers of deadly venom and bundles of rare herbs and roots.

The necromancer himself stood watching the boiling brew, his attention rapt. The dark liquid began to froth higher. With but a moment's hesitation he removed the amulet from his neck. A chill climbed his backbone at being even so barely separated, but it was necessary. Before the black froth reached the rim of the beaker, he lowered the amulet by its chain until serpent and eagle alike were covered. The silver chain grew colder, bitter metal ice searing his preternaturally long fingers. The froth sank, but the black liquid bubbled even more fiercely. The stone of the beaker began to glow red.

> "Hand of a living man, powdered when dry
> Blood of an eagle, no more to fly
> Eye of the mongoose, tooth of the boar
> Heart of a virgin, soul of a whore
> Burn to their blackness, heat till they boil
> Dip in the periapt, confounding the roil."

Hands shaking with haste, Amanar removed the amulet. He wanted to wipe it dry on the instant and replace it about his neck, but this stage of the spell was critical. With long bronze tongs he lifted the stone beaker. Nearby, atop a white marble pedestal, was a small, clear crystal coffer, fragile seeming against even that smooth stone. Deliberately the mage tilted the tongs, pouring the boiling liquid over the gleaming box.

The words he muttered then were arcane, known only to him among the living. The scalding mixture struck the small coffer. The crystal shrieked as if it would shatter in ten thousand pieces. The liquid seemed to gather itself to fly away in steam. As if from a great distance, screams echoed in the room. Mongoose and boar. Virgin and whore. Abruptly there was silence. The noxious mix was gone, no drop of it remaining. The crystal walls of the coffer now contained gray clouds, shifting and swirling as if before a great wind.

Breathing heavily, Amanar set the beaker and tongs aside. Confidence was flowing back into him. The haven, however temporary, was prepared. He wiped the amulet clean, inspecting it minutely before placing it once more about his neck.

From below rose the dolorous tone of a great bronze gong. Smiling, the mage unbarred the door and took up the crystal coffer beneath his arm. The gong echoed hollowly again.

Amanar made his way directly to the alabaster-walled audience chamber, its domed ceiling held aloft by carven ivory columns as thick as a man's trunk. Behind his throne reared a great serpent of gold. The arms of the throne were hooded vipers of Koth, the legs adders of Vendhya, all of gold. As he surveyed the assemblage before him, the necromancer allowed no particle of his surprise to touch his face. The S'tarra he had expected knelt with heads bowed, while five young women he had definitely not expected, in gossamer silks, hands bound behind their backs, were forced to prostrate themselves before the throne.

Amanar sat, carefully holding the crystal coffer on his lap. "You have that which I sent you for?" he said.

Sitha stepped forward. "They brought this, master." The S'tarra Warden presented an ornate casket of worked gold, the lid set with gemstones.

The mage forced himself to move slowly, but still his fingers trembled as he opened the casket. One by one, four jewels the like of which no man had ever seen, mounted in pendants of silver or gold, were casually tossed on the mosaic floor. A blood-red pearl the size of a man's two thumbs. A diamond black as a raven's wing, and big as a hen's egg. A golden crystal heart that had come from the ground in that shape. A complex lattice of pale blue that could cut diamond. All were as nothing to him. His hand shook visibly as he removed the last, the most important. As long as the top joint of a man's finger, of midnight hue filled with red flecks that danced wildly as Amanar's palm cupped the stone, this was the pendant that must be kept from Morath-Aminee.

He waved the golden casket away. "Dispose of those trifles, Sitha." His S'tarra henchman bowed, and gathered the pendants.

Almost tenderly Amanar swathed the dark stone in silk, then laid it in the crystal coffer. When he replaced the lid, he breathed a sigh of relief. Safe, at last. Not even Morath-Aminee would be able to detect what was in there, for a time, at least. And before that could happen he would have found a new haven, far away, where the god-demon would never think to look.

Clutching the crystal box firmly, Amanar turned his attentions to the women lying before him with their faces pressed to the divers-colored tiles. They trembled, he noted with idle satisfaction.

"How came you by these women?" the mage demanded.

Surassa, who had led the foray, lifted a scaled head. The dark face was expressionless, the words sibilant. "Before Shadizar, master, we spoke the words you told us, and ate the powders, that the glamour might be on us, and none should see us enter."

"The women," Amanar said impatiently. "Not every last thing that happened." He sighed at the look of concentration that appeared in the S'tarra's red eyes. When they knew a thing by rote, it was difficult for them to separate one part.

"The palace, master," Surassa hissed finally. "We entered the palace of Tiridates unseen, but when we came to the place where that which you sent us to seek was to be, only the casket was to be found. Taking the casket, we searched then the palace. Questioning some, and slaying them for silence, we found the pendants about the necks of these women, and slew the men who were with them. Leaving then the palace, we found that, as you had warned us, the glamour had worn off. We donned the robes—"

"Silence," Amanar said, and the saurian creature's words ceased at once. For their limited intelligence he had commanded them to fetch the casket and all five pendants, fearing they might make a mistake in the pressure of the moment and bring the black diamond instead of that which he needed. Yet despite all his careful instructions they had managed to increase their risk of being caught by taking these women. Rage bubbled in him, made all the worse for knowing that punishing them would be like punishing dogs. They would accept whatever he did, and understand not a whit of why. The S'tarra, sensing something of his mood, shifted uneasily.

"Bring the women before me," the necromancer commanded.

Hastily the five women were pulled to their knees and the bare covering of their silks ripped away. With fearful eyes the kneeling, naked women watched Amanar rise. He walked thoughtfully down the line of them. Severally and together, they were beautiful, and just as important to him, their dread was palpable.

He stopped before a pale blonde with ivory satin skin. "Your name, girl?"

"Susa." He quirked an eyebrow, and she hastily added, "Master. I am called Susa, an it please you, master."

"You five are the dancing girls Yildiz sent to Tiridates?"

Her blue eyes were caught by his dark ones, growing more tremulous as he watched. "Yes, master," she quavered.

He stroked his chin and nodded. A king's dancing girls. Fitting for one who would come to rule the world. And when the last jot of amusement had been wrung from them, their puny souls could feed Morath-Aminee.

"Conan will free us," one of the girls suddenly burst out. "He will kill you."

Amanar walked slowly down the line to confront her. Slender and long of leg, her big, dark eyes stared defiance even as her supple body trembled. "And what is your name, girl?" His words were soft, but his tone brought a moan from her throat.

"Velita," she said at last.

He noted how her teeth had clamped lest she should say "master." There would be much pleasure in this one. "And who is this Conan who will rescue you?"

Velita merely trembled, but Surassa spoke. "Pardon, master, but there was one of that name spoken of in Shadizar. A thief who has grown troublesome."

"A thief!" Amanar laughed. "Well, little Velita. What shall I do about this rescue? Sitha, command the patrols, if they find this man Conan they are to bring me his skin. Not the man. Just the skin." Velita shrieked and crumpled forward to rest her sobbing head on her knees. Amanar laughed again. The other women watched him, terror-struck. But not enough, he thought. "Each night you will dance for me, all five of you. She who pleases me most will gain my bed for the night. The middle three will be whipped and sleep in chains. She who pleases me least . . ." he paused, feeling the anxiety grow " . . . will be given to Sitha. He is rough, but he knows still how to use a woman."

The kneeling women cast one horrified glance at the reptilian creature, now watching them avidly, and threw themselves prostrate, groveling, screaming, pleading. Amanar basked in the miasma of their terror. Surely this was what the god-demon felt when it consumed a soul. Stroking the crystal coffer and stroked by their shrieks, he strode from the chamber.

XIII

Conan eyed the ridge to the left of the narrow valley the bandits were traversing. There had been movement up there. Only a flicker, but his keen gaze had caught it. And there had been others.

He booted his horse forward along the winding trail to where Hordo rode. Karela was well to the front, fist on one red-booted thigh, surveying the mountainous countryside as if she headed an army rather than a motley band of two score brigands, snaking out behind her.

"We're being watched," Conan said as he came alongside the one-eyed bandit.

Hordo spat. "Think you I don't know that already?"

"Hillmen?"

"Of course." The lone eye frowned. "What else?"

"I don't know," Conan said. "But the one good chance I had, I saw a helmet, not a turban."

"The soldiers are still behind us," Hordo said

thoughtfully. "Talbor and Thanades will let us know if they begin to close."

The two bandits had been ordered to trail behind, keeping the Zamoran cavalry in sight. Conan refrained from suggesting they might have become affrighted apart from the band and fled, or that Karela was holding the soldiers in too much contempt. "Whoever they are, we'd best hope they don't attack us here."

Hordo looked at the steep, scrub-covered slopes rising on either side of the trail and grimaced. "Mitra! Pray they're not strong enough, though a dozen good men . . . ." He trailed off as Aberius appeared on the trail ahead, whipping his horse steadily.

"That looks ill," Conan said. Hordo merely grunted, and the two rode forward to reach Karela as the weasel-faced bandit galloped up.

"Hillmen," Aberius panted. Greasy sweat dotted his face. "Six score, maybe seven. Camped athwart the trail ahead. And they're breaking camp."

There was no need to discuss the danger. Kezankian hillmen admitted allegiance to no one but themselves, though both Turan and Zamora had tried futilely to subdue them. The fierce tribesmen's way with strangers was simple, short and deadly. One not of his clan, even another hillman, was an enemy, and enemies were for killing.

"Coming this way?" Karela said quietly. At Aberius' anxious nod she cursed under her breath.

"And the soldiers behind," Hordo growled.

Karela's green eyes flashed at the bearded man. "Do you grow frightened with age, Hordo?"

"I've no desires to be between the sledge and the stone," Hordo replied, "and my age has naught to do with it."

"Watch you don't become an old woman," she sneered. "We'll leave the trail, and let the hillmen and the soldiers exhaust themselves on each other. Mayhap we'll have a good view from the ridge."

Conan laughed, and tensed as the red-haired woman rounded on him with her hand on her sword. If he was forced to disarm her—he did not think he could kill her, even to save his own life—he would certainly have to fight Hordo as well. And likely the rest of the brigands, who had gathered a short distance down the rocky trail.

"Your idea of letting them fight among themselves is a good one," he said, "but if we try to take horses up these slopes we'll be at it still a week hence."

"You've a better plan, Cimmerian?" Her voice was sharp, but she had loosed her grip on her jeweled tulwar.

"I have. Most of the band will ride back along the trail and up one of the side canyons we've passed."

"Back toward the soldiers?" Hordo protested.

"The hillmen have trackers, too!" Aberius shrilled. "Once they pick up our trail, and they will, it's us that'll have to fight them, not the accursed Zamorans!"

"I trust there's more to your plan," Karela said softly. "If you turn out to be a fool after all . . . ." Her words trailed off, but there was a dangerous glint in her tilted eyes. Conan knew she would not forgive the shame of having taken a fool to her bed.

"I said most of the band," the big Cimmerian went on calmly. "I will take a few men forward to where the hillmen are."

Aberius' laugh was scathing, and frightened. "And defeat all seven score? Or perhaps you think your mild face and dulcet tones will turn their blades aside?"

"Be silent!" Karela commanded. She touched her full lips with her tongue before going on in a quieter voice. "If you're a fool, Conan, you're a brave one. Speak on."

"I'll attack the hillmen, all right," Conan said, "but as soon as they know I'm there, I'll be away. I'll lead them past where the rest have turned off the trail, straight to the soldiers. While they're fighting, I and who comes with me will slip away to rejoin you and the others."

"One or the other will have your guts for saddle ties," Aberius snorted.

"Then they'll have yours, too," Karela said. "And mine. For you and I will accompany him." The man's pinched face drew tighter, but he said nothing. Conan opened his mouth to protest; she cut him off. "I lead this band, Cimmerian, and I send no man to danger while I ride to safety. Accept that, or I'll have you tied across your saddle, and you can accompany the others."

A chuckle rumbled up from Conan's massive chest. "There's no sword I'd rather have beside me than yours. I only thought that without you there, those rogues might keep on riding right out of the mountains."

After a moment she joined his laughter. "Nay,

Conan, for they know I'd pursue them to Gehanna, if they did. Besides, Hordo will keep my hounds in line. What's the matter with you, bearded one?''

Hordo stared at her with grim eyes. "Where the Red Hawk must bare her blade," he said flatly, "there ride I."

Conan waited for another blast of the red-haired bandit's temper, but instead she sat her horse staring at Hordo as if she had never seen him before. Finally she said, "Very well, though you're like to lose your other eye if you don't listen to me. Get the rest on their way."

The one-eyed man bared his teeth in a fierce grin and whirled his horse back down the trail.

"A good man," Conan said quickly.

Karela glared. "Do not upbraid me, Cimmerian."

The mass of brigands clattered down the twisting trail and were soon lost to sight. Hordo booted his horse back up to where Conan and the others waited.

"Think you the watchers will take a hand in this, Conan?" the bearded brigand asked.

"What watchers?" Karela demanded. Aberius let out a low moan.

Conan shook his head. "Men on the hillside, but not to concern us now, I think. If they numbered enough to interfere, we'd know it already."

"Hordo, you knew of this and didn't tell me?" Karela said angrily.

"Do we wait here talking," Conan asked, "or do we find the hillmen before they find us?"

For a reply Karela kicked her horse into a gallop

up the trail.

"If her mind were not on you, Cimmerian," Hordo growled, "she'd not need to be told." He spurred after the Red Hawk.

Aberius looked as if he wanted to ride back after the other bandits, but Conan pointed ahead. "That's the way."

The weasel-faced brigand showed his teeth in a snarl, and reluctantly turned his horse after the other two. Conan rode in close behind, forcing him to a gallop.

As soon as they reached the others, Conan drew his sword and rested it across his muscular thighs. With thoughtful looks Karela and Hordo did the same. On that narrow trail, often snaking back on itself with screening escarpments of stone, they would be on the hillmen without warning. If the hillmen did not come on them the same way. Aberius lagged back, chewing his lip.

Abruptly they rounded a sharp bend, and were into the camp of the hillmen. There were no tents, but dark, hook-nosed men in turbans and dirty motley bent to strap bedrolls while others kicked dirt over the ashes of their fires. A thick, bow-legged man, his bare chest crossed by a belt that held his tulwar, saw them first, and an ululating cry broke from his throat. For a bare moment every man in the camp froze, then a shriek of "Kill them!" sent all rushing for their horses.

Conan pulled his horse around as soon as the shout rose. There was no need to do more to ensure being followed. "Back," he said, forcing his horse against those of Karela and Hordo. Aberius seemed to have broken free already. "Back, for your lives."

Karela sawed her reins, brought her horse around, and then all three were pounding back the way they had come. Conan kept an eye behind. For the twists of the trail he could see little, but what he saw told him the hillmen had been quicker to horse than he had hoped. The lead horseman, a burly man with his beard parted and curled like horns, flashed into and out of sight as the trail wound round boulders and rock walls. When they reached the soldiers, they must be far enough ahead to distinguish themselves from the fierce tribesmen, though not far enough to allow too many questions.

Conan looked ahead. Karela was stretching her black out as much as the trail would allow, and Hordo rode close behind her, using his quirt to urge greater speed from her mount. If Conan could buy them a tenth of a glass at one of these narrow places . . . . As the Cimmerian rode between two huge, round boulders, he abruptly pulled his horse around. A quick glance showed that neither of the others had noticed. A few moments, and he would catch up to them.

The fork-bearded hillman galloped between the boulders, raised a wavering battlecry, and Conan's blade clove turban and skull to his shoulders. Even as the man fell from his saddle-pad, more turbanned warriors were forcing their way into the gap. Conan's sword rose and fell in murderous butchery, its steel length stained quickly red, blood running onto his arm and spattering across his chest.

Of a sudden he was aware of Karela, sword flashing, trying to force her way in beside him. Her red hair stood about her head like a mane, and battle light shone in her green eyes. Behind, Conan could hear Hordo calling for her to come back. Her curved blade took a hillman's throat, then another's slash cut one of her reins. A lance pinked her mount, and it reared, screaming and twisting, ripping the other rein from her hand.

"Take her, Hordo!" Conan cried. He brought the flat of his blade down across the rump of her great black horse, earning himself a bloody slash across his chest for his inattention to the hillmen. "Take her to safety, Hordo!"

The big, one-eyed brigand gathered in her dangling rein and spurred down the trail, pulling her horse behind. Conan heard her shouts fading. "Stop, Hordo! Derketo shrivel your eye and tongue! Stop this instant, Hordo! I command it! Hordo!"

Conan had no time to watch, though, for he was engaged again even as she shouted. The hillmen tried to force their way through by sheer weight of numbers, but only two men at a time would fit into the gap, and when more tried they fell before Conan's whirlwind blade. There were six men down beneath the prancing hooves, then seven. Eight. A horse stumbled on a body and reared. The savage cut Conan had intended for the hook-nosed rider half-severed the horse's neck. It fell kicking beneath the hooves of the next horse, and that one went down as well, its rider catapulting from the saddle to lose his turbanned head to the mighty

Cimmerian's broadsword.

The rest of the swarthy riders fell back from that bloody passage, blocked now with dead to the height of a man. Raised tulwars and shouted threats of what would be done when Conan was taken told him they had not given up, though. He edged his horse back. Once he was gone they would clear away the dead, tumbling men and horses alike by the trail, and follow to avenge their honor. But he had gained the time he needed.

The Cimmerian pulled his horse around and booted it into a gallop. Behind him the blood-curdling cries still rose.

XIV

By the time Conan rejoined the other two, Karela was controlling her horse awkwardly with the single rein, and Hordo was assiduously avoiding her savage glare.

"Where's Aberius?" Conan said. There had been no sign of the man along the way.

Karela thrust a murderous look at the big Cimmerian, but there was no time to speak, for as he spoke they rounded a bend, and there ahead was the Zamoran cavalry column. The officer in the lead raised his hand to signal a halt as the three reached him. Some of the mailed men eyed Conan's bloody sword and loosened their own in their scabbards.

"Ho, my lord general," Conan said, bowing to the blocky, sunburnt officer. His armor showed more wear than any general's ever had, the Cimmerian thought, but flattery never hurt, and it could never be piled on too deeply. Though perhaps it might go better with the officer who joined them then, slender and handsome even beneath his dirt.

"Captain," the blocky officer said, "not general. Captain Haranides." Conan suddenly hoped the hillmen showed quickly. The dark eyes that regarded him from beneath that russet-crested helm were shrewd. "Who are you? And what are the lot of you doing in the Kezankians?"

"My name is Crato, noble captain," Conan said, "late guard on a caravan bound from Sultanapur, as was this man, Claudo by name. We had the misfortune to fall among hillmen. The lady is Vanya, daughter of Andiaz, a merchant of Turan who took passage with us. I fear that we three are all who survived. I also fear the hillmen are at our heels, for I looked back not long since and saw them on the trail behind."

"Merchant's daughter!" the young officer crowed. "With those bold eyes? If that wench is a merchant's daughter, I'm King of Turan." The captain's mouth tightened, but he kept silent. Conan could see him watching their reactions. "What say you, Crato? What price for an hour of the jade's time?"

Conan tensed, waiting for her to draw her sword, but she merely pulled herself haughtily erect. "Captain Haranides," she said coldly, "will you allow this man to speak so? My father may be dead, but I yet have relatives who have the ear of Yildiz. And in these months past I hear that your Tiridates wishes to be friends with King Yildiz." The captain still said nothing.

"Your pardon, noble sir," Conan said, "but the hillmen . . . ." Where were they, he wondered.

"I see no hillmen," the young officer said sharply. "And I've heard of no caravans since those seven that disappeared. More likely you're brigands yourselves, who had a falling out with the rest of your band. Perhaps being put to the question will loosen your tongues. The bastinado—"

"Easily, Aheranates," the captain said. Abruptly he wore a warm smile for the three. "Speak more easily. I'm sure these unfortunates will tell us all they know, if only . . . ." The smile froze on his face, then melted. "Sheol!" he thundered. "You've brought them straight to us!"

Conan looked over his shoulder and would have shouted for joy if he dared. The hillmen sat their horses in a startled knot not two hundred paces distant. But already the shock of seeing the soldiers was wearing off, and curved tulwars were being waved above turbanned heads. Ululating cries of defiance floated toward the cavalry.

"Shall we retreat?" Aheranates asked nervously.

"Fool!" the hook-nosed captain spat. "An we turn away, they'll be on our backs like vultures on dead meat. Pass the word—but quietly!—that I'll give no signal, but when I ride forward every man is to charge as if he had a lance up his backside. Move, lieutenant!" The slender officer licked his lips, then started down the column. Haranides turned a gimlet eye on Conan as he eased his sword. "I hope you can use that steel, big man, but in any case, you stay close to me. If we're alive when this is over, there are questions I want to ask."

"Of course, noble captain," Conan said, but

Haranides was already spurring forward. Howling, the cavalry column poured after him up the trail. Screaming hillmen charged, and in an instant the two masses of men were locked in a maelstrom of flashing steel and blood.

Karela and Hordo turned away from the battle and rode for a narrow gorge that let off the trail. Conan hesitated, staring at the combat. Haranides might well have tried to kill him, had the captain known who he was, but this leading the man to his death suddenly festered inside the tall Cimmerian.

"Conan," Hordo called over his shoulder, "what are you waiting for? Ride before someone sees us going." The bearded ruffian continued to suit his actions to his words, following close behind his auburn-haired leader.

Reluctantly Conan rode after them. As they made their way up the sheer-walled cut in the dark granite, the sounds of killing seemed to follow them.

For a long time they rode in silence, till the battle noises had long since faded. The narrow passage opened into a canyon that meandered back to the east. Conan and Karela each rode locked in their own sour silence. Hordo looked from one to the other, frowning. Finally he spoke, with false jollity.

"You've a facile tongue, Conan. Why, you near had me believing my name was Claudo, for the bland look in those blue eyes of yours when you said it."

"A thief had best have a facile tongue," Conan grunted. "Or a bandit. And speaking of facile tongues, what happened to that snake Aberius? I have seen him not since before we met the hillmen.''

Hordo forced a laugh with a worried glance at Karela, whose face looked like stormclouds on the horizon. ''We encountered the craven well down the path. He said he was guarding our backtrail, to keep our retreat open.''

Conan growled deep in his throat. ''You should have slit the coward's throat.''

''Nay. He has too many uses in him for that. I sent him to find the rest of the band, and to tell them to make camp. Can I but puzzle out how these canyons go, we'll be back to them soon.''

''This is my band, Conan!'' Karela suddenly snapped. ''I comand here! The Red Hawk!''

''Then if you think Aberius should escape his cowardice,'' Conan replied gruffly, ''let him. But I'll not change my mind on it.''

She tried to jerk her horse around to face him, but her single rein made the big black take a dancing sidestep instead. The auburn-haired bandit made a sound that in another woman Conan would have called a sob of frustration. But of course such was unlikely from her.

''You fool barbarian!'' she cried. ''What right had you to send me—me!—to safety? Giving my reins to this one-eyed buffoon! Whipping my horse as if I were some favored slave girl who must be kept from danger!''

''That's what you're angry about?'' Conan said incredulously. ''With but one rein left, you were easy meat for the next hillman's blade.''

''You made that decision, did you? It was not yours to make. I choose when and where I fight, and how much risk I'll face. I!''

"You're the most ungrateful person at having your life saved that I've ever met," Conan grumbled.

Karela shook her fist at him, and her voice rose to an enraged howl. "I do not need you to save my life! I do not want you to save my life! Of all men, you least! Swear to me you will never again lift a hand to save my life or my freedom. Swear it, Cimmerian!"

"I swear it!" he answered hotly. "By Crom, I swear it!"

Karela nodded shortly and got her horse moving again with violent kicks and much tugging at her one rein. The bare brown rock through which they rode, layered in places with much faded colors, fitted Conan's mood well. Hordo dropped back to ride beside the muscular youth.

"Once I liked you not at all, Conan," the one-eyed man said in a voice that would not carry forward to Karela. "Now, I like you well, but still I say this. Leave us."

Conan cast a sour eye at him. "If there be leaving to do, you do it. And her, with the rest of her band. I have a seeking here, remember?"

"She'll not turn aside, despite hillmen, or soldiers, or demons themselves. That's the trouble, or what comes of it. That, and this oath, and a score of things more. Emotion rules her head, now, and not the other way round, as always before. I fear what this means."

"I did not ask for the oath," Conan replied. "If you think her temper runs away with her, speak to her, not me."

The bearded bandit's hands gripped his reins till his knuckles were white. "I do like you, Conan, but bring you harm to her, and I will carve you as a Kethan carves stone." He booted his horse ahead, and the three traveled once more in heavy silence.

Long shadows stretched across the mountain valleys by the time they found the bandit camp, among huge boulders at the base of a sheer cliff. Despite the crisp coldness of the air, the scattered fires were small, and placed among the boulders so as to lessen the chance of being seen. Karela's red-striped pavilion stood almost against the towering rock wall.

"I'll see you in my tent, Conan," the red-haired woman said. Without waiting for an answer, she galloped to the pavilion, gave her horse into a bandit's care, and disappeared inside.

As Conan dismounted, he found a knot of bandits gathering about Hordo and him. Aberius was among them, though not in the forefront.

"Ho, Aberius," the Cimmerian said. "I'm glad to see you well. I thought you might have been injured in holding the trail open for us." Some of the rough-faced men snickered. Aberius bared his teeth in what might have been meant to be a grin, but his eyes were those of a rat in a box. He said nothing.

"The hillmen are taken care of, then?" a Kothian with one ear asked. "And the soldiers?"

"Slitting each other's weazands," Hordo chuckled. "They're no more concern to us, not in this world."

"And I've no concern for the next," the Kothian laughed. Most of the others joined in. Conan noted Aberius did not.

"On the morrow, Aberius," Conan said, "you'll take up the trail again, and in a day or two we'll have the treasure."

The pinch-faced brigand had started at the sound of his name. Now he licked his lips before answering. "It cannot be. The trail is lost." He flinched as the other bandits turned to stare at him. "It's lost, I say."

"But only for the moment," Conan said. "Isn't that right? We'll go back to that valley where the hillmen were camped, and you'll pick it up again."

"I tell you it isn't so simple." Aberius shifted his shoulders and tugged nervously at his dented iron breastplate. "While on the trail I can tell a rock disturbed by a horse from one that merely fell. Now I'm away from the trail. If I go back, they'll both look the same."

"Fool!" someone snarled. "You've lost us the treasure."

"All this way for naught," another cried.

"Cut his throat!"

"Slit Aberius' gullet!"

Sweat beaded the man's narrow face. Hordo stepped forward quickly. "Hold, now! Hold! Can you track these men, Talbor? Alvar? Anyone?" Heads were shaken in reluctant denial. "Then open not your mouth against Aberius."

"I still say he is afeared," Talbor muttered. "That is why he cannot find the tracks again."

"I'm not affrighted of any man," Aberius said hotly. He licked his lips once more. "Of any man." There was a peculiar emphasis to the last word.

"Of what, then?" Conan said. For a moment he thought Aberius would refuse to answer, then the man spoke in a rush.

"On the mountain slope, after we four rode forward, I saw a . . . a thing." His voice gained fervency as he spoke. "Like a snake, it was, yet like a man, too. It wore armor, and carried a sword, and flame shot from its mouth twice the length of a sword. As I watched it signaled for more of its kind to come forth. Had I not ridden to half-kill my horse, I'd be dead at those creatures' hands."

"If it had the flame," Conan muttered, "what need had it for the sword?" Some of the others began to murmur fearfully, though, and even those who were silent had unease on their faces.

"Why did you not speak of this before?" Hordo demanded.

"There was no need," Aberius replied. "I knew we would soon leave, since the tracks are lost. We must leave soon. Besides, I thought you would misbelieve me."

"There are strange things under the sky," Conan said. "I've seen some of them, myself. But I've never seen anything that could not be killed with cold steel." Or at least, very few, he amended to himself. "How many of these things did you actually see, Aberius?"

"Only the one," Aberius admitted with obvious reluctance. "But it summoned more, and I saw them moving beyond the rocks. There could have been a hundred, a thousand."

"Yet all in all," Hordo said, "you saw but one. There cannot be many of them, else we'd have heard before. A thing like that would be talked of.

"But," Aberius began.

"But nothing," Hordo barked. "We'll keep a wary eye for these creatures of yours, but on the morrow we see if you can tell a horse track from horsemoss."

"But I told you—"

"Unless you all want to give up the treasure," the one-eyed bandit went on as if the smaller man had not spoken. Loud objections went up on every side. "Then I'll talk to the Red Hawk, and at dawn we'll move. Now go get something into your bellies."

One by one the bandits drifted away to their fires. Aberius went last of all, casting a dark look at Conan as he went.

XV

While Hordo stumped off to the red-striped pavilion, Conan found a spot where he could sit with his back to a massive boulder and no one could come at him unseen. That look from Aberius had spoken of knives in the back. He got out his honing stone and broadsword and began to smooth the nicks made by hillmen's chainmail. The sky became purple, and lurid red streamers filled the jagged western horizon. He was putting the finishing touches to his blade's edge when the one-eyed brigand stormed out of Karela's tent.

The bearded man stalked to within a few feet of Conan, obviously ill at ease. Hordo rubbed his bulbous nose, muttering under his breath. "A good habit, that," he said finally. "I've seen more than one good man die because an untended notch in his blade left him with a stump the next time it took a good blow."

Conan laid the broadsword across his thighs. "You didn't come to talk of swords. What does she say about tomorrow?"

"She wouldn't even listen to me." Hordo shook his bearded head. "Me, who's been with her from the first day, and she wouldn't listen."

"No matter. On the morrow, you turn back, and I go on. Perhaps she's right not to risk these snake-men on top of all else."

"Mitra! You don't understand. I never got to speak of the creatures, or of Aberius' denial he can find the trail again. She paced like a caged lioness, and would not let me say two words together." He tugged at his beard with both hands. "Too long have I been with her," he muttered, "to be sent on such an errand. Zandru, man, it's because you didn't come when she ordered that she's ready to bite heads off. And her temper worsens every minute you sit here."

Conan smiled briefly. "I told her once I was no hand at obedience."

"Mitra, Zandru, and nine or ten other gods whose names escape me at the moment." Hordo let out a long sigh and squatted with his thick arms crossed on his knees. "Another time I wouldn't mind wagering on which of you will win, but not when I might be shortened a head for being in the middle."

"There's no talk of winning or losing. I'm in no battle with her."

The side of the one-eyed man's mouth that was not drawn into a permanent sneer grimaced. "You're a man, and she's a woman. There's battle enough. Well, what happens, happens. But remember my warning. Harm her, and it's you will be shorter a head."

"Since she's angry with me, talk her into turning

back. That will give you what you want. Her away from me." He did not add that it would also give him what he wanted, and relieve him of the necessity of stealing the pendants from the bandits.

"The temper she's in, 'tis more likely she'll order you staked out again, and begin again where first we were."

Conan touched his sword; his steel blue eyes were suddenly cold. "This time I'll collect my ferryman's fee, Hordo."

"Speak not of ferryman's fees," the other man muttered. "An she decides so . . . I'll get you away in the night. Bah! This talk of what will happen and what may happen is building towers of sand in the wind."

"Then let us talk on other things," Conan said with a laugh that did not touch his eyes. He believed the one-eyed brigand did indeed like him, but he would not trust his life to that where the need of going against Karela's commands was concerned. "Think you Aberius made these snakemen out of air, to cover his wanting to turn back?"

"He tells the truth with a face that shouts lie, yet this time I think he may actually have seen something. That's not to say it was what he says it was. Ah, I know not, Conan. Snakes that walk like men." The bearded bandit shivered. "I begin to grow old. This chasing after a king's treasure is beyond me. I'd settle for a good caravan with guards who have no wish to die."

"Than talk her into turning back. 'Tis almost full dark. I'll leave the camp tonight, and in the morning, with me gone, there will be no trouble in it."

"Much you know," Hordo snorted. "With the humor on her now, she'd order us to pursue, and slay any who would not."

The flap of the striped pavilion opened, and Karela emerged, her face almost hidden by the hood of a scarlet cloak that covered her to the ground. She moved purposefully toward the two men through the deepening purple twilight. The cookfires made small pools of light among the boulders.

Hordo got to his feet, dusting his hands nervously. "I . . . must see to the horses. Good luck to you, Conan." He hurried away, not looking in the direction of the approaching woman.

Conan picked up his sword again and bent to examine the blade. It must needs be sharp, but the razor-edge some men boasted of would split against chain mail and quickly leave naught but a metal club. He became aware of the lower edge of Karela's crimson cloak at the corner of his vision. He did not look up.

"Why did you not come to my tent?" she demanded abruptly.

"I had need to tend my sword." With a final examination of the edge, he stood and sheathed the sword. Her tilted green eyes glared up at him from within the shelter of her hood; his sapphire gaze met hers calmly.

"I commanded you to come to me! We have much to discuss."

"But I will not be commanded, Karela. I am not one of your faithful hounds."

Her gasp was loud. "You defy me? I should have known you would think to supplant me. Do not think simply because you share my bed—"

"Be not a fool, Karela." The big Cimmerian made an effort to keep a rein on his temper. "I have no designs on your band. Command your rogues, but do not try to command me."

"So long as you ride behind the Red Hawk—"

"I ride with you, and beside you, as you ride with and beside me. No more than that for either of us."

"Do not cut me off, you muscle-bound oaf!" Her shout rang through the camp, echoing from tall boulders and the looming cliff. Bandits at the cook fires, and currying horses, turned to stare. Even in the dimness Conan could see that her face had colored. She lowered her voice, but her tone was acid. "I thought that you were the man I sought, a man strong enough to be the Red Hawk's consort. Derketo blast your soul! You're naught but a street thief!"

He caught her swinging hand before it could strike his cheek, and held it easily despite her struggles. Her scarlet cloak gaped open, revealing that she wore nothing beneath. "Again you break your oath, Karela. Do you hold your goddess in such contempt as to believe she will not punish a foresworn oath?"

Abruptly the auburn-haired woman seemed to realize the spectacle they were making before her brigands. She gathered her cloak together with her free hand. "Release me," she said coolly. "Rot your soul, I will not say please."

Conan loosened his grip, but it was not her plea that caused him to do so. As she tore her wrist free the hairs on the back of his neck were rising in an unpleasantly familiar fashion. He stared through the now black sky at the mountains around them. The stars were glittering bright points, and the moon had not yet risen. The mountains were formless deepenings of the night's shadows.

"Imhep-Aton follows still," he said quietly.

"I may allow you some liberties in private, Conan," Karela grated, rubbing her wrist, "but never again in public are you to . . . . Imhep-Aton? That's the name the possessed man spoke, that night in the camp. The sorcerer's name."

Conan nodded. "It was he who spoke to me first of the pendants. If not for the man he sent to kill me that night, I'd have delivered them to him, once I had them, for the price agreed. Now he has no more claim on me, or on the pendants."

"How can you be sure it is him, and not a hillman, or just the weight of night in these mountains pressing on you?"

"I know," he said simply.

"But—" Abruptly she stared past him, green eyes going wide in shock, mouth dropping open.

Conan spun, broadsword leaving its scabbard as he turned to knock aside the thrust of a spear in the hands of a demon-like apparition. Red eyes glowed at him from a dark scaled face beneath a ridged helmet. A harsh cry hissed at him from a fanged mouth. The big Cimmerian allowed himself no time for surprise. His return blow from the parry opened the creature from crotch to neck, black blood bubbling forth as it fell.

Already that sibilant battle cry was going up around the camp. Men leaped to their feet around the fires, on the border of panic as scores of scaly-skinned warriors poured out of the night. Alvar stared, and screamed as a spear pierced him through the chest. A swarthy Iranistani turned to flee and had his spine severed by a massive battle-ax in claw-fingered hands. Bandits darted like rats searching for an escape.

"Fight, Crom blast you!" Conan shouted. "They can die, too!"

He ran toward the slaughter in the camp, looking for Karela. Almost at once he spotted her in the middle of the fighting. From somewhere she had acquired a tulwar, though not her jeweled blade. Her cloak now dangled, bunched, from her left hand as a snare to catch other's weapons, and she danced naked through the butchery, red hair streaming, a fury from the Outer Dark, her curved sword drinking ebon blood.

"Up, my hounds!" she screamed. "Fight, for your lives!" Roaring, Hordo dashed in behind her to take a spear in the thigh that had been meant for her back. The one-eyed brigand's blade sought his reptilian attacker's heart, and even as the creature was falling he tore the spear from his leg and waded into the fray, blood over his boot.

Before Conan loomed another of the scaled men, his back to the Cimmerian, his spear raised to transfix Aberius, who lay on the ground with bulging eyes, his gap-toothed mouth open in a scream. Battles are not duels. Conan slammed his sword through the creature's back to stand out a foot from its chest. While it still stood, death-shriek bubbling forth, he planted a booted foot on its agony-arched back to tug his blade free.

The saurian killer fell twitching across Aberius,

who screamed again and wriggled free with a glare at Conan as if he wished the Cimmerian were in the scaled one's place. The weasel-faced bandit grabbed the dying creature's spear, and for a bare second the two men stared at one another. Then Aberius darted into the fighting, shouting, "The Red Hawk! For the Red Hawk!"

"Crom!" Conan bellowed, and plunged into the maelstrom. "Crom and steel!"

The battle became a kaleidoscoping nightmare for the Cimmerian, as all battles did for all warriors. Men battling scaled monsters flickered before him and were gone, still locked in their death struggles. The cloud of battles covered his mind, loosing the fury of his wild north country, and even those scaled snake-men who faced him knew fear before they died, fear at the battle light that glowed in his blue eyes, fear at the grim, wild laughter that broke from his lips even as he slew. He waded through them, broadsword working in murderous frenzy.

"Crom!" If these scaly demons were to pay his ferryman's fee, he would set it high. "Crom and steel!"

And then there were none left standing among the night-shrouded boulders save those of human kind. Conan's broad chest was splattered with inky blood, mixing with his own in more than one place. He looked about him wearily, the battle fury fading.

Reptilian bodies lay everywhere, some twitching still. And among them were no few of the bandits. Hordo hobbled from wounded brigand to wounded brigand, a red-stained rag twisted about his thigh, offering what aid he could do those who still could use it. Aberius sat hunched by a fire, leaning on his spear. Other bandits began to make their dazed way in from the darkness.

Karela strode across the charnel ground to the Cimmerian, the cloak discarded, tulwar still gripped firmly in her hand. He was relieved to note that none of the blood that smeared her round breasts was her own.

"It seems Aberius saw nothing after all," she said when she faced him. "At least we know now what you felt watching you. I could wish you had gotten your warning somewhat earlier."

Conan shook his head. It was no use explaining to her how he knew it had not been the gaze of these things he felt on him. "I wish I knew whence they—"

He broke off with a sudden oath, and bent to examine the boots of one of the dead creatures. They were worked in the pattern of an encircling serpent, its head seeming surrounded by rays. Hurriedly he went to another body, and still others. All wore the boots.

"What takes you, Conan?" Karela demanded. "Even if you need boots, surely you could never wear something that came from these."

"No," he replied. "Those who stole the pendants from Tiridates' palace wore boots worked with a serpent." He tugged one of the boots from a narrow foot and tossed it to her.

She stepped aside to let it fall with a grimace of distaste. "I've had my fill and more of those things. Conan, you can't believe these . . . these whatever they are, entered Shadizar and left, unhindered. The City Guard is blind, I'll grant, but not as blind as that."

"They wore hooded robes that covered them to their fingertips. And they left the city at night, when the guards on the gates are half asleep at best. They could have entered the night before and remained hidden until it was time to do their work at the palace."

"It could be as you say," Karela admitted reluctantly. "But what help that is to us, I cannot see."

Hordo limped up and stood glaring at Conan. "Two score men and four, Cimmerian. That's what I led into these accursed mountains on this mad quest of yours. Full fifteen are food for worms this night, and two more like not to last till dawn. Thank whatever odd gods you pray to, we took a pair of them alive. The amusement of putting them to the question will keep you from being staked out in their place. And I'll tell you, for all my liking, if they tried I'm not sure I'd stop them."

"Prisoners?" Karela said sharply. "I've little love for these creatures dead, none alive. Give them to the men now. Come dawn we'll be riding out of these mountains."

"We abandon the treasure, then?" The one-eyed bandit sounded more relieved than surprised. "Fare you well, then, Conan, for I see this will be the last night we spend in company."

Karela turned slowly to give the Cimmerian an unreadable look. "Do we part, then?"

Conan nodded reluctantly, and with a rueful glare at Hordo. He had not meant her to find out so soon. In fact, his plan had been to leave in the night, with one of the prisoners for a guide, and let her discover him gone come morning.

"I continue after the pendants," the Cimmerian said.

"And that girl," Karela said flatly.

"Company," Hordo muttered, before Conan could speak further.

Toward them marched those of the bandits who were able to walk, not one man without at least one bloody bandage, and every one with his weapon in hand. Aberius marched at their head, using his spear like a walking staff. The others wore purposeful looks on their faces, but only he had a spiteful smile. Ten paces from where Conan stood with Karela and Hordo, they stopped.

Hordo started forward angrily, but Karela put a hand on his arm. He stopped, but his glare promised reckonings another time. Karela faced the gathering calmly, hand on hip and sword point planted firmly on the ground.

"Not hurt too badly, eh, Aberius?" she said with a sudden smile. The weasel-faced man seemed taken aback. He had a scratch down his cheek, and a piece of rag about his left arm. "And you, Talbor," she went on before anyone could speak. "Not as hard a night's work as you've had. Remember when we took that slaver's caravan from Zamboula, only they'd doubled the guard for fear of those quarry slaves they had bound for Ketha? I mind carrying you away from that across my saddle, with an arrow through you, and—"

"That's of no matter now," Aberius snapped. Hordo lurched forward, snarling, but Karela stopped him with a gesture. Aberius seemed to relax at that, and his smile became more satisfied. "No matter at all, now," he repeated smugly.

"Then what is of matter?" she asked.

Aberius blinked. "Has the Red Hawk suddenly
lost her vision?" A few of the men behind him
laughed; the others looked grim. "More than a
third of our number dead, and not a coin in anyone's purse to see for it. We were going to steal
some pendants from a few pilgrims. Now we've
followed them all the way into these accursed
mountains, and might follow to Vendhya with
naught to show for it. Hillmen. Soldiers. Now,
demons. It's time to go back to the plains, back to
what we know."

"I decide when to turn back!" Karela's voice
was suddenly a whip, lashing them. "I took you
from the mud, robbing wayfarers for a few coppers, and made you feared by every caravan that
leaves Shadizar, or Zamboula, or Aghrapur itself!
I found you scavengers, and made you men! I put
gold in your purses, and the swagger in your walks
that make men step wide of you and women
wriggle close! I am the Red Hawk, and I say we go
on, and take this treasure that was stolen from a
king!"

"You've led us long," Aberius said. "Karela."
The familiarity of the name brought a gasp from
the red-haired woman, and a growl from Hordo.
Suddenly she seemed only a woman. A naked
woman. Aberius licked his lips. Lecherous lights
appeared in the eyes of the men behind him.

Karela took a step back. Conan could read every
emotion that fled across her face. Rage. Shame.
Frustration. And finally the determination to sell
her life dearly. She took a firmer grip on her tul-

war. Hordo had unobtrusively slipped his blade from its sheath.

If he had half a brain, Conan told himself, he would slip away now. After all, he owed her nothing. There was the oath not to save her, too. Before the brigands knew what was happening, he could be gone into the night, with one of the prisoners to guide him to the pendants. And Velita. With a sigh, he stepped forward.

"I do not break my oath," he said softly, for Karela's ears alone. "It's my own life I'm saving." He walked down to confront Aberius and the rest with a friendly smile, though the casual-seeming way his hand rested on his sword hilt was deceptive.

"Do not think to join us, Conan," Aberius said. There was considerable satisfaction in his smile. "You stand with them."

"I thought we all stood together," the Cimmerian replied. "You do remember the reason we came, don't you? Treasure? A king's treasure?"

The narrow-faced bandit spat, barely missing Conan's boot. "That's well out of our reach, now. I'll never find that trail again."

Conan let his smile broaden. "There's no need. These creatures you've killed tonight wear boots with the same markings as those who stole the pendants and the rest from Tiridates' palace. You can rest assured they serve the same master."

"Demons," Aberius said incredulously. "The man wants us to fight demons for this treasure." A mutter of agreement rose from the others, but Conan spoke quickly on his heels.

"What demons? I see creatures with the skins of

snakes, but no demons.'' Protests broke out; Conan did not allow them to form. "Whatever they look like, you killed them tonight.'' He caught each man's eye in turn. "You killed them. With steel, and courage. Do demons die from steel? And you've bound two of them. Did they mutter spells and make you disappear? Did they fly away when you put ropes on them?'' He looked sideways at Aberius, and grinned widely. "Did they breathe flame at you?''

Laughter rippled through the brigands, and Aberius colored. "It matters not! It matters not, I tell you! I still cannot find the trail, and I've not heard a word from these monsters that any can understand.''

"I said there's no need to find the trail again,'' Conan said. "At dawn we'll contrive to let these two escape. You can track them easily enough.''

"They're both wounded,'' Aberius protested desperately. "Like as not, neither will last an hour.''

"It's still a chance.'' Conan let his voice swell. "A chance for a king's treasure in gold and jewels. Who's for gold? Who's for the Red Hawk?'' He risked unsheathing his sword and raising it overhead. "Gold! The Red Hawk!''

In an instant every man save Aberius was waving his weapon in the air. "Gold!'' they bellowed. "Gold!'' "The Red Hawk!'' "Gold!''

Aberius twisted his thin mouth sourly. "Gold!'' he shouted, pushing his spear aloft. "The Red Hawk!'' His beady eyes glared murder at Conan.

"Good, then!'' Conan shouted over their cries. "Off with you, to rest and drink! Till dawn!''

"Dawn!" they roared. "Gold!"

Conan waited until they were well on their way back to the fires, then returned to Karela. She stared at him as if stricken. He put out a hand to touch her, but she jerked her arm away and stalked toward her tent without a word. Conan stared after her in consternation.

"I said once you had a facile tongue," Hordo said, sheathing his sword. "You've more than that, Conan of Cimmeria. Belikes you'll be a general, someday. Mayhap even a king. If you live to get out of these mountains. If any of us do."

"What's the matter with her?" Conan demanded. "I told her I did this for me, not her. I did not break the oath she demanded."

"She thinks you try to supplant her," Hordo replied slowly. "As chief of the band."

"That's foolish!"

Hordo did not seem to hear. "I hope she does not yet realize that what was done tonight can never be undone. Mitra grant her time before she must know that."

"What are you muttering about, you one-eyed old ruffian?" Conan said. "Did one of those blows tonight addle your brains?"

"You do not see it either, do you?" The bearded man's voice was sad. "What has been shattered can be mended, but the cracks are always there, and those cracks will break again and again until there is no mending."

"Once there's gold in their purses, they'll be as loyal as they ever were. On the morrow, Hordo, we must bury these creatures as well as our own dead.

There must be no vultures aloft to warn whoever sent them out.''

''Of course.'' Hordo sighed. ''Rest you well, Cimmerian, and pray you we live to rest another night.''

''Rest you well, Hordo.''

After the one-eyed bandit disappeared toward the camp fires, Conan peered toward Karela's pavilion, beneath the loom of the cliff. Her shadow moved on the striped walls. She was washing herself. Then the lamps were extinguished.

Muttering curses under his breath Conan found a cloak and wrapped himself in it beneath the shelter of a boulder. Rest you well, indeed. Women!

Imhep-Aton rose from his place on the mountainside above the bandit camp and turned into the darkness. When he reached a place where the shadows against the stone seemed to darken, he walked on, through the shadow-wall and into a large, well-lit cave. His mount and his packhorse were tethered at the rear of it. His blankets were spread by the fire where a rabbit roasted on a spit. Nearby sat the chest containing the necessities of his thaumaturgies.

The mage rubbed his eyes, then stretched, massaging the small of his back. One spell had been needed to gain the eyes of an eagle, a second to make the night into day to his sight, still a third to let him hear what was said in the camp. Maintaining all three at once had given him a pain that ran from his head all the way down his backbone.

Yet it was worth the discomfort. The fools thought they ruled where their horses' hooves trod. He wondered what they would think if they knew they were but dogs, to corner a bear and die holding its attention while he, the hunter, moved in for the kill.

Laughing, the necromancer bent to his supper.

XVI

Seated on his golden serpent throne, Amanar watched the four dancing girls flexing their sinuosities across the mosaic floor for his enjoyment. Naked but for golden bells at ankles and wrists, they spun and writhed with wild abandon, in the sweat of fear for his displeasure, the tinkle of the bells a counterpoint to the flutes of four human musicians who kept their eyes on their own feet. There were few human servants within the keep, and none ever raised their eyes from the ground.

Amanar luxuriated in the fear he felt emanating from the four women, enjoying that as much as he did the luscious curves they flaunted shamelessly before him. The fifth girl, golden-eyed Yasmeen, had been the first to find herself given screaming to Sitha—threats produced more fear if it was known they would be carried out—and she had somehow managed to cut her own throat with the huge S'tarra's sword.

It had been all the necromancer could do to keep

her alive long enough to be sacrificed to Morath-Aminee, and there had been little pleasure for him in the haste of it. He had taken precautions to make certain there would be no repetition of the unfortunate incident. Through lidded eyes Amanar watched his possessions dance for his favor.

"Master?"

"Yes, Sitha?" the mage said without shifting his gaze. The heavily muscled S'tarra stood bowed at one side of the throne, but its scarlet eyes watched the dancing girls greedily.

"The map, master. It flashes."

Amanar uncoiled from the throne and strode out of the chamber with Sitha at his heels. The girls continued to dance. He had given no command to cease, and they dared not without it.

Close beside the throne chamber was a small room with only two furnishings. A silver mirror hung on one gray stone wall. Against the other a great sheet of clear crystal leaned on a polished wooden frame, etched with a map of the mountains surrounding the keep. In the crystal a flashing red light moved slowly along a valley, triggered by the wards Amanar had set. Lower animals would not set off the warning, nor would his S'tarra. Only men could do that.

Turning to the mirror Amanar muttered cryptic words and made cabalistic gestures that left a faint glow in the air. As the glow faded, the silver mirror grew clear as a window, a window that looked down from an eagle's height on men riding slowly along a mountain valley.

One of the men made a gesture, as if pointing to something on the ground. They were tracking.

Amanar spoke further esoteric phrases, and the vision of the mirror raced ahead, seeking. Like a falcon sensing prey, the image stopped, then swooped. On a badly wounded S'tarra, stumbling, falling, rising to struggle forward again. Amanar returned the mirror to the mounted party that followed his servant.

Near thirty men, well armed, and one woman. The mage could not tell whether the woman or a heavily muscled youth with fierce blue eyes commanded. Amanar rubbed his chin thoughtfully with an over-long hand.

"The girl Velita, Sitha," he said. "Fetch her here immediately."

The big S'tarra bowed himself from the room, leaving Amanar to study the image in the mirror. S'tarra used their wounded, those too badly hurt to heal, as fresh meat. This one would not have been allowed to leave his patrol; therefore the patrol no longer existed. Since these men followed, it was likely they had destroyed the patrol, and that was no small feat. It was also unlikely that they followed to no purpose.

"The girl, master." Sitha appeared in the door grasping Velita by her hair so that the dark-eyed girl perforce must walk on the balls of her feet. Her hands hung passively at her sides, though, and she shivered in terror both of that which gripped her and of the man she faced.

"Let her down," Amanar commanded impatiently. "Girl, come here and look into this mirror. Now, girl!"

She stumbled forward—though with her grace it seemed more a step of her dancing—and gasped when she saw the images moving before her. For a moment the necromancer thought she would speak, but then her jaw tightened and she closed her eyes.

"You spoke a name once, girl," Amanar said. "A man who would rescue you. Conan. Is that man among these you see?" She did not move a muscle, or utter a sound. "I mean the man no harm, girl. Point him out to me, or I will have Sitha whip you."

A low moan rose in her throat, and she opened her large eyes long enough to roll them in terror at the huge S'tarra behind her. "I cannot," she whispered. Her body trembled, and tears streamed down her face in silent sobs, but she would speak no more.

Amanar made an exasperated noise. "Fool girl. All you do is delay me for a few moments. Take her, Sitha. Twenty strokes."

Fanged mouth open in a wide grin, the massive S'tarra gathered her hair once more in its fist, lifting her painfully as they left. Tears rolled down her face all the harder, yet still her sobs were soundless.

The mage studied the images further. She had actually answered his question, in part at least, though she likely thought she had protected the man. But she had named this Conan a thief, and thieves did not ride with more than a score of armed men at their backs.

From within his serpent-embroidered black robe he produced the things he needed for this simple task. A red chalk scribed a five-pointed star on the stone floor. From a pouch he poured a small mound of powder on each of the points. His left hand stretched forth, and from each fingertip a spark flew to flare the powders to blinding flame. Five thin streams of acrid red smoke rose toward the distant ceiling.

Amanar muttered words in a dead tongue, made a gesture with his left hand. The smoke was suddenly sucked back down onto the pentagram, swirling and billowing as if whipped by a great wind, yet confined to the five-pointed star. He spoke one further word, and with a sharp crack the smoke was gone. In its place was a hairless gray shape no higher than his knee. Vaguely ape-like in form, with sharply sloping forehead and knuckles brushing the stone floor, its shoulders bore bony wings covered with taut gray hide.

The creature chattered at him, baring fangs that seemed to fill half its simian face, and sprang for the mage. At the boundary of the pentagram it suddenly shrieked, and was thrown back in a shower of sparks to crumple in the center of the star. Unsteadily it rose, claws clicking on the stone. The bat-like wings quivered as if for flight. "Free!" it barked shrilly.

Amanar's lip curled in disgust and anger. He was far beyond dealing with these minor demons personally. That the girl had forced him to it was a humiliation he would assuage personally, to her great discomfort.

"Free!" the demon demanded again.

"Be silent, Zath!" the necromancer commanded. The gray form recoiled, and Amanar allowed himself a small smile. "Yes, I know your name. Zath! An you fail to do as I command, I'll use the power that gives me. Others of your kind have from time to time annoyed me, and have found themselves trapped in material bodies. Bodies of solid gold.'' Amanar threw back his head and laughed.

The ape-like creature shuddered. Its dead-white eyes watched the sorcerer malevolently from beneath bony eyebrow ridges, but it said, ''Zath do what?''

''These two,'' Amanar said, touching the images of Conan and Karela. ''Discover for me their names, and why they follow one of my S'tarra.''

''How?'' the demon shrilled.

''Play no games with me,'' Amanar snapped. ''Think you I do not know? If you are close enough to an ordinary man to hear his speech, you can hear his thoughts as well. And you may as well stop trying me. You know it will not work.''

The demon chattered his fangs angrily. ''Zath goes.'' With a thunderous clap, it disappeared. A wind ruffled Amanar's robe as air rushed into the pentagram.

The sorcerer dusted his hands as though he had touched something demeaning, and turned back to the mirror. For a time the images rode on, then suddenly one of their number pointed aloft. Consternation swept across their faces. Crossbows were raised, bolts loosed at the sky.

A snap sounded in the chamber, and the ape-like demon was back in the pentagram, flexing its wings and fondling a crossbow quarrel. ''Try to kill Zath,'' it giggled, and added contemptuously, ''With iron.'' The demon amused itself by poking the quarrel through its bony arm. The crossbow arrow left no wound.

"What of that which I sent you for?" Amanar demanded.

The demon glared at him a moment before speaking. "Big man named Conan. Woman named Karela, called Red Hawk. They come for pendants, for girl. Free!"

Amanar smiled at the images on the mirror, recovering now from their encounter with Zath and riding on. The lovely Velita's thief, and the famed Red Hawk at the same time, with her band. There were many uses to which such beings could be put.

"Ahead of these people," he said to the demon without taking his eyes from the mirror, "is one of my S'tarra. It is wounded, but yet lives. You may feed. Now, go." The necromancer's smile was far from pleasant.

The slopes of the twisting valley steepened and grew bleaker as the bandits rode. Conan eyed a thornbush, of which there were even fewer here than had been along the trail earlier. It was stunted and bent as if something in air or soil distorted the dark branches into an unwholesome simulacrum of the plant it had once been. All the scrub growth they passed grew more like that the further they went along the wounded snake-creature's trail.

"Fitting country," Hordo muttered just loud enough for Conan to hear. His lone eye watched Karela warily, where she rode at the column's head. "First snake-men, then that flying Mitra-alone-knows-what."

"It didn't hurt anyone," Conan said flatly, "and it went away." He was not about to say anything that might dissuade the others from turning back, but at the same time he could not entirely dispel his own sense of unease.

"It was hit," the one-eyed man went on. "Two bolts at least, but never a quiver out of it. 'Tis only luck the rest of these rogues didn't turn tail on the moment."

"Mayhap you should turn back, Hordo." He twisted in his saddle to peer down the line of mounted bandits straggled behind him on the winding valley floor. Greed drove them forward, but since the strange creature was seen flying above them, seeming to follow them, every man watched the gray skies and stony slopes with sullen eyes. From time to time a man would touch his bandaged wounds and look thoughtfully back the way they had come.

Conan shook his black-maned head at the bearded brigand. "If she says she has decided to turn back, they'll follow her gratefully; if she pushes on, they'll begin dropping away one by one."

"You of all men should know she'll not turn from this trail. Not so long as you go on."

Conan was spared answering by a loud hail from Aberius. The weasel-faced bandit had been riding ahead of them to track the wounded snake-creature. Now he sat his horse where the trail wound around a rock spire ahead, waving his arm over his head.

"Halloo!"

Karela galloped forward without a word.

"I hope he's lost the track," Hordo muttered. Conan booted his horse ahead. After a moment the one-eyed man followed.

The red-haired woman turned her horse aside as

Conan rode up. He looked at what Aberius had been showing her. The reptilian creature they had been following lay sprawled on its back, dead, in the shadow of the stone spire. Its chain mail had been torn off, and its chest ripped open.

"Scavengers have been at it already," Hordo muttered. "It's too bad the other one crawled off somewhere to die." He did not sound as if he thought it too bad at all.

"No vultures in the sky," Conan said thoughtfully. "And never have I heard of jackals that rip out a heart and leave the rest."

Aberius' horse whinnied as he jerked at the reins. "Mitra! The Cimmerian's right. Who knows what slew him? Perhaps that foul thing that flew over us and took no mind of crossbow bolts." His beady eyes darted wildly, as if expecting the apparition to appear again, from behind a rock.

"Be silent, fool!" Karela snapped. "It died of the wounds it took last night, and your approach frightened a badger or some such off its feeding."

"It makes no matter," Aberius said slyly. "I can track this carrion no further."

The woman's green-eyed gaze was contemptuously amused. "Then I've no more need of you, have I? I'll wager I can find where it was going myself."

"It's time to leave these accursed mountains." The pinch-faced man swiveled his head to the other bandits, waiting down the trail. Enough fear of the Red Hawk remained to keep them back from her council.

Karela did not deign to acknowledge his whine. "Since loosing its bonds, the creature has kept a straight line. When the twists of the land took it aside, it found its way back again. We'll keep the same way."

"But—" Aberius swallowed the rest of his words as Hordo pushed his horse closer. Karela started ahead, ignoring them.

"An I hear any tales," the one-eyed man grated, "other than that you frighted some slinking vermin from this corpse, I'll see you cold carrion beside it." Conan caught his eye as he turned to follow Karela, and for a moment the bearded bandit looked abashed. "She needs one hound at least to remain faithful, Cimmerian. The way is forward, Aberius. Forward, you worthless rogues!" he bellowed. He met Conan's eyes again, then kicked his horse into a gallop.

For a time Conan sat his horse, watching the faces of the passing brigands as they came in view of the bloody, scaled corpse. Each recoiled, muttering or with an oath, as he rounded the spire and got a clear look at what lay there, but the greed in their eyes was undiminished. They rode on.

Muttering his own oath, Conan spurred after Karela and Hordo.

XVII

Haranides wearily raised his hand to signal a halt to the bedraggled column behind him. The site among the boulders at the face of the cliff had been a camp. An attempt had been made to hide the face, but a thin tendril of smoke still rose from ashes not covered well enough with dirt.

"Dismount the men, Aheranates," the captain commanded, wincing as he did so himself. A hillman's lance had left a gouge along his ribs that would be a long time in healing. "Take a party of ten and see if you can find which way they went without mucking up the tracks too badly."

The slender lieutenant—Haranides could not help wondering how he had come through the fight without a scratch—touched his forehead stiffly in salute. "Sir." He sawed at his reins to pull his horse around and began telling off the men.

Haranides sighed. He was not in good odor with the lieutenant, which meant he would not be in good odor with the lieutenant's father, which meant . . . . Odor. He fingered the polished stone jar in his pouch. The perfume had seemed familiar to him, but it was not until he was beating aside a hillman's curved sword that he remembered where he had smelled it before. And knew that the red-haired jade who had come to 'warn' him of the tribesmen was the Red Hawk.

The problem was that Aheranates, too, knew that he had had her in his grasp and let her slip away. Once the fighting was done and wounds were tended as well they could be in the field, Haranides had ordered them along the trail of the three.

"Sir?" Haranides looked up from his brown study to find Resaro knuckling his forehead. "The prisoner, sir?"

When the butchery was over, they had found a hillman who had merely been stunned by a blow to the head. Now Haranides had great need to know what had brought such a body of tribesmen together. They normally formed much smaller bands for their raiding. It was necessary to know if he might find himself facing other forces as large. He grimaced in disgust. "Put him to the question, Resaro."

"Yes, sir. If the captain will pardon me for saying so, sir, that was a fine piece of work back there. The handful we didn't slice into dogmeat are likely still running."

"See to the prisoner," Haranides sighed. Resaro touched his forehead and went.

The man might think it fine work, the captain thought, and in the ordinary course of events it might have been considered so, but this was no ordinary patrol. Two hundred good cavalrymen had he led through the Gate to the Three Swords. After burying his dead, separating those too badly wounded to go on, and detaching enough healthy men to give the wounded a chance if they were attacked on their way out of the mountains, he had four score and three left. And he had neither the Red Hawk nor Tiridates' trinkets in hand. In eyes of king and counselor it would be those lacks that damned him.

A choked scream rose from where Resaro had the hillman. "Mitra blast Tiridates and the Red Hawk both," the captain growled under his breath. He walked into what had been the bandit camp, examining the ground between the looming boulders as much to keep his mind off the hillman's moans as in hope of finding anything of importance.

Aheranates found him standing where the pavilion had been. "Would I could see what she saw from here," Haranides said without looking at the slender man. "There is a wrong feel to this place. What happened here?"

"A battle. Sir." A supercilious smile curled the lieutenant's mouth at for once being ahead of Haranides. "Or, at least, a fight, but it must have been a big one. Hillmen attacked the bandits in camp and cut them up badly. We no longer need worry about the Red Hawk. An she still lives, she's screaming over a torture-fire about now."

"A very complete picture," the captain said slowly. "Based on what?"

"Graves. One mass grave that must hold forty or more, and seventeen single graves. They're upslope, to the north there."

"Graves," Haranides repeated thoughtfully. The hill tribes never acted in concert. In their dialects the words for 'enemy' and 'one not of my clan' were the same. But if they had found some compelling reason . . . . "But who won, lieutenant?"

"What?"

The hook-nosed captain shook his head. "Learn something about those you chase. None of the hill tribes bury their victims, and they take their own dead back to their villages so their spirits won't have to wander among strangers. On the other hand, if the bandits won, why would they bury the hillman dead?"

"But the bandits wouldn't bury tribesmen," Aheranates protested.

"Exactly. So I suggest you take a few men and find out what's in those graves." It was Haranide's turn to smile, at the consternation on the lieutenant's face.

As the slender youth began to splutter about not being a graverobber, a bowlegged cavalryman ran to a panting halt before them. The edge of a blood-stained bandage showed under his helmet. "Captain," he said nervously. "Sir, there's something maybe you ought to see. It's . . . ." He swallowed convulsively. "You'd best see for yourself, sir."

Haranides frowned. He could not think of anything that would put one of these tough soldiers in this taking. "Lead the way, Narses."

The soldier swallowed again, and turned back the way he had come with obvious reluctance. Haranides noted as he followed that Aheranates was clinging to his heels. He supposed that to the lieutenant's mind, even something that made a seasoned campaigner turn green was better than opening day-old graves.

Near a thornbush springing from the crevice between two boulders a pair of soldiers stood, making an obvious effort not to look into the narrow opening. From chain mail and helmet to hook nose and bandy legs, they were like Narses, and like him, too, in the tightness around their eyes and the green tinge about their lips.

Narses stopped beside the two and pointed to the cleft. "In there, sir. Saw a trail of . . . of blood, sir, leading in, so I looked, and . . . ." He trailed off with a helpless shrug.

The blood trail was clear to be seen, dried black smears on the rock, and on the stony ground beneath the bush.

"Clear the brush away," Haranides ordered irritably. Likely the bandits, or the tribesmen, had tortured someone and tossed the body here for the ravens. He liked looking at the results of torture even less than he liked listening to it, and if the men's faces were any indication, this was a bad job of it. "Get a move on," he added as the men fiddled with their swords.

"Yes, sir," Narses said unhappily.

Swinging their swords like brush knives, to the accompaniment of grumbled curses as thorns found the chinks of their chain mail and broke off in the flesh, the bush was hacked to a stump and the limps dragged clear of the crevice. Haranides put his foot on the stump and levered himself up to peer into the crevice. His breath caught in his throat.

He found himself staring straight into sightless,

inhuman eyes in a leathery scaled face. The fanged mouth was frozen in rictus, seemingly sneering at him. One preternaturally long bony hand, a length of severed rope dangling from the wrist, clutched with clawed fingers at a sword gash in chain mail stained with dried blood. All of its wounds appeared to be from swords, he noted, or at least from the sorts of weapons men bore.

"But then, what self-respecting vulture would touch it," he muttered.

"What is it?" Aheranates demanded.

Haranides climbed down to let the lieutenant take his place. "Did you see anything else up this way?" the captain asked the three soldiers.

A shriek burst from Aheranates' mouth, and the slender young officer half tumbled back to the ground. He stared wildly at the captain, at the three soldiers, scrubbing his mouth with the back of his hand. "Mitra's Holies!" he whispered. "What is that?"

"Not a hillman," Haranides said drily. With a sob the lieutenant stumbled a few steps and bent double, retching. Haranides shook his head and turned back to the soldiers. "Did you find anything?"

"Yes, sir," Narses said. He seemed eager to talk about anything but what was in the crevice. "Horse tracks, sir. Maybe a score or more. Came from the camp down there, right past . . . past here, and went off that way, sir." He flung a hand to the south.

"Following?" the captain mused half to himself.

"We must go back," Aheranates panted suddenly. "We can't fight demons."

"This is the first demon I ever saw killed by a sword," Haranides said flatly. He was relieved to see the momentary panic in the three soldiers' eyes fade. "Get that thing down from there," he went on, turning their looks to pure disgust. "We'll see if our hillman friend knows what it is."

Grumbling under their breath, the bow-legged cavalrymen climbed awkwardly into the cranny and worked the stiffened body free. Haranides started back while they were still lifting it down.

The hillman was spreadeagled between pegs in the ground, surrounded by cavalrymen betting among themselves on whether or not he would open up at the next application. From the coals of a small fire projected the handles of half a dozen irons. The smell of scorched flesh and the blisters on the soles of the hillman's feet and on his dark, hairless chest told the use to which the irons had been put.

Resaro, squatting by the tribesman's side, thrust an iron carefully into the fire. "He isn't saying much so far, sir."

"Unbelieving dogs!" the hillman rasped. His black eyes glared at Haranides above a long, scraggly mustache that was almost as dark. "Sons of diseased camels! Your mothers defile themselves with sheep! Your fathers—"

Resaro casually backhanded him across the mouth. "Sorry, sir. Be a lot worse done to one of us in his village, but he seems to take it personally that we expect him to talk, instead of just killing him outright."

"Never will I talk!" the hillman growled. "Cut off my hands! I will not speak! Pluck out my eyes!

I will not speak! Slice off—"

"Those all sound interesting," Haranides cut him off. "But I can think of something better." The black eyes watched him worriedly. "I'll wager the odds are good there's a hillman up there somewhere watching us right this minute. One of your lot, or another one. It doesn't matter. What do you think would happen if that man sees us turn you loose with smiles and pats on the back?"

"Kill me," the hillman hissed. "I will not talk."

Haranides laughed easily. "Oh, they'd kill you for us. A lot more slowly than we would, I suspect. But worst of all," his smile faded, "they'll curse your soul for a traitor. Your spirit will wander for all time, trapped between this world and the next. Alone. Except for other traitors. And demons." The hillman was silent, but unease painted his face. He was ready, Haranides thought. "Narses, bring that thing in there and show it to our guest."

The watching soldiers gasped and muttered charms as Narses and another carried the rigid corpse into the circle. Haranides kept his eyes on the hillman's face. The dark eyes slid away from the reptilian creature, then back again, abruptly so full of venom as to seem deadly.

"You know it, don't you?" the captain said quietly.

The hillman nodded reluctantly. His eyes were still murderous on Haranides. "It is called a S'tarra." His mouth twisted around the word, and he spat for punctuation. "Many of these thrice-accursed dung-eaters serve the evil one who dwells in the dark fortress to the south. Many men, and even women and children, disappear within those

light-forsaken stone walls, and none are seen
again. Not even their bodies to be borne away for
the proper rites. Such abominations are not to be
endured. So did we gather—'' The thin-lipped
mouth snapped shut; the tribesman resumed his
glare.

"You lie," Haranides sneered. "You know not the
truth, as your mother knew not your father. Hill
dogs do not attack fortresses. You cower in fear of
your women, and you would sell your children for a
copper."

The dark face had become engorged with rage as
Haranides spoke. "Loose me!" the tribesman
howled. "Loose me, drinker of jackal's urine, and I
will carve your manhood to prove mine!"

The captain laughed contemptuously. "With such
numbers as you had, you could not have taken a mud
hut held by an old woman and her granddaughter."

"Our strength was as the strength of thousands for
the righteousness of our cause!" the dark man spat.
"Each of us would have killed a score of the diseased
demon-spawn!"

Haranides studied the hillman's anger-suffused
eyes, and nodded to himself. That was as close as he
was likely to get to confirmation that there were no
more hillmen out. "You say they take people," he
said finally. "Do valuables attract them? Gold?
Gems?"

"No!" Aheranates burst out. Haranides rounded
on him angrily, but the slender man babbled on.
"We cannot pursue these . . . these monsters! Mitra!
'Twas the Red Hawk we were sent for, and if these
creatures kill her, good and well enough!"

"Erlik take you, Aheranates!" the captain grated.

The hillman broke in. "I will guide you. And you ride to slay the scaled filth," he spat, "I will guide you faithfully." Anger had been washed from his face by some other emotion, but what emotion was impossible to say.

"By the Black Throne of Erlik!" Haranides growled. Seizing Aheranates' arm he pulled the young lieutenant away from the prying eyes of the men, behind a massive boulder. The captain glanced around to make certain none of the others had followed. When he spoke his voice was low and forceful. "I've put up with your insolence, with foolishness, slyness, and pettiness enough for ten girls in a zenana, but I'll not put up with cowardice. Especially not in front of the men."

"Cowardice!" Aheranates' slender frame quivered. "My father is Manerxes, who is friend to—"

"I care not if your father is Mitra! Hannuman's stones, man! Your fear is so strong it can be felt at ten paces. We were sent to return with the Red Hawk, not with a rumor that she might possibly be dead somewhere in the mountains."

"You mean to go on?"

Haranides gritted his teeth. The fool could make trouble for him once they returned to Shadizar. "For a time, lieutenant. We may overtake the bandits. And if they have been captured by these S'tarra, well the hilltribes may consider their keep a fortress, but if they thought to take it with fewer than ten score, it's possible eighty real soldiers can do the task. In any event, I won't turn back until I'm sure the Red Hawk and the king's playthings are beyond my grasp."

"You've gone mad." Aheranates' voice was cold and calm, his eyes glazed and half-focused. "I have no other choice. You cannot be allowed to kill us all." His hand darted for his sword.

In his shock Haranides was barely able to throw himself back away from the lieutenant's vicious slash. Aheranates' eyes were fixed; his breath came in pants. Haranides rolled aside, and the other's blade bit into the stony ground where his head had been. But now the captain had his own sword out. He lunged up from the ground, driving it under the younger man's ribs to thrust out behind his shoulder.

Aheranates stared down incredulously at the steel that transfixed him. "My father is Manerxes," he whispered. "He . . . ." A bubble of blood formed on his lips. As it broke, he fell.

Haranides got to his feet, cursing under his breath, and tugged his sword free of the body. He started at a footstep grating on the rock behind him. Resaro stepped up to look down at Aheranates' body.

"The fool," Haranides began, but Resaro cut him off.

"Your pardon for interrupting, sir, but I can see as you're distraught over the lieutenant's death, and I wouldn't want you to say something, in anguish, so to speak, that I shouldn't ought to hear."

"What are you saying?" the hook-nosed captain asked slowly.

Resaro's dark eyes met his levelly. "The lieutenant was a brave man, sir. Hid the terrible wounds he took againsts the hillmen till it was too late for him, but I expect he saved us all. His father will be proud of him." He fumbled a rag from beneath his tunic. "You'd best wipe your sword, sir. You must have dropped it and got some of the lieutenant's blood on it."

Haranides hesitated before accepting the cloth. "When we get back to Shadizar, come see me. I'll need a good sergeant in my next posting. Now get the hillman on a horse, and we'll see if we can find the Red Hawk."

"Yes, sir. And thank you, sir."

Resaro knuckled his forehead and disappeared, but Haranides stood looking at the lieutenant's corpse. Whatever slight chance he might have had of surviving a return to Shadizar without the Red Hawk *and* the Tiridates' trinkets had died with that foppish young idiot. With a muttered oath he went to join his men.

XVIII

Conan's keen eyes swept the ridges as the bandit column wound its way along the floor of the narrow, twisting valley. Hordo was by his side, muttering unintelligibly beneath his breath, while Karela maintained her usual place ahead of them all. Her emerald cape was thrown back, and she rode with one fist planted jauntily on her hip. With the need for tracking past, Aberius was back with the rest of the brigands, riding strung out behind.

"She acts as if this is a parade," Hordo growled.

"It may be," Conan replied. He eased his broadsword in its worn shagreen sheath. His gaze still traversed the ridgelines, never stopping in any one place for long. "We have watchers, at least."

Hordo tensed, but he was too long in the trade of banditry to look around suddenly. He loosened his own blade. "Where are they?" he asked quietly.

"Both sides of the valley. I don't know how many."

"It won't take many in here," Hordo grumbled, eying the steep slopes. "I'll warn her."

"We both go," Conan said quickly. "Slowly, as if we're just riding forward to have a casual word." The one-eyed man nodded, and they kicked their mounts to a faster walk.

Karela looked around in surprise and irritation as they rode up on either side of her. Her mouth opened angrily.

"We're being followed," Hordo said before she could speak. "Along the ridges."

She glanced at Conan, then turned back to Hordo. "You're sure?"

"I'm sure," Conan said. Her back stiffened, and she faced forward again without speaking. He went on. "Half a glass past, I saw movement on the east ridge. I thought it was an animal, but now there are two to the east and three to the west, and they move together."

"Hannuman's stones," she muttered, still not looking at him. They rounded a bend in the trail, and whatever else she had to say was lost in a gasp.

In the center of the trail, only twenty paces from them, stood eight reptilian warriors like those they had killed, in chain mail and ridged helmets, bearing on their shoulders the four crossed poles of a bier. Atop the bier was a tall throne of intricately carved ivory, in which sat a man robed in scarlet. A white streak serpentined through his black hair. He held a long golden staff across his chest and bowed slightly without rising.

"I am called Amanar." His voice rang loudly against the precipitous slopes. "I welcome you, wayfarers."

Conan found he had his broadsword in hand, and noted from the corner of his eye that Karela and Hordo had their blades out as well. Amanar wore a smile, though it did not reach his strange, red-flecked black eyes, but the Cimmerian sensed evil there, evil beyond the scaled creatures that served him. There was nothing rational in his perception. It was a primitive intuition that came from bone and blood, and he trusted it all the more for that.

"Be not affrighted," Amanar intoned.

The sounds of sliding rock and gravel jerked Conan's gaze away from the man on the bier—he was shocked to realize the other had held his eyes thus—to find the abrupt rises to either side of the trail swarming with hundreds of the snake-men, many with javelins or crossbows. There were shouts from the bandits behind as they realized they were as good as surrounded.

"Rats in a barrel," Hordo growled. "Take a pull on the hellhorn for me, Conan, if you get to Gehanna first."

"What mean you by this?" Karela demanded loudly. "If you think to buy our lives cheaply—"

"You do not understand," the man on the bier interrupted smoothly. Conan thought he detected amusement. "The S'tarra are my servants. I greet what few strangers pass this way as I greet you, but betimes strangers are unscrupulous folk who think to use violence against me for all my friendliness. I find it best to remove all temptation by having my retainers near in sufficient numbers. Not that I suspect you, of course."

Conan was certain of the sarcasm in that last.

"What kind of man is served by minions such as these scaled ones?" He suspected the answer, whether he got it or not, was that he had encountered another magician.

Instead of a reply from Amanar, Karela snapped, "You forget who commands here, Cimmerian!" Her green-eyed glare transferred to the man in the scarlet robes, lessening not a whit in intensity. "Still, Amanar, it is not a question out of place. Be you a sorcerer to be served by these monsters?"

Gasps rose from the bandits, and their mutterings increased. Conan winced, for he knew how dangerous it was to confront a mage too openly. But Amanar smiled as he might at rambunctious children.

"The S'tarra are not monsters," Amanar said. "They are the last remnants of a race that lived before man, and gentle of nature despite their outward appearances. Before I came the hillmen hunted them like animals, slaughtered them. No, you have naught to fear from them, nor from me, though some bands which do not serve me sometimes fail to distinguish between the hillmen who hate them and others of humankind."

"We met such a band," Karela said.

Conan looked at the red-haired bandit sharply, but he could not tell whether she believed the man, or whether she attempted some deeper game.

"Praise be to all the gods that you survived," Amanar said piously. "Let me offer you the shelter of my keep. Your retainers may camp outside the walls and feel safe. Pray say you will be my guests. I have few visitors, and there is something I would speak to you of, which I think you will find to your advantage."

Conan looked at the S'tarra arrayed on the slopes above and wondered wryly how many refused Amanar's invitations.

Karela did not hesitate. "I accept gratefully," she said.

Amanar smiled—once more it did not touch his eyes—bowed slightly to her, and clapped his hands. The eight S'tarra bearing his ivory throne turned carefully and started up the trail. Karela rode after him, and Conan and Hordo quickly followed her. On the slopes of the narrow valley the S'tarra kept alongside the bandits, moving over the slanted ground with lizardlike agility. Honor guard, Conan wondered, or simply guard?

"How much of what he says do you believe?" Hordo said softly.

Conan glanced at the throned man leading them—he had experience of the acuity of wizards' hearing. Amanar seemed to be ignoring them. "Not a word," he replied. "That—S'tarra, did he call it?—was headed here."

The one-eyed man frowned. "If we turn suddenly, we could be free of his minions before they had ought but a crossbow shot or two at us."

"Why?" Conan laughed softly. "We came for the pendants, and what else we might find. He takes us into his very keep, right to them."

"I never thought of that," Hordo said, joining Conan's quiet laughter.

Karela looked over her shoulder, her tilted green eyes unreadable. "Leave the thinking to me, old one," she said flatly. "That beard leeches your brain." An uncomfortable silence fell over them.

XIX

As the narrow, twisting gorge they had followed so long debouched into a broader valley, they saw the Keep of Amanar. Ebon towers reared into the sky, their rounded sides seeming to absorb the afternoon sun. Black ramparts, crenellated and sprouting bartizans, grew from the stone of the mountain. A ramp led to the barbican, topped by troughs for pouring boiling oil on those who approached unwarily. Not even a thornbush grew in the stony soil surrounding it all.

Amanar gestured to the wide expanse of the valley below the fortress. "Camp your men where you will. Then come you inside, and I will speak with you." His bier was carried swiftly up the ramp, leaving the bandits milling at its foot.

"Find a spot for my hounds, Hordo," Karela said, dismounting and handing him her reins. Conan climbed down as well. Her green eyes sparkled dangerously. "What do you think you're doing, Cimmerian?"

"I'm not one of your hounds," he replied levelly. He started up the ramp, noting the guard positions on the walls. It would not be an easy place for a thief to enter.

The Cimmerian tensed as running boots pounded up behind him. Karela eased her pace to a walk beside him, her heavy breathing coming more from anger, he suspected, than exertion. "Conan, you don't know what you're doing here. You're out of your depth."

"I need to see what's inside, Karela. These walls could hold off an army. I may yet have to scale them in the night if we're to gain the pendants. Unless Amanar and his scaly henchmen have frightened you out of it."

"I haven't said that, have I? And I won't have you accusing me of cowardice!"

They stopped before the lowered portcullis. From behind the heavy iron bars, a S'tarra peered at them with red eyes that seemed to glow slightly in the shadows of the gateway. Two more stepped from the arched doorway of the barbican, pikes in hand.

"We are expected by Amanar," Conan said.

"I am expected," Karela said.

The S'tarra made a lifting gesture, and with a clanking of chain the grating began to rise. "Yes," it hissed. "The master said the two of you would come. Follow me." Turning on its heel, it trotted into the dark recesses of the fortress.

"How did he know we'd both come?" Karela said as they followed.

"I'm not the one out of my depth," Conan replied. Behind them the portcullis creaked shut. The muscular Cimmerian found himself hoping it would be as easy to get out as it had been to get in.

The granite-paved baileys of the fortress, the sable stone barracks and casemates, were as bleak as the exterior, but then the S'tarra led them through great iron-bound doors into the donjon, a massive obsidian cube topped by the tallest tower of the keep.

Conan found himself in a marble-walled hall with a floor mosaicked in rainbow arabesques. Silver sconces held golden dragon lamps, filling even the vaulted ceiling, carved with hippogriffs and unicorns, with lambent radiance. He nodded to himself with satisfaction. If Amanar lit his entry hall with such, he had wealth enough and more for Conan's needs. There was still the matter of Velita, though, and his oath to free her.

The S'tarra halted before tall doors of burnished brass, and knocked. The creature bent as if to listen, then, though Conan heard nothing, swung one weighty door open. The music of flutes and harps drifted out as the creature bowed, making a gesture for them to enter.

Conan strode in, Karela rushing so as not to seem to be following. He smiled at her, and she bared her teeth in return.

"Welcome," Amanar said. "Sit, please." He sat in an ornately carved chair beside a low ebony table, fondling his golden staff. Two similar chairs were arranged on the other side of the table.

The music came from four human musicians sitting cross-legged on cushions against the wall. They played softly, without looking at one another or raising their eyes from the floor. A woman appeared from behind a curtain with a silver tray holding wine. Her gaze, too, never left the costly carpets that covered the floor as she set the tray on the table, bowed to Amanar, and scurried silently from the room. Amanar seemed not to notice her. His red-flecked eyes were on Karela.

"I didn't know you had any human servants," Conan said. He sat on the edge of his chair, careful to leave his sword free.

Amanar swung his gaze to the Cimmerian, and Conan found himself hard-pressed not to look away. The scarlet flecks in the man's eyes tried to pull him into their inky depths. Conan gritted his teeth and stared back.

"Yes," Amanar said, "I have a few. Worthless things, totally useless unless they're under my eye. At times I have thought I might be better off if I simply gave them all to the hillmen." He spoke loudly, not seeming to care whether the musicians heard, but they played on without missing a beat.

"Why don't you use S'tarra servants, then?" Conan asked.

"They have limits. Yes, definite limits." The man with the odd white streak through his hair suddenly rubbed his hands together. "But come. Let us drink." No one moved to take one of the crystal goblets. "Do you yet distrust me?" There was a touch of mocking in his voice. "Then choose you any cup, and I will drink from it."

"This is ridiculous," Karela suddenly burst out, reaching for the wine.

Conan seized her wrist in an iron grip. "A sip from all three in turn," he said quietly. Amanar shrugged.

"Release me," Karela said quietly, but her words quivered with suppressed rage. Conan loosed his hold. For a moment she rubbed her wrist. "You've formed a bad habit of manhandling me," she said, and reached again for a goblet.

Amanar forestalled her by snatching the crystal cup from under her very fingers. "As your friend still mistrusts . . . ." Swiftly he sipped from each of the three goblets. "You see," he said as he set the last one back on the silver tray, "I do not die. Why should I bring you here to kill you, when I could have had the S'tarra bury you beneath boulders in the valley where we met?"

With an angry glare at Conan, Karela grabbed a goblet and drank, throwing her head back. Conan picked up another slowly, as Amanar took his. The fruity taste was a surprise. It was one of the heady wines of Aquilonia, costly so far from that western land.

"Besides," Amanar said quietly, "why should I wish harm to Conan, the thief of Cimmeria, and Karela, the Red Hawk?"

A scream burst from Karela. Conan bounded to his feet with a roar, crystal cup falling to the carpet as he drew his broadsword. Amanar made no move except to sway toward Karela, standing with her jeweled tulwar in hand, her head turning wildly as if seeking attackers. The dark man's heavy-lidded eyes half closed, and he inhaled deeply as if breathing in her perfume. The musicians played on unconcerned, eyes never lifting.

"Yes," Amanar murmured, leaning back in his chair. He appeared surprised to see Conan's sword. "Do you need that? There is only me, and I can hardly fight you with my staff." He extended the staff to tap Conan's blade. "Put it away and sit. You are in no danger."

"I'll stand," Conan said grimly, "until a few questions are answered."

"Conan was right," Karela whispered. "You're a sorcerer."

Amanar spread his hands. "I am what some men call a sorcerer, yes. I prefer to think of myself as a seeker of wisdom, wanting to bring the world a better way." He seemed pleased with that. "Yes. A better way."

"What do you want with us?" she said, taking a firmer grip on her curved sword. "Why did you bring us here?"

"I have a proposal to make to you. Both of you." The mage fingered his golden staff and smiled. Karela hesitated, then abruptly sheathed her blade and sat down.

"Before I put my sword up," Conan said, "tell me this. You know our names. What else do you know?"

Amanar seemed to consider before answering. "Quite incidentally to discovering your names, I discovered that you seek five dancing girls and five pendants. Searching further told me these were stolen from the palace of King Tiridates of Zamora. Why you seek them, most particularly why you seek them in the Kezankian Mountains, I do not know, however." His smile was bland, and Conan could see doubt spreading on Karela's face.

So much had already been revealed that the Cimmerian decided it could do little further harm to reveal a trifle more. "We came because the women and the gems were taken by S'tarra.'' He bridled at Amanar's answering laugh.

"Forgive me, Conan of Cimmeria, but the mere thought that S'tarra could enter Shadizar is ludicrous. The City Guard would kill them at sight, before they as much as reached the gates. Besides, my muscular friend, the S'tarra never leave the mountains. Never.''

Conan answered in a flat voice. "Those who entered Tiridates' palace wore the boots the S'tarra wear, the boots worked with a serpent.''

Amanar's laughter cut off abruptly, and his eyes lidded. Conan had the sudden impression of being regarded by a viper. "The boots," the sorcerer said at last, "are often taken by hillmen when they strip the S'tarra they have killed. I should imagine a caravan guard who killed a hillman during an attack and found a good pair of boots on him might take them. Who can say how far a pair of those boots might travel, or how many might be worn outside the mountains?" His voice was reasonable in the extreme, if devoid of color, but his black eyes challenged Conan to reject the explanation if he dared. The only sound in the room came from the musicians.

Karela abruptly broke the impasse. "Hannuman's stones, Conan. Would he have mentioned the gems in the first place if he had them?''

The young Cimmerian was suddenly aware of how foolish he must look. The musicians played their flutes and harps. Karela had retrieved her goblet from the carpet and poured more wine. Amanar sat with the long fingers of one hand casually caressing his golden staff. In the midst of this peaceful scene Conan stood sword in hand, balanced to fight on the instant.

"Crom!" he muttered, and slammed his blade into its sheath. He resumed his chair, ostentatiously sprawling back. "You spoke of a proposal, Amanar," he said sharply.

The mage nodded. "I offer you both . . . haven. When the City Watch searches too diligently for Conan the thief, when the Army of Zamora presses too hard against the Red Hawk, let them come here, where the hillmen keep the army away, and my fortress grants safety from the hillmen."

"From the kindness of your heart," Conan grunted.

Karela gave him a pointed look. "What would you require in return, Amanar? We have neither knowledge nor skills to be of use to a sorcerer."

"On the contrary," the mage replied. "The Red Hawk's fame is known from the Vilayet Sea to the Karpashian Mountains, and beyond. It is said that she would march her band into Gehanna, if she gave her word to do so, and that her rogues would follow. Conan is a thief of great skill, I am sure. From time to time I would ask you to perform certain . . . commissions for me." He smiled expansively. "There would, of course, be payment in gold, and I would in no way interfere with your, ah, professions."

Karela grinned wolfishly. "The caravan route to Sultanapur lies less than half a day to the south, does it not?"

"It does," Amanar laughed quietly. "And I'll not object if you should do business there. I may

even have some for you myself. But make not your
decision now. Rest, eat and drink. Tomorrow will
be time enough, or the next day.'' He got to his
feet, gesturing like a gracious host. ''Come. Let me
show you my keep.''

Karela rose with alacrity. ''Yes. I'd like very
much to see it.'' Conan remained where he was.

''You may keep your sword,'' the mage said
derisively, ''if you yet feel the need of protection.''

Conan sprang angrily to his feet. ''Lead on, sorcerer.''

Amanar looked at him searchingly, and the Cimmerian suddenly thought that he and Karela had
been placed on the two ends of a merchant's
balance scale. Finally the necromancer nodded
and, using his golden rod as a walking staff, led
them from the room. The musicians played on.

First the red-robed mage took them to the
heights of the outer curtain wall, its sheer scarp
dropping fifty feet to the mountain slope. Pike-
bearing S'tarra sentries in chain-mail hauberks fell
to their knees at Amanar's approach, but he did
not deign to acknowledge the obeisance. From
thence they went to the ebon parapet of the inner
rampart, where S'tarra crossbowmen in bartizans
could cut down any who managed to gain the outer
wall. From the banquette catapults could hurl great
stones. Atop the towers of the inner wall were ballistae, the arrows of which, as long as a man, could
pierce through horse and rider together on the
valley floor. Massive blocks of pitch-black stone
had been piled to build barracks where dwelt
S'tarra in their hundreds. The scaled ones knelt for
the mage, and followed Conan and Karela with

hungering rubiate eyes.

In the donjon itself, Amanar led them through floor after floor of many-columned rooms hung with cloth-of-gold and costly tapestries. Rare carpets covered mosaicked floors, and bore furnishings inlaid with nacreous mother-of-pearl and deep blue lapis-lazuli. Carven bowls of jasper and amber from far Khitai, great golden vases from Vendhya, set with glittering rubies and sapphires, silver ornaments adorned with golden chrysoberyl and crimson carnelian, all were scattered in profusion as if they were the merest of trinkets.

Human servants were few, and none that the Cimmerian saw ever raised his or her eyes from the floor as they sped by on their tasks. Amanar paid them less heed even than he did the S'tarra.

On the ground level of the donjon, as Amanar began to lead them to the door, Conan noticed an archway, its plain stonework at odds with the ornateness of all else they had seen within. The passage beyond seemed to slope down, leading back toward the mountain.

Conan nodded toward it. "That leads to your dungeons?"

"No!" Amanar said sharply. The black-eyed mage recovered his smile with an obvious effort. "That leads to the chambers where I carry out my . . . researches. None but myself may enter there." The smile remained, but the eyes with the strange red flecks became flat and dangerous. "There are wards set which would be most deadly to one who made the attempt."

Karela laughed awkwardly. "I, for one, have no

interest in seeing a magician's chambers.''

Amanar shifted his dark gaze to the red-haired woman. "Perhaps, someday, I will take you down that passage. But not for a time yet, I think. Sitha will show you out."

Conan had to control a desire to reach for his sword as a S'tarra fully as large as he suddenly stepped from a side passage. He wondered if the mage had some means of communicating with his servants without words. Such a thing could be dangerous to a thief.

The big S'tarra gestured with a long, claw-tipped hand. "This way," it hissed. There was no subservience in its manner toward them, but rather a touch of arrogance in those red eyes.

Conan could feel the eyes of the sorcerer on his back as he followed the dark-eyed man's minion. At the portcullis Sitha gestured without speaking for the heavy iron grate to be raised. From within the barbican came the creak of the windlass. Clanking chains pulled the grate to chest height on Karela. Sitha gestured abruptly, and the creak of the windlass ceased. The S'tarra's fanged mouth cracked in a mocking smile as it gestured for them to go.

"Do you not realize we are your master's guests?" Karela demanded hotly. "I'll—"

Conan grabbed her arm in his huge hand and pulled her protesting under the grate after him. It began to clank down at the very instant they were clear.

"Let's just be thankful to be out," Conan said, starting down the ramp. He saw Hordo waiting at the foot of it.

Karela strode angrily beside him, rubbing her

arm. "You muscle-bound oaf! I'll not take much more of this from you. I intend to see that Amanar punishes that big lizard. These S'tarra must learn proper respect for us, else my hounds will constantly be goaded into fighting them. I might even carve that Sitha myself."

Conan looked at her in surprise. "You intend to accept this offer? The Red Hawk will wear this sorcerer's jesses and stoop at his command?"

"Have you no eyes, Conan? Five hundred of the scaled ones he commands, perhaps more. My hounds could not take this keep were they ten times their number, and I will not waste them against its walls in vain. On the other hand, if all the gold that you and I and all my pack have ever seen in our lives were heaped in one pile it would not equal the hundredth part of what I saw within."

"I've *seen* a lot of gold," Conan snorted. "How much of it stuck to my fingers, and how much of this would, is another matter. This Amanar prates of a better way for mankind, but I've never met a sorcerer who did not tread a black path. Think you what he will ask you to do for his payment."

"A safe heaven," she snapped back, "close to the caravan route. No longer will I need to send my men off to hide as caravan guards when the army hunts us too closely. No longer must I play the fortuneteller while I wait to rejoin them. These things are worth much to me."

The Cimmerian snarled deep in his throat. "They mean naught to me. The Desert is haven enough. I came here to steal five pendants, not to serve a practitioner of the black arts."

They reached the bottom of the ramp, and Hordo looked from one to the other of them.

"You two arguing again?" the one-eyed man growled. "What had this Amanar to say?"

The two ignored him, squaring off at one another.

Karela bit off her words. "He does not have the pendants. Remember, it was he who first mentioned them. And I saw no more than a handful of women among his servants, not one of whom looked to be your dancing girl."

"You talked of the pendants?" Hordo said incredulously.

Conan spared the bearded bandit not a glance. "You believe the man? A sorcerer? He'd have us think the mountains filled with tribes of S'tarra, whole nations of them, but that wounded one we followed was coming here. He knows of the pendants because his minions stole them."

"Sorcerer!" Hordo gasped. "The man's a sorcerer?"

Karela's green eyes flashed to the one-eyed man, the blaze in them so fierce that he took a step back. "Show me where you've camped my hounds," she snapped. "I'll see they're bedded properly." She stalked away without waiting for a reply.

Hordo blinked at Conan. "I'd best go after her. She's going the wrong way. We'll talk later." He darted after the red-haired woman.

Conan turned to look back up at the fortress. Dimly, through the grate of the portcullis, he could make out a shape, a S'tarra, watching him. Though he could distinguish no more than it was there, he knew it was Sitha. Fixing what he could remember of the keep's interior in his head, he went in search of the others.

XX

A gibbous moon crept slowly over the valley of the Keep of Amanar while purple twilight yielded to the blackness of full night. And blackness it was, except about the fires where the bandits huddled well away from the keep, for the pale light of the moon seemed not to enter that maleficent vale.

"I've never seen a night like this," Hordo grumbled, tipping a stone jar of *kil* to his mouth.

Conan squatted across the fire from the one-eyed brigand. It was a larger blaze than he would have built, but Hordo as well as the others appeared to be trying to keep the night at bay.

"It is the place, and the man," the Cimmerian said, "not the night."

His eyes followed Karela for a moment, where she moved among the other fires stopping at each for a word, and a swallow of *kil*, and a laugh that more often than not sounded strained on the part of the men. She had decked herself in her finest, golden breastplates, emerald girdle, a crimson cape

of silk and her scarlet thigh-boots. Conan wondered whether her attire was for the benefit of the
others, or if she, too, felt the oppression of the
darkness that pressed against their fires.

Hordo scrubbed his mouth with the back of his
hand and tossed another dried dung-chip on the
fire. "A sorcerer. To think we would ever serve
such. She won't let me tell them, you know. That
this Amanar's a mage, I mean." He added yet
another chip to the blaze.

Conan edged back from the heat. "Soon or late,
they'll find out." He checked the position of the
moon, then laughed to himself. In that valley there
might as well be no moon and a sky full of rain
clouds. A good night for a thief.

"More *kil*, Cimmerian? No? More for me,
then." The one-eyed man turned the stone jar up
and did not lower it until it was dry. "It'd take vats
of this to comfort my bones this night. A mage.
Aberius darts his eyes like a ferret. He'll bolt the
first chance he sees. And Talbor says openly he'd
ride out on the instant, could he find two coppers
to steal."

"Why wait for the coppers?" Conan asked.
"You like this thing as little as Aberius or Talbor.
Why not ride out on the morrow?" It was in his
mind that by dawn Amanar might not be so friendly toward the bandits. "You can persuade her if
anyone can, and I think a night like this would be
halfway to convincing her for you."

"You do not know her," Hordo muttered,
avoiding the Cimmerian's blue-eyed gaze. "Once a
thing is in her mind to do, she does it, and there's
an end to it. And what she does, I do." He did not

sound particularly happy about that last.

"I think I'll take a walk," Conan said, rising.

Hordo's lone eye stared at him incredulously. "A walk! Man, it's black as Ahriman's heart out there!"

"And it's hot as the gates of Gehanna here," Conan laughed. "If you build that fire any higher, you'll melt." He walked into the night before the other man could say more.

Once away from the pool of light cast by the fires—not far in that strange, malevolent night—he stopped to let his eyes adjust as best they could. By touch he checked the Karpashian dagger on his left forearm, and slung his sword across his back. He had no rope or grappel, but he did not think he would need either.

After a time he realized that he could see, in a fashion. The full moon, glowing blue-green in the sky, should have lit the night brightly. The thin, attenuated light that in truth existed flickered unnaturally. Objects could only be detected by gradations of blackness, and in that dark lambence all appeared to quiver and move.

Quickly he started toward the fortress, biting back a string of oaths as rocks turned beneath his feet on the slope and boulders loomed out of the black, often to be detected first by his outstretched hands. Then the wall of the keep reared before him, as if the black of the night had been concentrated and solidified.

The gargantuan stones of that wall seemed to form an unbroken vertical plane, yet were there finger- and toe-holds to be found by a man who knew where to look. Conan moved up that sheer escarpment heedless of the infinite darkness beneath him, and the rocks that would dash his life out if his grasp slipped.

Short of the top of the wall he stopped, clinging like a fly, massive body flattened tightly against the ebon stone. Above him the S'tarra sentries' boots grated closer, and past. In an instant he scrambled through the embrasure, across the parapet, and let himself down over the inner edge. The climb down into the other bailey was easier, for that side of the wall had not been designed with the intent of stopping anyone from scaling it.

His feet found the paving stones, and he squatted against the wall to get his bearings. Scattered lamps, brass serpents with wicks burning in their mouths, cast occasional pools of light within the fortress. The heavy iron-strapped gates letting into the inner bailey stood open, and apparently unguarded. But that would be a dangerous assumption to make. He was choosing a spot to scale the inner rampart when a movement caught his eye.

From the shadows to his left down the wall a man darted across the bailey. As he passed through the meager light cast by a serpent lamp Conan recognized Talbor. So the man was not waiting to find his two coppers to steal. The Cimmerian only hoped the other raised no alarm to make his own task more difficult. Talbor ran straight to the open gate into the inner bailey and passed through.

Conan forced himself to wait. If Talbor was taken it would be no time for him to be halfway up the inner wall. No alarm was raised. Still he waited, and still there was no sound.

The Cimmerian uncoiled from his crouch and walked across the bailey, carefully avoiding the sparse pools of light from the serpent lamps. If glimpsed, he would be no more than another moving shadow, and it was rapid motion that drew the eye at night. He slowed, examining the gateway carefully. The guardpost was empty.

He went through the gate at the same slow walk and crossed the inner bailey. From the walls behind he could hear the tread of sentries' boots, their pace unchanging.

As he approached the huge cube of the donjon he chose his entry point. Best, because highest, would have been the single black tower that rose into the darkness at one corner, but he had seen in the daylight that whatever mason had constructed it had been a master. He had been able to detect no slightest crack between the carefully fitted stones. It reminded him uncomfortably of the Elephant Tower of the necromancer Yara, though that had glittered even in the dark where this seemed one with the night.

The walls of the donjon itself presented no such problem, though, and he quickly found himself squeezing with difficulty through an overly broad arrowslit on the top level. Once inside he swiftly drew his sword. A single oil lamp on the wall was lit; he began to examine his surroundings.

The purpose of the room he could not fathom. Its only furnishing, other than tapestries on the walls, seemed to be a single high-backed chair of carved ivory set before a gameboard, one hundred squares of alternating colors set in the floor. Pieces in the shapes of bizarre animals, each as high as his

knee, were scattered about the board. He hefted
one, and grunted in surprise. He had thought it
gilded, but from its weight it had to be of solid
gold. Could he depart with two or three of those,
he would have no need of the pendants. Even one
might do.

Regretfully he set the piece, a snarling, winged
ape-creature, back on the board. He must yet find
Velita, and to attempt to do so burdened with that
weight would be madness. With great care he
cracked the door. The marble-walled hall was
brightly lit by silver lamps. And empty. He slipped
out.

As he moved along that corridor, its floor red-
and-white marble lozenges in an intricate pattern,
he realized that he moved through a strange silence. He had entered many great houses and
palaces in the dead of night, and always there was
some sound, however slight. Now he could have
moved through a tomb in which no thing breathed.
Indeed, as he cautiously examined room after
room he saw no living thing. No S'tarra. No
human servant. No Velita. He hurried his pace,
and went down curving alabaster stairs to the next
floor.

Through two more floors he searched, and the
opulence he saw paled the golden figures to insig-
nificance. A silver statue of a woman with sapphires for eyes, rubies for nipples and pearls for the
nails of her fingers. A table encrusted with diamonds and emeralds till it cast back the light of
silver lamps a hundredfold. A golden throne set
with a king's ransom in black opals.

And then he was peering into a room, plain beside the others for merely being paneled in amber and ivory, peering at a pair of rounded female buttocks. Their owner knelt, naked, with her back to the door and her face pressed to the floor. The muscular youth found himself smiling at the view, and sternly drew his mind back to the matter at hand. She was the first living soul he had seen, and human rather than S'tarra.

One quick stride took him to the bent form; a big hand clasped over her mouth lifted her from the floor. And he was staring into Velita's large, liquid brown eyes.

"Come, girl," he said, loosing his hold, "I was beginning to think I'd never find you."

She threw her arms around him, pressing her soft breasts against his broad chest. "Conan! You did come. I never really believed, though I hoped and prayed. But it's too late. You must go away before Amanar returns." A shudder went through her slim form as she said the name.

"I swore to free you, didn't I?" he said gruffly. "Why are you kneeling here like this? I've seen no one else at all, neither S'tarra nor human."

"S'tarra are not allowed in the donjon when Amanar isn't here, and humans are locked in their quarters unless he desires them." She tilted her head up, and her voice dropped to a whisper. "I didn't betray you, Conan. Not even when Sitha whipped me. I would not tell Amanar who you are."

"It's over, Velita," he said.

She seemed not to hear. Tears trembled on her long lashes. "He became enraged. For my punishment several times a day, without warning, I am commanded to come to this room and kneel until I am told to leave. When I hear footsteps I never know if I am to be sent back to my mat, or if it is Amanar. Sometimes he merely stands, listening to me weep. I hate him for making me fear him so, and I hate myself for weeping, but I can't help it. Sometimes he beats me while I kneel, and if I move the punishment begins again."

"I'll kill him," Conan vowed grimly. "This I swear to you on pain of my life. Come, we'll find the pendants, and I'll take you away this night."

The lithesome naked girl shook her small head firmly. "I cannot go, Conan. I am spell-caught."

"Spell-caught!"

"Yes. Once I tried to escape, and my feet carried me to Amanar. Against my will I found myself telling him what I intended. Another time I tried to kill myself, but when the dagger point touched my breast my arms became like iron. I could not move them, even to set the knife down. When they found me Amanar made me beg before he would free me."

"There must be a way. I could carry you away." But he saw the flaw in that even as she laughed sadly.

"Am I to remain bound the rest of my life for fear of returning to his place? I don't know why I even tried to take my life," she sighed heavily. "I'm sure Amanar will kill me soon. Only Susa and I remain. The others have disappeared."

The big Cimmerian nodded. "Mages are not easily killed—this I know for truth—but once dead their spells die with them. Amanar's death will free you."

"Best you take the pendants and go," she said. "I can tell you where they are. Four are in the jeweled casket, in a room I can show you. The fifth, the one I wore, is in the chamber where he works his magics." She frowned and shook her head. "The others he tossed aside like offal. That one he wrapped in silk and laid in a crystal coffer."

The memory of the stone came back to Conan. A black oval the length of his finger joint, with red flecks that danced within. Suddenly he seized Velita's arms so hard that she cried out. "His eyes," he said urgently. "That stone is like his eyes. In some way it is linked to him. He'll free you rather than have it destroyed. We'll go down to his thaumaturgical chamber—"

"Down? His chamber is in the top of the tower above us. Please release me, Conan. My arms are growing numb."

Hastily he loosed his grip. "Then what lies at the end of that passage that seems to lead into the mountain?"

"I know not," she replied, "save that all are forbidden to enter it. His chamber is where I said. I've been taken to him there. Would the gods had made him like Tiridates," she added bitterly, "a lover of boys."

"Then we'll go up to his chamber," Conan said. She shook her head once more. "What's the matter now?" he asked.

"There is a spell on the stairway in the tower whenever he is out of the donjon. Truly he trusts no one, Conan. One of the human servants climbed that stair while Amanar was gone to meet you." She shivered and buried her face against his chest. "He screamed forever, it seemed, and none could get close even to end his misery."

He smoothed her hair awkwardly with a big hand. "Then I must enter the donjon when he is here. But if he isn't here now, Velita, where is he?"

"Why, in your camp of bandits. I heard him say that the night might affright them, so he has taken them rare wines and costly viands for a feasting."

Conan raised his hand helplessly. It seemed the gods conspired against him at every turn. "Velita, I must go back to the camp. If he suspects I'm here . . . ."

"I know," she said quietly. "I knew from the first you could not take me with you."

"Does not my standing here tell you my oath-sworn word is good? I will see Amanar dead, and you free."

"No!" she cried. "Amanar is too powerful. You'll die to no purpose. I release you from your oath, Conan. Leave these mountains and forget that I exist."

"You cannot release me from an oath sworn before gods," he said calmly, "and I will not release myself from one sworn on my life."

"Then you will die. Yet I do pray that somehow you will find a way. Please go now, Conan. I must await Amanar's return, and I don't want you to see me . . . ." The slender girl's head dropped, and her shoulders quivered with sobs.

"I swear!" Conan grated. Almost wishing to find himself face to face with the sorcerer, he strode from the room.

XXI

As Conan approached the bandit camp he was struck with the sounds of raucous laughter and drunken, off-key singing. Stumbling into the light he stared in amazement. The brigands were in full carouse. Hook-nosed Reza squatted with a whole roast in his hands, tearing at it with his teeth. Aberius staggered past, head tilted back and a crystal flagon upturned. Half the wine spilled down his chest, but the weasel-faced man laughed and tossed the costly vessel to shatter against the rocky ground. Hordo swung his tulwar in one hand, a golden goblet in the other, roaring an obscene song at the moon. Every man sang or laughed, ate or drank, as was his wont and his mood, belching and wiping greasy fingers on his robes, gulping down costly Aquilonian wines like the cheapest tavern swill.

Through the midst of the revelry Karela and Amanar approached Conan. She held a crystal goblet like a lady of high degree, but there was a

stagger to her walk, and the mage had his long arm
about her slim shoulder. Amanar had pushed back
her scarlet cape so that his elongated fingers
caressed her silken flesh in a possessive manner.
Remembering Velita, Conan was both disgusted
and offended, but he knew he must yet control his
temper until the pendant was in his grasp.

"We wondered where you were," the red-haired
woman said. "Look at this feast Amanar has
brought us. This has cured the fit of sulking that
had taken my hounds."

Amanar's dark eyes were unreadable. "There is
little to see even in daylight, Conan of Cimmeria,
and few men care to wander here in the night.
What did you find to interest you in the darkness?"

"They built the fires too hot for my northern
blood," Conan replied. He eyed the way those long
fingers kneaded Karela's shoulder. "That's a
shoulder, mage," he said with more heat than he
had intended, "not a lot of bread dough."

Karela looked startled, and Amanar laughed.
"The hot blood of youth. Just how old are you,
Cimmerian?" He did not remove his hand.

"Not yet nineteen," Conan said proudly, but he
was saddened to see the change in Karela's eyes. He
had seen the same in other women's eyes, women
who thought a man needed a certain number of
years to be a man.

"Not yet nineteen!" Amanar choked on his own
laughter. "Practically a beardless youth for all his
muscles. The Red Hawk, the great robber of
caravans, has robbed a cradle."

She shrugged off the mage's arm, her tilted green

eyes glowing dangerously. "A barbar boy," she muttered. Then, in a louder voice, "I have considered your offer, Amanar. I accept."

"Excellent," the sorceror said with a satisfied smile. He rubbed the side of his long face with the golden staff and regarded Conan. "And you, young Cimmerian who likes to wander in the dark? Despite your youth my offer to you yet holds, for I think there must be skill in those massive shoulders."

Conan managed to force a smile onto his lips. "I need to think longer. In a day or two, as you first spoke of, I will give you my answer."

Amanar nodded. "Very well, Cimmerian. In a day or two we shall see what your future will be." His red-flecked eyes turned to Karela with a caressing gaze that made Conan's flesh crawl. "You, my dear Karela, must come to the keep on the morrow. Without the young Cimmerian, of course, as he has not yet made up his mind. We must have a number of long private discussions concerning my plans for you."

Conan longed to smash his fist into that dark face but instead he said, "Perhaps you'll speak of some of those plans to us all. Knowing what they are might help me decide, and some of these others as well."

Karela's head had been turning between the two men with a comparing gaze, but at that she jerked rigidly erect. "My hounds go where I command, Cimmerian!"

A sudden silence fell, laughter and song all dying away. Conan looked around for the cause and found Sitha standing at the edge of the light, clutching a great double-bladed battle-ax across its broad chest. Red eyes glowed faintly as it surveyed the men around the fires, and they shifted uneasily, some loosening their weapons in their scabbards. The S'tarra's lipless mouth curled back from its fangs in what might have been meant for a smile. Or a sneer.

"Sitha!" Amanar said sharply.

Looking neither to left nor right, the S'tarra strode through the camp to kneel at Amanar's feet. At an impatient gesture Sitha rose and leaned close to whisper in its master's ear.

Conan could catch no sound of what was said, nor read anything on the mage's dark face, but Amanar's knuckles grew white on his golden staff, telling Conan the man found the news displeasing. Talbor, Conan thought. Amanar gestured for his minion to be silent.

"I must leave you," the mage said to Karela. "A matter requires my attention."

"Not trouble, I hope," she said.

"A small matter," Amanar replied, but his mouth was tight behind his close-cropped beard. "I will see you on the morrow, then. Rest well." He turned his attention to Conan. "Think well on your decision, Cimmerian. There are worse things than what I offer. Sitha." The sorcerer strode from the camp, his S'tarra minion at his heels.

With the departure of the scaled creature the noise level of the camp began to rise again quickly. Hordo staggered up to Conan and Karela.

"I do not like those things," the one-eyed brigand said unsteadily. He still held his bared tulwar and the now-empty golden goblet, and he swayed as he spoke. "When are we to leave this accursed valley and be about what we know? When are we for the caravan routes?"

"You're drunk, my old hound," Karela said affectionately. "Find yourself a place to sleep it off, and we'll talk in the morning."

"I entered the keep tonight," Conan said quietly.

Karela's green eyes locked with his sapphire gaze. "You fool!" she hissed. Hordo stared with his mouth open.

"He has the pendants," the Cimmerian went on, "and the women. At least, he has two of the women. The other three have disappeared. It's my belief he killed them."

"Killed slave girls?" Hordo said, scandalized. "What sort of man does a thing like that? Even a sorcerer . . . ."

"Keep your voice down," Karela snapped. "I told you not to bandy that word about until I gave you leave. And you, Conan. What's this nonsense you're babbling? If the women are gone, likely he sold them. Or was your precious Velita one of them?"

"She was not," Conan growled back. "And why should she still raise your hackles? You know there's nothing between us, though there seems to be quite a bit between you and Amanar, from the way he was fondling you."

"No!" Hordo protested, putting a hand on her shoulder. "Not Amanar. Not with you. I'll admit I thought better of you taking Conan to your bed, but—"

Face flaming, Karela cut him off sharply. "Be silent, you old fool! What I do, and with whom, is my business!" Her eyes flung green daggers at Conan, and she stalked away, snatching a flask from Aberius as she passed him.

Hordo shook his massive head. "Why did you not speak, Conan? Why did you not stop her?"

"She's a free woman," Conan said coldly. His pride was still pricked by the way she had accepted Amanar's arm about her. "I have no claim on her. Why didn't you stop her?"

"I'm too old to have my liver sliced out," Hordo snorted. "Your Velita was truly in the keep, then? I wonder you didn't take her, and the pendants, and ride from this place." He swept his curved sword in an arc that took in all the dark outside the firelight.

"She's spell-caught," Conan sighed, and told him how he had found Velita, and what she had said.

"So he lied to us," the bearded man said when Conan finished. "And if about the pendants and the women, about what else?"

"About everything. I had thought to tell her about what he's done with Velita, to show him for the man he is, but now I think she'd believe I made it up."

"And likely tell Amanar about it, to amuse him with your jealousy. Or what she'd see as jealousy," he added quickly as the big Cimmerian youth glared at him. "What am I to do, Conan? Even now I cannot abandon her."

Conan lifted his broadsword an inch free of its sheath and slammed it back again. "Keep your sword sharp, and your eye open." His steely gaze took in the motley rogues sprawled drunkenly around the fires. "And have these hounds of hers ready to move at an instant. Without letting her or Amanar discover it, of course."

"You don't ask much, do you, Cimmerian? What are you going to do?"

Conan peered through the darkness toward the fortress before answering. Even in that over-powering blackness those massive walls seemed blacker still. "Kill Amanar, free Velita, steal the pendants, and return to Shadizar, of course. Trifles like that."

"Trifles like that," Hordo groaned. "I need another drink."

"So do I," Conan said softly. The night weighed heavily on his broad shoulders. This valley would be a poor place to die.

XXII

The strange darkness lingered in the valley, resisting morning and fading to a gray dawn only after the blood-red sun stood well above the mountaintops. It was mid-morning before full daylight came, but Conan alone noticed in the bandit camp, for the others lay sprawled in drunken stupors. As the sun at last sucked the last canescence from the valley air, the Cimmerian made his way to the spring that bubbled from a cleft not far from the camp.

Scooping water in his cupped hands, he drank, and made a disgusted sound in his throat. Though cold, the water was flat and lifeless, like everything else in the barren and forboding rift. He contented himself with splashing it on his face, and settled to observe the valley.

On the battlements of the keep S'tarra moved, but nothing else stirred except vultures making slow circles in the distance. Conan wondered grimly how Velita had fared at Amanar's return.

The sorcerer seemed not to know how far Conan's nocturnal peregrinations had taken him—at least, there was no sign of alarm, no squads of S'tarra sent for him—but that spoke not at all to her faring.

"Tonight," the muscular youth vowed.

Aberius, tottering up to fall on his knees beside the spring, glanced incuriously at him. The man's usual hostility seemed momentarily expelled by wine fumes. The weasel-faced bandit dashed a few handfuls of water over his head and staggered away to be replaced by Hordo, who threw himself at full length by the spring and plunged his head into the pool.

Just as Conan was about to go over and pull him out, the one-eyed man lifted his head and peered at the Cimmerian through dripping hair and beard. "Has this water no taste," he mumbled, "or did my tongue die last night?"

"Both," Conan chuckled. Hordo groaned and lowered his head once more to the water, but this time only far enough to drink. "Have you seen Talbor this morning, Hordo?"

"I've seen nothing this morning but the insides of my own eyelids. Let me decide in peace whether I desire to live or not."

"Talbor was inside the fortress last night, when I was."

Hordo lifted himself on his elbows, flipping water at his face with spatulate fingers. "Such a thing to tell a man with my head. Do you think that's why Amanar was summoned to the keep?"

Conan nodded. "Talbor's not in the camp. I checked at first light."

"He could have stolen what he wanted, taken a horse, and be halfway out of the Kezankians by now," the other man protested. "He's not as particular as you. He'd not insist on Tiridates' playpretties, and a dancing girl besides."

"You could be right," Conan said flatly.

"I know," Hordo sighed. "I don't believe it, either. So is he dead, or is he in the sorcerer's dungeon? And what do we tell her?"

"We wait to see what Amanar tells her. His S'tarra outnumber us at least twenty to one, and those are odds I bet small coins on."

He got to his feet as Sitha appeared at the port-cullis and came down the black granite ramp. The tall S'tarra carried neither ax nor sword that Conan could see. It reached the bottom of the incline and set off at a brisk pace across the gray, boulder-strewn valley floor toward the bandit camp. Conan started down the rocky slope to meet it, and Hordo scrambled to his feet to follow.

When Conan walked into the camp, the scaled creature was the center of a ring of brigands. No weapons were in hand, he was relieved to see, but the human eyes there were far from friendly. And who could say of Sitha's?

Hordo pushed past Conan to confront the S'tarra. "What's this, then? Does your master send a message for us?"

"I come for myself," Sitha hissed. It stood half a head taller than the burly one-eyed bandit, taller even than Conan, and if there was no expression in those sanguine eyes there was certainly contempt in the sibilant voice. A padded gambeson and chain-mail hauberk covered it to the knees, but it wore no helmet. "I am Sitha, Warden of the S'tarra, and I come to pit myself against you."

Aberius, behind Conan, laughed uneasily. "Without so much as a dagger?"

Sitha bared its fangs. "My master would not be pleased, an I slew you. We will pit strength at the stones."

"Stones?" Hordo said. "What stones?"

The S'tarra spun on its booted heel, motioning for them to follow. In a muttering file they did, down the valley away from the keep to a spot where boulders had been arranged to form a rough circle half a hundred paces across. The ground between had been smoothed and leveled, and in the center of the circle lay two rough spheres of dark granite. Conan estimated the smaller at twice the weight of a man, the larger at half again as much.

"Lift one of the stones," Sitha said. "Any one of you." It flashed bare fangs again, briefly. "Any two of you."

"Hordo!" someone called. "Hordo's strongest!"

Aberius eyed the stones, then Karela's one-eyed lieutenant. "Who'll wager?" he cried, his narrow face taking on a malicious smile. "Who thinks old Hordo can lift the small stone?"

"Old Hordo, is it?" Hordo spat.

He bent to the lesser of the huge stones as a babbling knot formed around Aberius to get their wagers marked. The burly man threw his arms about the stone, fitting his hands carefully to the undercurves, and heaved. The scar running from under his eye-patch whitened with strain, and his eye bulged. The round stone stirred. Abruptly his hands slipped, and he staggered back with an oath.

"Mitra!" the one-eyed brigand panted. "There's no way to get a good grip on the accursed thing." Chortling, Aberius collected his winnings.

"Your strongest cannot lift it," Sitha hissed. "Can two of you do it? Let any two try." His scathing glance took in Conan, but the Cimmerian said nothing.

Reza and another hawk-nosed Iranistani, named Banidr, pushed forward. Aberius began again to hawk his wagering. Those who had lost the first time were now quickest to press their coins at him.

Reza and Banidr conferred a moment, dark heads together, then squatted, one on either side of the stone. Pressing their forearms in under the lower curve of the stone sphere, each grasped the other's upper arm. Their closeness to the stone forced them into spraddle-legged stances. For a moment they rocked back and forth, counting together, then suddenly tried to heave themselves erect. Veins popped forth on their foreheads. The stone lifted. A finger breadth. A handwidth. Banidr cried out, and in an instant the stone had forced their arms apart, torn loose their grips, and thumped to the ground. Banidr fell back, clutching himself. Arguments broke out as to whether the two had lifted the stone far enough or not.

"This!" Sitha's shout riveted the bandits, drying their arguments in mid-word. "This I mean by lifting the stone!" The S'tarra bent over the large granite ball, locked its arms about it, and straightened as easily as if it had been a pebble. Gasps broke from the bandits as it started toward them; they parted before it. Five paces. Ten. Sitha let the stone fall with a crash, and turned back to the dumbstruck men. "That I mean by lifting." Peals of hissing laughter broke between its fangs.

"I'll have a try," Conan said.

The S'tarra's laughter slowed and stopped. Red eyes regarded Conan with open contempt. "You, human? Will you try to carry the stone back to its place, then?"

"No," the young Cimmerian said, and bent to the larger stone.

"Two to one he fails," Aberius cried. "Three to one!" Men eyed Conan's massive chest and shoulders, weighed the odds, and crowded around the weasel-faced man.

Conan squatted low to get his arms below the largest part of the big stone. As his fingers felt for purchase on the rough sphere, he found Sitha's frowning gaze on him.

With a sudden roar, the big Cimmerian heaved. His mighty thews corded, and his joints popped with the strain. The muscles of his broad back stood out in stark relief, and his massive arms knotted. Slowly he straightened, every fiber quivering as he came fully erect. His eyes met Sitha's once more, and snarling, the S'tarra took a backward step. With great effort Conan stepped forward, back bowed under the strain. He took another step.

"Conan," someone said softly, and another voice repeated, louder, "Conan!"

Teeth bared by lips drawn back in a rictus of effort, Conan went forward. Now his eyes were locked on the stone Sitha had carried.

Two more voices took up the cry. "Conan!"

Five more. "Conan!" Ten. "Conan!" The shouts were flung back from the mountain slopes as a score of throats hurled forth their chant with his every step. "Conan! Conan! Conan!"

He came level with the other stone, took one step more, and let the great sphere fall with a thunderous thud that every man there felt in his feet. Conan's shoulder joints creaked as he straightened, looking at Sitha. "Will you try to take my stone back?"

Cheering bandits darted between a glowering Aberius, parting with all his former winnings and more, and Conan, some clasping his hand, others merely wanting to touch his arm. Sitha's hands twitched in front of its chest as if clutching for the thick haft of a battle-ax.

Of a sudden the bronzen tones of a great gong broke from the fortress and echoed down the valley. Sitha whirled at the first tone and broke into a run for the black keep. The gong pealed forth again, and again, its hollow resonance rolling against the mountains. Atop the ebon ramparts of the keep S'tarra ran.

"An attack?" Hordo said, bewildered. The bandits crowded in close behind the one-eyed man, their exuberance of moments before already dissipated. Some had drawn their swords.

Conan shook his head. "The portcullis is open, and I see no one near the ballistae or catapults. Whatever's happening, though . . . ." He let his words trail off as Karela galloped up to face them, one fist on a scarlet thigh-boot.

"Are the lot of you responsible for this?" she demanded. "I heard all of you bellowing like oxen in a mire, then this infernal gong began." As she spoke the tolling ceased, though the ghost of it seemed yet to hang in the air.

"We know no more than you," Hordo replied.

"Then I'll find out what's happening," she said.

"Karela," Conan said, "do you not think it best to wait?"

Her green eyes raked him scornfully, and without a word she spun her horse and galloped toward the fortress. The big black's hooves rang on the black granite of the ramp, and after a moment's delay she was admitted.

Minutes later the portcullis opened once more. Sitha's massive form, helmeted and bearing the great battle-ax, galloped through the gate, followed by paired columns of mounted S'tarra. Conan counted lances as they streamed down the incline and pounded across the valley towards a gorge leading north.

"Three hundred," the Cimmerian said after the last S'tarra had disappeared. "More wayfarers, do you think?"

"So long as it's not us," Hordo replied.

Slowly the bandits returned to the cold ashes of their campfires, breaking into twos and threes to cast lots or dice. Aberius began maneuvering three clay cups and a pebble atop a flat rock, trying to entice back some of the silver he had lost. Conan settled with his back to a tilted needle of stone, where he could watch both the keep and the gorge into which Sitha had led the S'tarra. The day stretched long and flat, and except when Hordo brought him meat and cheese and a leather flagon of thin wine Conan did not change his position.

As the sanguinary sun sank on the western mountain peaks, the S'tarra returned, galloping from the same knife-sharp slash in the valley by which they had left.

"No casualties," Hordo said, coming up beside Conan as the S'tarra appeared.

Conan, once more counting lances, nodded. "But they took . . . something." Twenty riderless horses were roped together in the middle of the column, each bearing a long bundle strapped across it.

A spark of light in the east caught the Cimmerian's eye, a momentary glitter that flashed against the shadows of mountains already caught in twilight and was gone. It flashed again. Frowning, he studied the slopes around the valley. High above them, to the north, another spark flared and was gone.

"Think you Amanar knows the valley is watched?" Hordo asked.

"You use that eye," Conan said approvingly. The S'tarra rode up the long incline to the fortress, the portcullis creaking open to let them ride in without slowing. "I worry more about who does the watching."

The one-eyed brigand let out a long, low whistle between his teeth. "Who? Now that's a kettle of porridge to set your teeth on edge."

Conan knew the choices of who it could be—hillmen, the army, Zamoran or Turanian, or Imhep-Aton—but he was not certain which would be worst for him and for the bandits, or even if those two would be the same. Time ran short for him. "I mean to bring Velita out of the keep tonight, Hordo. It may mean trouble for you, but I must do it.''

"I've half a memory of you saying as much last night," Hordo mused. Karela appeared, riding slowly down the ramp from the fortress. "Almost I wish you would, Cimmerian. 'Twould give the excuse to get her away from this place, away from the sorcerer.''

Karela reached the bottom of the ramp and turned her big black toward the camp. She rode with one fist on her hip, her callimastian form swaying with the motion of the horse. The bloody sun was half obscured behind the peaks, now, yet enough remained to bathe her face in a golden glow.

"And if she will not go," Conan said, "you'll follow where she leads, be it a hillman's torture fire or Amanar's diabolic servitude.''

"No more," Hordo replied sadly. "My last service to the Red Hawk, and it must be so, will be to tie her to her saddle and take her to safety." His voice hardened suddenly. "But it will be me, Conan. No other will raise a hand to her while Hordo yet lives. Not even you.''

Conan met the fierce single-eyed gaze levelly. On the one hand, an oath not lift a hand to save her; on the other, how could he stand and watch her die? It was a cleft stick that held his tongue.

Karela reined in before the two men, raising a hand to shield her eyes as she peered at the mountain-shrouded sun. "I had not realized I was so long with Amanar," she murmured, shifting her green eyes to them. "Why are you two glaring at each other like a pair of badgers? I thought you now were almost fraternal in your amity."

"We stand in concord, Hordo and I," Conan
said. He stretched up his hand, and the other man
grasped it, pulling him to his feet.

"We'll give them a good turn, eh, Cimmerian,"
Hordo said, "before we go under."

"We'll drink from golden goblets in Aghrapur
yet," Conan replied soberly.

"What do you two babble about?" Karela
demanded. "Gather my hounds, Hordo. I'll speak
to them before that accursed dark comes on us."

With a quick nod Hordo darted ahead to
assemble the bandits. Karela looked at Conan as if
she wanted to speak, then the moment passed.
There was much to say, he thought, but he would
not speak first. He started after Hordo, and
moments later heard her horse following slowly.
She made no effort to catch up.

XXIII

"Do you want gold?" Karela shouted. "Well, do you?"

She stood atop a boulder as high as a man's head, crimson-thigh-booted feet well apart, fists on hips, her hair an auburn mane. She was magnificent, Conan thought, from his place at the back of the semicircle of brigands who listened to her. Just looking at her was still enough to make his mouth grow dry.

"We want gold," Reza muttered. A few others echoed him. Most watched silently. Aberius had a thoughtful look in his beady eyes, making him look even more sly and malicious than usual. Hordo stood beside the flat-topped boulder, keeping a worried watch on the brigands and Karela both. The fires of the camp surrounded them, holding off the twilight.

"Do you like being chased into hiding by the army?" she cried.

"No!" half a dozen voices growled.

"Do you like spending half a year at guards' wages?"

"No!" a dozen shouted back at her.

"Well, do you know the caravan route is less than half a day south of here? Do you know that a caravan is coming along that route, bound for Sultanapur? Do you know that in three days time we'll take that caravan?"

Roars of approval broke from every throat. Except Aberius, Conan noted. While the others waved fists in the air, shouted and pounded each other on the shoulder, Aberius' look grew more thoughtful, more furtive.

"And the army won't hound us," she went on loudly, "because we'll come back here till they give up. The Zamoran Army are not men enough to follow where we go!"

The cheering went on. The bandits were too caught up in imagining the Zamorans less brave than they to think too closely on how brave they themselves were. Karela raised her hands above her head and basked in their adulation.

Hordo left his place by the boulder and came around to where Conan stood. "Once more, Cimmerian, she has us in the palm of her hand. You don't suppose this could . . . ."

Conan shrugged as the one-eyed man trailed off doubtfully. "You must do as you will." Hordo still looked uncertain. Conan sighed. He would not like seeing the burly bandit dead. Purple twilight was already giving way, night falling as if the inky air had jelled. The bandits around Karela continued their cheering. "I'll be away, now," the Cimmerian went on, "before they notice my going."

"Fare you well," Hordo said quietly.

Conan slipped into the caliginous night. Scudding clouds obscured the lustrous moon as he hurried along the stony slope. Before the full mantle of night enfolded that tenebrous vale, he wanted to be as close to the walls of the fortress as he could.

Abruptly he stopped, broadsword coming firmly into his hand. No sound had reached his ear, no glimmer of motion caught his eye, but senses he could not describe told him there was something ahead of him.

The darkness ahead seemed suddenly to split, fold and thicken, and there was an elongated shadow where there had been none. "How did you know?" came Imhep-Aton's low voice. "No matter. Truly now your usefulness is ended. Your pitiful efforts are futile, but as a rat scurrying beneath the feet of warrior in battle may cause him to trip and die, so may you discommode those greater than yourself."

The darkling shape moved toward Conan. He could see no weapon but an outstretched hand.

Of a sudden rock behind him grated beneath a boot. Conan dropped to a full squat, felt rather than saw a pike thrust pass above his head. Grasping his sword hilt with both hands he pivoted on his left foot, striking for where the pike-wielder must be. He felt the point of his blade bite through chain mail and flesh at the same moment that he saw his attacker's red eyes glowing in the night. The falling pike struck him on the shoulder, the rubiate glow faded, and he was tugging his sword free of a collapsing body.

Desperately Conan spun back, expecting at any moment to feel the sting of Imhep-Aton's steel, but before him he saw three shadowy shapes now, locked in combat. A sibilant shriek broke and was cut off, and one of the shadows fell. The other two fought on.

A cascade of small stones skittering down the slope heralded the arrival of more S'tarra. On the fortress walls torches began to move, and the great gong tolled into the dark. The portcullis began to clank noisily open.

Conan could see two pairs of glowing eyes now, approaching him slowly, well separated. Could the beings see in that dark, he wondered. Could they recognize him? He would not take the chance. The shining sanguinary eyes were located thusly, he calculated, so the pikes must be held so.

Silently, with a prayer to Bel, god of thieves, the Cimmerian sprang toward the closer S'tarra, his sword arcing down for where he hoped the pike was. With a solid chunk his blade bit into a wooden pike-haft. He kicked with the ball of his foot, and got a hissing grunt in reply. Reversing the swing of his broadsword, he spun it up and then down for the joining of neck and shoulder. The grunt became a scream.

Conan threw himself to one side as the second pike slashed along his ribs. The dying S'tarra grappled with him as it fell, pulling him to the ground. The other stood over him, triumph heightening the glow of its eyes. A howl burst from its fanged mouth as the Cimmerian's steel severed its leg at the knee, and the S'tarra fell beside the first. There was no time for precision. Like a cleaver Conan's blade split between those red eyes.

From the fortress pounding feet were drawing

nearer. Quickly Conan jerked his sword free and ran into the night. The bandit camp had been roused as well. As he ran closer he could see them gathered at the edge of the light from their fires, peering toward the keep, where the gong still sounded. He circled around the camp and, cutting a piece from his breechclout, wiped his sword and sheathed it before striding in.

The brigands' eyes were all toward the sounds of S'tarra approaching; none but Hordo saw him enter. Conan tossed the scrap of rag, stained with black blood, into a fire and snatched a cloak from his blankets to settle around his shoulders and hide the gash in his side.

"What happened?" Hordo whispered as Conan joined the others. "You're wounded!"

"I never reached the keep," Conan replied quietly. "S'tarra were waiting. And I discovered who watched from the mountain." He remembered the second light. "As least, I think I did. Later," he added as the other started to question him further. S'tarra were entering the camp, Sitha at their head.

The bandits backed away, muttering, as the reptilian creatures strode into the firelight. Only Karela stood her ground. Arms crossed beneath her round breasts, the red-haired woman confronted the massive bulk of Sitha. "Why do you come here?" she demanded.

"S'tarra have been slain this night," Sitha replied. Its crimson eyes ran arrogantly from her ankles to her face. "I will search your camp and question your men to see if any were involved." The bandits' muttering became angry; sword hilts were grasped.

"You may die trying," Karela said coldly. "I'll not have my camp searched by such as you. And if your master has questions, I'll answer them of him, but not of his cattle." She spat the last word, and Sitha quivered, claw-tipped hands working convulsively on the haft of the huge battle-ax.

"You may find," Sitha hissed malevolently, "that answering questions for my master is even less pleasant than answering them for me." It spun abruptly on its heel and stalked from the circle of light, followed by the rest of the S'tarra.

When the last of them disappeared into the dark, Karela turned to face the bandits. "If any of you were involved in this," she said sharply, "I'll have your ears." Without another word she strode through them and disappeared into her striped pavilion.

Hordo let out a long breath and pulled Conan aside. "Now what happened out there?" The brigands were breaking up into small knots, discussing the night's events in low voices. Aberius stood alone, watching Conan and Hordo.

"I slew three S'tarra," Conan said, "and Imhep-Aton slew two. Or was perhaps himself slain, but I don't believe that."

Hordo grunted. "He who sent the man Crato against you? A second sorcerer in this Mitraforsaken valley is ill news indeed. I must tell her."

Conan grabbed the one-eyed man's arm. "Don't. She may well tell Amanar, and I do not think these two have any good will towards each other. Whatever comes between them may give you the chance to get her away from here."

"As with the hillmen and the soldiers," Hordo said slowly, "you will bring the two to combat while we slip away. But I think me being caught between two sorcerers may be worse than being caught between the others." He barked a short laugh. "I tell you again, Cimmerian, if you live, you'll be a general. Mayhap even a king. Men have risen from lower stations to become such."

"I have no desire to be a king," Conan laughed. "I'm a thief. And Imhep-Aton, at least, has no animosity toward you or Karela." Though the same, he reflected, could hardly be said of himself. "The keep is too much stirred for me to enter this night. I fear Velita must bear another day of Amanar. Come, let us find a bandage for my side and a flagon of wine."

Speaking quietly together the two men walked deeper into the bandit camp. Aberius watched them go, tugging at his lower lip in deep thought. Finally he nodded to himself and darted into the night.

XXIV

The sun, Conan estimated, stood well past the zenith. It was the day after his fight with the S'tarra, and Karela was once more closeted with Amanar for the entire morning. The bandits slept or drank or gambled, forgetting the ill of the night in the light of the sun. Conan sat cross-legged on the ground, honing his blade as he watched the black keep. To conceal his bandaged wound, he had donned a black tunic that covered him to below the hips. He lay the blade across his knees as a S'tarra approached.

"You are called Conan of Cimmeria?" the creature hissed.

"I am," Conan replied.

"She who is called Karela asks that you come to her."

There had been no further attempt to question the bandits about the occurrences in the night. Conan could not see how he might be connected with them now. He rose and sheathed his sword.

"Lead," he commanded.

The big Cimmerian tensed while passing through the gate, but the guards gave him no more than a flicker of their lifeless red eyes. In the donjon the S'tarra led him a way he did not know, to huge doors that Conan realized to his shock were of burnished gold. A great reptilian head was worked in each, surrounded by what appeared to be rays of light. The S'tarra struck a small silver gong hanging from the wall. Conan's neckhairs stirred at the great doors swung open with no human agency that he could see. The S'tarra gestured for him to enter.

With a firm tread Conan walked through the open doors; they swung shut almost on his heels with a thump of finality. The ceiling of the great room was a fluted dome, supported by massive columns of carved ivory. Across the mosaic floor Amanar sat on a throne made of golden serpents, while another burnished serpent reared behind it, great ruby eyes regarding all who approached. The mage's robe, too, was gold, seemingly of ten thousand tiny scales that glittered in the light of golden lamps. Human musicians filed out by a side door as Conan entered. The only other present was Karela, standing beside Amanar's throne and drinking thirstily from a goblet.

She lowered the goblet in surprise at the sight of Conan. "What are you doing here?" she demanded. The chamber was cool, yet perspiration dampened her face, and her breath came quickly.

"I was told you sent for me," Conan said. Warily he placed a hand on his sword.

"I never sent for you," she said.

"I took the liberty," Amanar said, "of using your name, Karela, to ensure the man would come."

"Ensure he'd come?" Puzzled, Karela swung her green eyes from Conan to the mage. "Why would he not?"

Amanar pursed his lips and touched them with his golden staff. His eyes on Conan seemed amused. "This night past were five of my S'tarra slain."

Conan wondered from which direction the S'tarra would come. There could be a score of doors hidden behind those ivory columns.

"You think Conan did this killing?" Karela said. "I spoke to you of this matter this morning, and you said nothing."

"Sometimes," the dark sorcerer said, "it is best to wait, to let the guilty think they will escape. But I see you require proof." He swung his staff against a small crystal bell that stood in a silver stand beside the throne.

At the chime the door through which the musicians had departed opened again. Aberius hesitantly entered the chamber, his eyes darting from Conan to the throne, as if measuring the distance to each. He rubbed his palms on the front of his yellow tunic.

"Speak," Amanar commanded.

Aberius' pointed face twitched. He swallowed. "Last night, before the gong sounded, I saw this Conan of Cimmeria leave our camp." His beady black eyes avoided Karela. "This surprised me, for all of us think the darkness of the nights here strange, and none will go out in them. None other

did, that night as before. Conan returned after the
alarm, with a wound on his side. I'll warrant
there's a bandage beneath that tunic.''

"Why did you not come to me, Aberius?"
Karela said angrily. Her piercing gaze shifted to the
Cimmerian. "I said, Conan, that I'd have the ears
of any man involved, and I—"

"I fear," Amanar interrupted smoothly, "that it
is I who must set this man's punishment. It is me he
has offended against. You, Aberius," he added in
a sharper tone, "go now. The gold agreed upon
will be given as you leave."

The weasel-faced bandit opened his mouth as if
to speak, closed it again, then suddenly scurried
from the room. The small door closed behind him.

"Why, Conan?" Karela asked softly. "Is that
girl worth so much to you?" She squeezed her eyes
shut and turned away. "I give him to you," she
said.

Conan's blade slipped from its sheath with a
rasping whisper. "You reckon without me," the
Cimmerian said. "I give myself to no one."

Amanar rose, holding the golden staff across his
chest like a scepter. "Extend your life, Cimmerian.
Prostrate yourself and beg, and I may have mercy
on you." He started forward at a slow walk.

"Dog of a sorcerer," Conan grated, "come no
closer. I know your mage's tricks with powders
that kill when breathed." The golden-robed man
came on, neither speeding nor slowing. "I warn
you," Conan said. "Die then!"

With the speed of a striking falcon the big
Cimmerian youth lunged. Amanar's staff whipped
up; hissing, a citron vapor was expelled from its

tip. Conan held his breath and plunged through the cloud. His sword struck Amanar's chest, piercing to the hilt. For a bare moment Conan stood chest to chest and eye to eye with the mage. Then his muscles turned to water. He tried to cry out as he toppled to the mosaic floor, but there was no sound except the thud of his fall. His great chest labored for breath, and his every muscle twitched and trembled, but not at his command.

The sorcerer stood above him, viewing him with the same dispassion he might exhibit at a bird found dead in the keep. "A concentrated derivative from the pollen of the golden lotus of Khitai," he said in a conversational tone. A thin smile curled his lips cruelly. "It works by contact, not by breathing, my knowledgeable thief. The paralysis grows if no antidote is applied, deeper and deeper until life itself is paralyzed. I am told one feels oneself dying by inches."

"Amanar," Karela gasped, "the sword!" She stood by the throne, a trembling hand pressed to her lips.

The sorcerer looked at the sword as if he had forgotten it pierced his chest. Grasping the hilt he drew it from his body. The blade was unbloodied. He seemed pleased with her shock. "You see, my dear Karela? No mortal weapon can harm me." Contemptuously he dropped the sword almost touching Conan's hand.

The Cimmerian strained to reach the leather-wrapped hilt, but his arms responded only with drug-induced tremors.

Amanar emitted a blood-chilling laugh and casually moved the sword even closer with his foot, until the hilt touched Conan's twitching hand. "Even before Aberius betrayed you, Cimmerian, I suspected you in the slaying, though two of the dead displayed certain anomalies. You see, Velita betrayed you also." His dark laugh was like a saw on bone. "The *geas* I placed on her commanded her to tell me if you saw her, and she did, though she wept and begged me to kill her rather than let her speak." He laughed again.

Conan tried to curse, but produced only a grunt. The man would die, he vowed, if he had to return as a shade to do the deed.

The sorcerer's cold, lidded eyes regarded him thoughtfully. The red flecks in their black depths seemed to dance. "You rage, but do not yet fear," he said softly. "Still, where there is such great resistance, there must be great fear once the resistance is shattered. And you will be shattered, Cimmerian."

"Please," Karela said, "if he must die, then kill him, but do not torture him."

"As you wish," Amanar said smoothly. He returned to the throne and struck the crystal bell once more.

This time Sitha appeared from the small door through which Aberius had left. Four more S'tarra followed, bearing a litter. Roughly they lifted Conan onto the bare wood and fastened him with broad leather straps across his massive chest and thighs. As they were carrying him out Conan heard Amanar speak.

"There is much we must speak of, my dear Karela. Come closer."

The door swung shut.

XXV

As the litter was carried through the donjon, one mailed S'tarra at each corner and Sitha leading, Conan lay seemingly quiescent. For the moment struggle was futile, but he constantly attempted to clench his right hand. If he could make even that beginning . . . . The hand twitched of its own volition, but no more. He fought to keep breathing.

The litter was carried from a resplendent corridor through an archway and down rough stone stairs. The walls, at first worked smooth, became raw stone, a passage hacked from the living rock beneath the dark fortress. Those who went thither no longer had a care for mosaics or tapestries.

The crude corridor leveled. Sitha pounded a huge fist against an iron-strapped door of rough wood. The door opened, and to Conan's surprise, a human appeared, the first he had seen in the keep who did not keep his eyes on the ground.

The man was even shorter than Conan, but even more massive, heavy sloping muscles covered with thick layers of fat. Piggish eyes set deep in a round, bald head regarded Conan. "So, Sitha," he said in a surprisingly high-pitched voice, "you've brought Ort another guest."

"Stand aside, Ort," Sitha hissed. "You know what is to be done here. You waste time."

Shockingly, the fat man giggled. "You'd like to cut Ort's head off, wouldn't you, Sitha, with that ax of yours? But Amanar needs Ort for his torturing. You S'tarra get carried away and leave dead meat when there's questions yet to be asked."

"This one is already meat," Sitha said contemptuously. Casually the S'tarra turned to smash a backhand blow to Conan's face. Ort giggled again.

Blood welled in Conan's mouth. Chest heaving, he fought to get painful words out. "Kill—you—Sitha," he gasped.

Ort blinked his tiny eyes in surprise. "He speaks? After the vapor? This one is strong."

"Strong," Sitha snarled. "Not as strong as I!" Its fist crashed into Conan's face, splitting his cheek. For a moment the S'tarra stood with fist upraised, fangs bared, then lowered its claw-tipped hand with an obvious effort. "Put him in his cell, Ort, before I forget the master's commands."

Giggling, Ort led the procession into the dungeons. Grim ironbound doors lined the rough stone walls. Before one Ort stopped, undoing a heavy iron lock with a key from his broad leather belt. "In here," he said. "There's another in there already, but I'm filling up."

Quickly, under Sitha's direction, the other S'tarra unstrapped Conan from the litter and carried him into the cell, a cubicle cut in the rock as crudely as the rest of the dungeon. As chains were being fastened to the Cimmerian's wrists and ankles he saw his fellow prisoner, chained in the same fashion to the far wall, and knew a second of shock. It was the Zamoran captain he had tricked into combat with the hillmen.

As the other S'tarra left, Sitha came to stand over Conan. "Were it left to me," it hissed angrily, "you would die now. But the master has use of you yet." From a pouch at its belt it took a vial and forced it between the Cimmerian's teeth. Bitter liquid flowed across his tongue. "Perhaps, Cimmerian, when the master has your soul, this time he will let me have what remains." With a sibilant laugh Sitha shoved the empty vial back into his pouch and strode from the cell. The thick door banged shut.

Conan could feel strength flowing slowly back into his limbs. Weakly he pushed himself to a sitting position and leaned against the cool stone of the cell wall.

The hook-nosed Zamoran captain watched him thoughtfully with dark eyes. There were long blisters on his arms, and others were visible on his chest where his tunic was ripped. "I am Haranides," he said finally. "Whom do I share these . . . accommodations with?"

"I am called Conan," the Cimmerian replied. He tested the chains that fastened his manacles to the wall. Three feet and more in length, the links of them were too thick for him to have burst even had he his full strength, and he was far from that as yet.

"Conan," Haranides murmured. "I've heard that name in Shadizar, thief. Would I had known you when we met last."

Conan shifted his full attention to the Zamoran. "You remember me, then, do you?"

"I'm not likely to forget a man with shoulders like a bull, especially when he brought me near ten score hillmen for a present."

"Did you indeed follow us, then? I would not have done it save for that."

"I followed you," Haranides replied bitterly. "Rather, I followed the Red Hawk and the trinkets she took from Tiridates. Or was it you, thief, who entered the palace and slew like a demon?"

"Not I," Conan said, "nor the Red Hawk. 'Twas S'tarra, the scaled ones, who did it, and we followed them as you followed us. But how came you to this pass, chained to the wall in Amanar's dungeon?"

"From continuing my pursuit of the red-haired wench when a wiser man would have returned to Shadizar and surrendered his head," the captain said. "Half a mountain of rock poured into the gorge by those things—S'tarra, you call them? No more than twenty of my men escaped. We had a hillman for a guide, but whether he led us into a trap, or perished beneath the stone, or even got away entirely, I know not."

"You got not those burns from falling rock."

Haranides examined his blisters ruefully. "Our jailor, a fellow named Ort, likes to entertain himself with a hot iron. He's surprisingly agile for one of his bulk. He'd strike and leap away, and in these," he rattled his chains, "neither could I attack nor escape him."

"If he comes again with his irons," Conan said eagerly, "perhaps in dodging from the one he will come close enough for the other to seize."

He pulled one of his chains to its fullest extent and measure with his eye. With a disgusted grunt he again slumped against the stone wall. There was room enough and more between him and the other man for Ort to leap and dodge as he would. The fat torturer could stand within a finger's breadth of either man with impunity. He realized the other man was frowning at him.

"It comes to me," Haranides said slowly, "that already I have told you more than I told Ort. How came you to be chained like an ox, Conan?"

"I misjudged the wiliness of a sorcerer," Conan replied curtly.

It rankled still, the ease with which he had been taken. He seemed to remember once calling himself a bane of wizards, yet Amanar had snared him like a three-years child. While Karela watched, too.

"Then you were in his service?" Haranides said.

Conan shook his head irritably. "No!"

"Perhaps you are in his service still, put in here to extract information more easily than good Ort."

"Are your brains moon-struck?" Conan bellowed, lunging to his feet. His chains left him paces short of the other man. At least, though, he had regained enough strength to stand. With a short laugh he sank back. "A cell is no place for a duel, and we can't reach each other besides. I'll ask you to watch your speaking, though. I serve no sorcerer."

"Perhaps," Haranides said, and he would say no more.

Conan made himself as comfortable as the bare stone floor and rough wall would permit. He had slept in worse conditions in the mountains as a boy, and of his own free will. This time he did not sleep, though, but rather set his mind to escape, and to the killing of Amanar, for that last he would do if his own life were extinguished in the same moment. But how to kill a man who could take a yard of steel through his chest and not even bleed? That was a weighty question, indeed.

Some men, he knew, had amulets which were atuned to them by magicks, so that the amulet could be used for good or ill against that man. The Eye of Erlik came to mind, which bauble had at last brought down the Khan of Zamboula, though not by its sorceries. That the pendant which Velita had worn nestled between her small breasts was a watch for Amanar's evil eyes was to the Cimmerian proof that it too was such an amulet. It could be used to kill Amanar, he was sure, if he but knew the way.

But first must come escape. He reviewed what he had seen since being carried to the dungeon, what Ort had said, what Haranides had told him, and a plan slowly formed. He settled to wait. The patience of the hunting leopard was in him. He was a mountain warrior of Cimmeria. At fifteen he had been one of the fierce Cimmerian horde that stormed the walls of Venarium and sacked that border city of Aquilonia. Even before that had he been allowed his place at the warriors' council fires, and since then he had traveled far, seen kingdoms and thrones totter, helped to steady some and topple others. He knew that nine parts of fighting was knowing when to wait, the tenth knowing when to strike. He would wait. For now. The hours passed.

At the rattle of a key in the massive iron lock Conan's muscles tensed. He forced them to relax. His full strength was returned, but care must be taken.

The door swung outward, and two S'tarra entered, dragging Hordo unconscious between them. Straight to the third set of chains they took him, and manacled him there. Without looking at either of the other two men they left, but the door did not close. Instead, Amanar came to stand in the opening. The golden robe had been replaced by one of dead black, encircled with embroidered golden serpents. The mage fingered something on his chest through the robe as he surveyed the cell with cold black eyes.

"A pity," he murmured, almost under his breath. "You three could be more use to me than all of the rest together, with the sole exception of Karela herself, yet you all must die."

"Will you imprison us all, then?" Conan said, jerking his head at Hordo. The one-eyed bandit stirred, and groaned.

Amanar looked at him as if truly realizing he were present for the first time. "No, Cimmerian. He meddled where he should not, as you did, as the man Talbor did. The others remain free. Until their usefulness ends."

Haranides' chains clinked as he shifted. "Mitra

blast your filth-soaked soul," the captain grated.

The ebon-clad sorcerer seemed not to hear. His strange eyes remained on Conan's face. "Velita," he said in a near whisper, "the slave girl you came to free, awaits in my chamber of magicks. When I have used her one last time, she will die, and worse than die. For if death is horrible, Cimmerian, how much more horrible when no soul is left to survive beyond?"

The big Cimmerian could not stop his muscles from tensing.

Amanar's laugh curdled marrow in the bone. "Interesting, Cimmerian. You fear more for another than for yourself. Yes, interesting. That may prove useful." His hellborn laugh came again, and he was gone.

Haranides stared at the closed door. "He fouls the air by breathing," he spat.

"Twice now," Conan said softly, "have I heard the taking of a soul spoken of. Once I knew a man who could steal souls."

The captain made the sign of the horns, against evil. "How did you know such a man?"

"He stole my soul," Conan said simply.

Haranides laughed uncertainly, not sure if this were a joke. "And what did you do than?"

"I killed him, and took back my soul." The Cimmerian shivered. That reclaiming had not been easy. To risk the loss again, perhaps past reclaiming, was fearful beyond death. And the same would happen to Velita, and eventually to Karela, could he not prevent it.

Hordo groaned again, and sat up, sagging his

broad back against the stone wall. At the clank of his chains he stared at his manacles, then closed his eye.

"What happened, Hordo?" Conan asked. "Amanar had you brought hence by S'tarra, saying you meddled. In what?"

Hordo's scarred face contracted as if he wished to cry. "She was gone so long from the camp," he said finally, "and you, that I became concerned. It was near dark, and the thought that she must either remain the night in this place or find her way to camp through that blackness . . . . At the gate they let me in, but reluctantly, and one of the scaled ones ran calling for Sitha. I found the chamber where thrice-accursed Amanar, may the worms feast long on him, sat on his throne of golden serpents." His one eye closed again, but he spoke on, more slowly. "Musicians played, men, though their eyes never left the floor. Those snake-skinned demon-spawn came, and beat me down with clubbed spears. The mage shouted for them to take me alive. Two of them I killed, before my senses went. Two, at least, I know."

He fell silent, and Conan prodded him. "Surely Amanar didn't have you imprisoned merely for entering his throne room?"

The bearded face contorted in a grimace of pain, and Hordo moaned through clenched teeth. "Karela!" he howled. "She danced for him, naked as any girl in a zenana, and with as wild an abandon! Karela danced naked for the pleasure of that . . . ." Sobs wracked his burly form, choking off his words.

The hackles stood on Conan's neck. "He will

die, Hordo," he promised. "He will die."

"This Karela," Haranides said incredulously, "she is the Red Hawk?"

Redfaced, Hordo lunged to the full extent of his chains. "She was ensorceled!" he shouted. "She knew me not. Never once did she look at me, or cease her dancing. She was spell-caught."

"We know it," Conan said soothingly.

The one-eyed man glared at Haranides. "Who is this man, Conan?"

"Don't you recognize him?" The Cimmerian laughed. "Haranides, the Zamoran captain we introduced to the hillmen."

"A Zamoran officer!" Hordo snarled. "Can I get my hands free, at least I'll rid the world of one more soldier before I die."

"Think you so, rogue?" Haranides sneered. "I've killed five like you before breaking fast in the morning." The bandit and the captain locked murderous gazes.

"Forgetting your chains for the moment," Conan said conversationally, "do you intend to do Amanar's work for him?"

The glares shifted to him. "We're going to die anyway," Hordo growled.

"Die if you want," Conan said. "I intend to escape, and let Amanar do the dying."

"How?" Haranides demanded.

The Cimmerian smiled wolfishly. "Wait," he said. "Rest." And despite their protests he settled down to sleep. His dreams were of strangling Amanar with the black pendant's chain.

XXVI

Karela woke and looked about her in confusion. She lay on a silk-draped couch, not in her pavilion, but in an opulent room hung with scarlet silken gauze. Silver bowls and ewers stood on a gilded table, and the finest Turanian carpet covered the floor. Sunlight streamed in through a narrow window. She was in Amanar's keep, she realized, and at the same moment realized she was naked.

"Derketo!" she muttered, sitting up quickly.

Her head spun. Had she taken too much wine the night before? For some reason she was sure she had spent a night inside the fortress. There was a vague memory of wild music, and a girl's sensual dancing. She put a hand to her forehead as if to wipe away perspiration, and jerked it back down with another oath. The room was cool; she was cool. Quickly she rose to search for her clothing.

Her golden breastplates and emerald girdle were carefully laid out on her scarlet cloak, atop a chest at the foot of the couch. Her crimson thigh-boots stood before the chest, and her jeweled tulwar leaned against it. She dressed swiftly.

"Who was that girl?" she muttered beneath her breath as she tugged the last boot on, pulling the soft red leather almost to the top of her thigh. The dance had been shamelessly abandoned, almost voraciously carnal.

But why should that be important, she wondered. More important was to see that she watched her drinking in the future. She did not trust Amanar enough to spend another night in that keep. Her cheeks flamed, only partly with anger. She was lucky she had not wakened in his bed. Not that he was not handsome, in a cruel fashion, and powerful, which had its own attractions, but that would be a matter of her own choosing.

The door opened, and Karela was on her feet, tulwar in hand, before she realized it. She looked in consternation at the girl who entered, head down, not looking at her, with a tall, wooden-handled silver pitcher on a tray. Why was she so jumpy, she thought, resheathing the curved blade. "I'm sorry, girl. I didn't mean to scare you."

"Hot water, mistress," the girl said in a toneless voice, "for your morning ablutions." Still without raising her eyes she set the tray on the table and turned to go. She seemed unaffected by being greeted with a sword.

"A minute," Karela said. The girl stopped. "Has anyone come asking for me at the portcullis? Hordo? A bearded man with an eye-patch?"

"Such a man was taken to the dungeons, mistress, this night past."

"The dungeons!" Karela yelped. "By the tits of

Derketo, why?"

"It was said, mistress, that he was discovered attempting to free the man Conan, and also that he had many golden ornaments in a sack."

The red-haired woman drew a shuddering breath. She should have expected something of the kind, should have guarded against it. Hordo and Conan had become close—sword-brothers, the hillmen called it—and men, never truly sane in her opinion, were at their maddest in such relationships. Still, for her most loyal hound, she must do something.

"Where is your master, girl?"

"I do not know, mistress."

Karela frowned. There had been a slight hesitation before that answer. "Then show me to the dungeons. I want to speak to Hordo."

"Mistress, I . . . I cannot . . . my master . . . ." The girl stood staring at the floor.

Karela grabbed the girl's chin, twisting her face up. "Look at me . . . ."

Her breath caught in her throat. The girl might have been called beautiful, except that there was no single line of expression or emotion on her face. And her brown eyes were . . . empty was the only word Karela could think of. She pulled her hand away, and had to resist the desire to wipe it on something. The girl dropped her eyes again immediately on being released. She had made no slightest resistance then, and she stood waiting now.

"Girl," Karela said, making her tone threatening, "I am here, and your master is elsewhere. Now show me to the dungeons!"

The girl nodded hesitantly, and led the way from the room.

She had been on the topmost level of the keep, Karela discovered as they took curving marble stairs, seeming to hang suspended in air, down to the ground floor. In a small side corridor the girl stopped before a plain stone archway that led onto rough stone steps. She had not raised her eyes in the entire journey, and Karela did not really want her to.

"There, mistress," the girl said. "Down there. I am not permitted to descend."

Karela nodded. "Very well, girl. If trouble comes of this for you, I'll intercede with your master."

"The master will do as he will do," the girl replied in her toneless voice. Before Karela could speak again, she had scurried away and was gone around a corner.

Taking a deep breath, and with a firm grip on her sword, the red-haired bandit descended the stairs until she came to an iron-strapped door. On this she pounded with her sword hilt.

The door was opened by a huge, fat man in a stained yellow tunic. She presented her blade to his face before he could speak. At least this one did not stare at the ground, she thought, though perhaps he should to hide his face.

"The man Hordo," she said. "Take me to where he is confined."

"But Amanar," the fat man began. Her sword point indented his neck, and his piggy eyes bulged. "I'll take you to him," he stammered in a high-pitched voice, and added, "Mistress."

Blade against his backbone, she followed him down the crudely cut corridor. He fumbled with the keys at his belt, and unlocked one of the solid wooden doors.

"Over there," she ordered, gesturing with her sword. "Where I can see you. And do you move, I'll make a capon of you, if you're not one already."

Anger twisted his suety face, but he moved as she directed. She pulled open the door and stared at the three men inside. Conan, Hordo, and one who looked vaguely familiar to her. All three looked up as the door swung open.

"You came!" Hordo cried. "I knew you would!"

Her green eyes rested on the broad-shouldered Cimmerian. His gaze, like twinned blue agates, regarded her impassively. She was relieved to see he still lived, and angry that she was relieved. The hard planes of his unlined face were handsome, it was true, and he was virile—her cheeks colored—but he was a fool. Why did he have to oppose Amanar? Why could he not forget that girl, Velita? Why?

"Why?" she said, and immediately pulled her gaze to Hordo. "Why did you do it, Hordo?"

The one-eyed bandit blinked at her in bewilderment. "Do what?"

"Steal from Amanar. Try to free this other fool." She jerked her head at Conan without looking at him again.

"I stole nothing," Hordo protested. "And I knew not that Conan was imprisoned until I was chained beside him."

"Then you were brought here for no reason?" she said derisively. Hordo was silent.

"He," Conan began, but Hordo cut him off with a shout.

"No, Cimmerian!" He added, "Please?" and the word sounded as if it were carved from his vitals.

Karela looked at the two men in consternation. Their eyes met, and Conan nodded. "Well?" she demanded. Neither man spoke. Hordo would not meet her gaze. "Derketo take you, Hordo. I should have you flogged. Can I talk Amanar into releasing you, I may yet."

"Release us now," Hordo said quickly. "Ort has the keys. You can—"

"You!" she said sharply. "It's you I'll try to free. I have no interest in these others." She felt Conan's eyes on her, and could not look at him. "Besides, it may do you good to sit here and worry as whether or not I can talk Amanar into releasing you to me." She gestured to the fat jailer with her sword. "You! Close the door." She stepped back to keep him under her eye and blade as he moved to do so.

"Karela," Hordo shouted, "leave this place! Leave me! Take horse and—" The door banged shut to cut him off.

As the fat man turned from locking the massive door, she laid her curved blade against his fat neck. Her eyes were glittering emerald ice. "If I find you have not taken good care of him," she said coldly, "I'll carve that bulk away to see if there's a man inside." Contemptuously she turned her back and stalked from the dungeon.

By the time she reached the top of the rude stone stairs her brain was burning. Amanar had no right. Conan was one thing, Hordo quite another. She would maintain the discipline of her hounds, and she had no intention of letting the mage usurp her authority in this fashion. She strode through the ornate halls of the black donjon, still clutching her sword in her anger.

One of the S'tarra appeared before her, blinking in surprise at the weapon in her hand. "Where is Amanar?" she demanded.

It did not speak, but its red eyes twitched toward a plain arch. She remembered Amanar saying that the passage beyond led to his thaumaturgical chambers. In her present mood, bearding the sorcerer there was just what she sought. She turned for the arch.

With a hissed shout, the mailed S'tarra leaped for her, and jumped back just in time, so that her blade drew sparks across the chest of its hauberk.

"Follow," she growled, "and you'll never follow anything again."

Its rubiate eyes remained on her face, but it stood still as she backed down the sloping passage, lined with flickering torches set in plain iron sconces. The corridor was longer than she had suspected. The archway, and the S'tarra still standing there, had dwindled to mere specks by the time her back came up against a pair of tall wooden doors.

The doors were carved with a profusion of serpents in endless arabesques, as were the stone walls of the corridor, though this had not been so high up. She thought she might be under the very heart of the mountain. Pushing open one of the doors, she went in.

The room was a great circle, surrounded by shadowed columns. The floor was a mosaic of a strange golden serpent. On the far side of the room, Amanar whirled at her entrance. Sitha, crouching near the mage, half rose.

"You dare to enter here!" Amanar thundered.

"I dare anything," she snapped, "while you have Hordo chained . . ." What was beyond the black-robed sorcerer finally impressed itself on her. The red-streaked black marble altar. The slim blonde girl bound naked to it, rigid with terror. "By the black heart of Ahriman," Karela swore, "what is it you do here, mage?"

Instead of answering, the cold-eyed man traced a figure in the air, and the figure seemed to stand glowing as he traced, stirring some buried memory deep inside her. Behind her eyes she felt something break, like a twig snapping. She would teach him to play his magical tricks with her. She started for the dark man . . . and stared down in amazement at feet that would not move. They did not feel held, they had full sensation, but they would not move.

"What wizardry is this?" she demanded hoarsely. "Release me, Amanar, or—"

"Throw the sword aside," he commanded.

She stifled a scream as her arm obeyed, sending the jewel-hilted tulwar skittering across the mosaicked floor to ring against a column.

Amanar nodded in satisfactio. "Remove your garments, Karela."

"Fool," she began, and her green eyes started

with horror as her slim fingers rose to the golden pin that held her scarlet cloak and undid it. The cloak slid from her shoulders to the floor. "I am the Red Hawk," she said. It was little more than a whisper, but her voice rose to a scream. "I am the Red Hawk!"

She could not stop watching with bulging eyes as her hands removed the golden breastplates from her heavy round breasts and casually dropped them, unfastened the emerald girdle that rode low on her flaring hips.

"Enough," Amanar said. "Leave the boots. I like the picture they present." She wanted to weep as her hands returned quiescent to her sides. "Beyond these walls," the black-robed man went on, "you are the Red Hawk. Inside them, you are . . . whatever I want you to be. I think from now on I will keep you thus when you are with me, aware of what is happening. Your fear is like the rarest of wines."

"Think you I'll return once I am free?" she spat. "Let me get a sword in my hand and my hounds about me, and I will tear this keep down about your head."

His laughter sent shivers along her bones. "When you leave these walls, you will remember what I tell you to remember. You will go believing that we conferred, on this matter or that. But when once again within this donjon, you will remember the true nature of things. The Red Hawk will grovel at my feet and crawl to serve my pleasure. You will hate it, but you will obey."

"I'll die first!" she shouted defiantly.

"That will not be permitted," he smiled coldly.

"Now be silent." The words she was about to speak froze on her tongue. Amanar produced a knife with a gilded blade from beneath his robe and tested its edge with his thumb. "You will watch what occurs here. I do not think Susa will mind." The girl on the altar moaned. The sorcerer's red-flecked black eyes suddenly held Karela's gaze as a viper holds the gaze of a bird. She could feel those eyes reaching into the very depths of her. "You will watch," Amanar said softly, "and you will begin to learn the true meaning of fear." He turned back to the altar; his chant rose, cutting into her mind like a knife. Flaming mists began to form.

Karela's green eyes bulged as if they would start from her head. She would not scream, she told herself. Even if she had a voice she would not scream. But her flanks and the rounded slopes of her breasts were of a sudden slick with sweat, and in her mind there was gibbering terror.

XXVII

"Conan!" Haranides shouted. "Conan!" The three men still lay chained to the walls of the cell beneath Amanar's keep.

Conan opened one eye, where he lay curled as comfortably as he could manage on the stone. "I'm sleeping," he said, and closed it again.

The Cimmerian estimated that a full day and more had passed since Karela had come to their cell, though there had been no food and but threee pannikins of stale water brought to their cell.

"Sleeping," Haranides grumbled. "When do we hear of this escape plan of yours?"

"The Red Hawk," Hordo said hopefully. "When she sets me free, I'll get the rest of you out. Even you, Zamoran."

Conan sat up, stretching until his shoulder joints cracked. "If she were coming, Hordo," he said, "she'd have been here long since."

"She may yet come," the one-eyed man muttered. "Mayhap she took my advice and rode away."

Conan said nothing. His best hope for Karela was that she had accepted Amanar's word for Hordo's crimes and was even then in the bandit camp, surrounded by the men she called her hounds.

"In any case," Haranides said, "we cannot put our hopes on her. Even if she gets you free, bearded one, you heard her say she'd do nothing for the Cimmerian and myself. I think me she is a woman of her word."

"Wait," Conan said. "The time will come."

A key rattled in the lock.

"'Tis Ort who's come," Haranides growled. "With his irons, no doubt."

"Ort?" Hordo said. "Who is—"

The heavy, iron-strapped cell door slammed open, and the fat jailer stood in the opening. Behind him was a brazier full of glowing coals, and from the coals projected the wooden handles of irons, their metal ends already as bright red as the coals they nestled among.

"Who's to be first?" Ort giggled.

He snatched an iron from the fire and waved its fiery tip at them. Hordo put his back against the wall, teeth bared in a snarl. Haranides crouched, ready to spring in any direction, so far as his chains would let him. Conan did not move.

"You, captain?" Ort said. He feinted toward Haranides, who tensed. "Ort likes burning officers. Or you, one-eye?" Giggling, he waggled the glowing iron at Hordo. "Ort could give you another scar, burn out your other eye. And you, strong one," he said, turning his pig-eyed gaze on Conan, "think you to sit unconcerned?"

Suddenly Ort darted at the Cimmerian, red-hot iron flashing, and danced back. A long blister stood on Conan's shoulder. Awkwardly he raised one arm to cover his head, and huddled against the wall, half turning his back on the man with the burning iron. The other three men all stared at the big youth incredulously.

"Fight him!" Haranides shouted, and had to throw himself back to avoid a vicious slash of the iron that would have taken him across the face.

"Face him like a man, Conan," Hordo urged.

Cautiously Ort dashed again to strike and retreat, curiously agile on his feet. Conan groaned as a second blister grew across his shoulders, and pressed himself tighter to the stone.

"Why he is no man at all," Ort giggled. The nearly round jailor swaggered closer, to stand over Conan raising his blazing weapon.

A roar of battle rage broke from Conan's throat, and his mighty thews pushed him from his crouch. One hand seized Ort's bulk, pulling him closer; the other looped its chain about the jailor's neck, catching at the same time a desperately flung hand. Biceps bulging, he jerked the heavy iron chain tight, fat flesh bulging through the links. Ort's tiny eyes, too, bulged from that fat face, and his feet scrabbled desperately at the bare stone floor. The jailor had but one weapon, and he used it, stabbing again and again with the burning iron at the Cimmerian's broad back.

The stench of burning flesh rose as the fiery rod seared Conan's muscles, but he locked the pain from his mind. It did not exist. Only the man before him existed. Only the man whose eyes were staring from his fat face. Only the man he must kill. Ort's mouth opened in a futile attempt to breathe, or perhaps to scream. His tongue protruded through yellowed teeth. The chain had almost disappeared into the fat of his neck. The iron dropped, and breath rattled in Ort's throat and was silent. Conan put all his strength into one last heave, and there was the crack of a breaking neck. Slowly he unwound the chain, freeing it with some difficulty, and let the heavy body fall.

"Mitra!" Haranides breathed. "Your back, Conan! I could not have stood it a tenth so long."

Wincing, Conan bent to pick up the iron. He ignored the dead man. To his mind all torturers should be treated so. "The means of our escape," he said, holding Ort's weapon up. Its metal was yet hot enough to burn, but the glow had faded.

Carefully Conan fit the length of the iron through a link of the chain a handsbreadth from the manacle on one wrist. He took a deep breath, then twisted, the iron one way, his wrist the other. The manacle cut into the just-healed wounds left from his being staked out by the bandits, and blood trickled over his hand. The other two men held their breath. With a sharp snap the chain broke.

Laughing, Conan held up his free wrist, the manacle still dangling a few inches of chain, and the iron. "I'd hoped the heat hadn't destroyed the temper of the metal. It would have broken instead of the chain, otherwise."

"You hoped," Hordo wheezed. "You hoped!" The bandit threw back his shaggy head and laughed. "You bet our freedom on a hope, Cimmerian, and you won.''

As quickly as he could Conan broke the rest of his chains, and those of the other men. As soon as Hordo was free, the bearded man leaped to his feet. Conan seized his arm to stop him from rushing out.

"Hold hard," the Cimmerian said.

"The time is gone for holding hard," Hordo replied. "I go to see to the Red Hawk's safety."

"To see to her safety?" Conan asked. "Or to die by her side?"

"I seek the one, Cimmerian, but I'll settle for the other."

Conan growled deep in his throat. "I'll not settle for death on S'tarra pikes, and if you will you're useless to me. And to Karela. Haranides, how many of your men do you think still live? And will they fight?"

"Perhaps a score," the captain replied. "And to get out of these cells they'll fight Ahriman and Erlik both."

"Then take you the jailer's keys, and free them. If you can take and hold the barbican, we may live yet."

Haranides nodded. "I'll hold it. What will you be doing, Cimmerian?"

"Slaying Amanar," Conan replied. Haranides nodded gravely.

"What about me?" Hordo said. The other two had been ignoring him.

"Are you with us?" Conan asked. He barely waited for Hordo's nod before going on. "Rouse the bandits. Somehow you must get over the wall without being seen, and bring them up the ramp before the catapults can fire on them. You must kill S'tarra, you and Karela's hounds, and set as many fires as you can within the keep. Both you and Haranides must wait my signal to move, so we are all in position. When the top of the tallest tower in the keep begins to burn, then ride."

"I'll be ready," Hordo said. "It is taught that no plan of battle survives the first touch of battle. Let us hope ours is different."

"Fare you well, Haranides," Conan said; then he and Hordo were hurrying from the dungeon.

At the top of the stone stairs, as they entered the donjon itself, a S'tarra rounded the corner not two paces from them. Hordo's shoulder caught the creature in its mailed midriff, and Conan's balled fist broke its neck. Hurriedly Conan pressed the S'tarra's sword on Hordo, taking a broadbladed dagger for himself. Then they, too, parted.

The way to Amanar's chamber atop the tower was easy to find, Conan thought. All one did was climb stairs until there were no more stairs to climb, sweeping marble arcs supported on air, polished ebon staircases wide enough to give passage to a score of men and massive enough to support an army.

And then there was only a winding stone stairway, curving around the wall of the tower with no rail to guard its inner drop. With his foot on the bottom step Conan paused, remembering Velita's tale of a spell-trap. Were Amanar not within the keep, Conan's next step could mean his bloody death by darkling sorceries. A slow death, he recalled. But if he did not go up, others would die at Amanar's hands even if he did not. He took a step, then a second and third before he could think, continuing to place one foot in front of another until he was at the top, staring at an iron-bound door.

A sigh of relief left him. Too, there was use in the knowledge that Amanar was within the keep. But this was not a way he cared to go about collecting information.

He opened the door and stepped into a room where evil soaked the walls, and the very air seemed heavy with sorcerous portent. Circular the room was, without windows and lined with books, but there was that about the pale leather of those fat tomes that made the Cimmerian want not to touch them. The tattered remains of mummies, parts of them ripped away, lay scattered across tables among a welter of beakers, flasks, tripods, and small braziers with their fires extinguished to cold ash. Jars of liquid held distorted things that might once have been parts of men. A dim light was cast over all by glass balls set in sconces around the walls that glowed with an eerie fire.

But Velita was not there. In truth, he admitted to himself, he had no longer expected her to be. He could, at least, avenge her.

Quickly he located the crystal coffer of which she had spoken. It sat in a place of honor, on a bronze tripod standing in the center of the room. Carelessly he tossed the smoky lid aside to shatter on the stone floor, rummaged in the silken wrappings, and lifted out the silver-mounted black stone on its fine silver chain. Within the stone red flecks danced, just as in Amanar's eyes.

Tucking the pendant behind his wide leather belt

he searched hurriedly for anything else that might
be of use. He was ready to go when he suddenly
saw his sword, lying among a litter of thaumaturgical devices on one of the tables. He reached
for it . . . and stopped with his hand hovering
above the hilt. Why had Amanar brought the
sword to this peccant chamber? Conan had had
experience of ensorceled swords, had seen one kill
the man who grasped it at the command of
another. What had Amanar done to his blade?

The door of the room banged open, and Sitha
sauntered in, fanged mouth dropping open in
surprise at seeing Conan. Conan's hand closed
over the swordhilt in an instant and brought the
blade to guard. At least, he thought with relief, it
had not killed him so far.

"So, Cimmerian," Sitha said, "you have escaped." Almost casually it reached to a jumble of
long, mostly unidentifiable objects, and produced
a spear with a haft as thick as a man's wrist. The
point was near a shortsword in length. "The
master cannot punish me for killing you here, in
this place."

"You must do the killing first," Conan said.
And he must set a fire. Soon. He circled, trying to
get the tables out from between them. Reach was
the S'tarra's advantage. Sitha moved in the op-
posite direction, spear held warily.

Abruptly the bronze gong began to toll. Sitha's
red eyes flickered away for just a moment; Conan
bent, caught the edge of a long table with his
shoulder, and heaved it over. Sitha leaped back as
the heavy table crashed where his feet had been.
Beakers of strange powder and flagons of multi-

colored liquids shattered on the floor. Acrid fumes rose from their mixing. The tolling continued, and now could be heard the faint sounds of shouting from the walls. Could Haranides or Hordo have decided not to wait, he wondered.

"My master sent me hence for powders," Sitha hissed. "Powders he thinks will increase the fear in the sacrifice." On the last word he lunged, the spear point darting for Conan's head.

The Cimmerian's broadsword beat the thrust aside, and his riposte slashed open the creature's scaled chin. Sitha leaped back from the blow, putting an elongated hand to the bloody gash and letting out a string of vile oaths.

"You still don't seem to have killed me," Conan laughed.

Sitha's sibilant voice became low and grating. "The sacrifice, Cimmerian, is that girl you came to this valley for. Velita. I will watch your face before I kill you, knowing you know she dies."

A berserker rage rose in the Cimmerian. Velita alive. But to remain that way only if he got there in time. "Where is she, Sitha?"

"The chamber of sacrifice, human."

"Where's this chamber of sacrifice?" Conan demanded.

Sitha bared his fangs in a derisive laugh. With a roar Conan attacked. The berserker was on him. He jumped up, caught a foot on the edge of the overturned table, and leaped down on the S'tarra's side. The spearpoint slashed his thigh while he was in midair, but his slashing sword, driven by the fury of a man who meant to kill or die, but to do it *now*, sliced through the haft. Conan screamed like a hunting beast as he attacked without pause, without thought for his own defense, without allowing time for Sitha to do else but stumble back in panic. His second cut, almost a continuation of the first, severed the S'tarra's right arm. Black blood spurted; a shriek ripped through those fangs. The third blow bit into Sitha's thick neck, slicing through. Those red eyes glared at him, life still in them, for a bare moment as that head toppled from the mailed shoulders. Blood fountained, and the body fell.

Panting with reaction, Conan looked about him. There was still the fire to . . . . Where the arcane powders and liquids had mixed among shattered fragments of stone and crystal, yellow flames leapt up, emitting an acrid cloud. In seconds the fire had seized on the overturned table, igniting it as though the wood had been soaked in oil from a lamp.

Choking and coughing, Conan stumbled from the chamber. Behind him flames roared; air stirred already in the body of the tower, drifting upward. Soon that necromanical chamber would be a furnace, and the tower top would flare for the signal. The tollings of the bronze gong rolled forth. If the signal were still needed.

Quickly the Cimmerian found his way from the tower, to a room with a window overlooking the keep and the valley beyond. His jaw dropped. On the ramparts S'tarra scurried with their weapons like ants in a stirred hill, and to good reason, for the valley floor swarmed with near a thousand turbanned hillmen, mounted and armed with lance and tulwar.

Where Haranides and Hordo were, Conan had

no idea. Their plan was gone by the wayside, but he might still save Velita if he could find the sacrificial chamber. But where in the huge black keep to begin? Even the donjon alone would take a day to search room by room. A sudden thought struck him. A chance, a small, bare chance, for her.

Pantherine strides took him down alabaster halls and marble stairs, past startled S'tarra scurrying on appointed tasks and so afraid to stop him. Like a hawk he sped, straight to the plain stone arch and the sloping passage beyond that Amanar had falsely claimed led to his thaumaturgical chambers.

Conan ran down that passage leading into the very heart of the mountain, arms and legs pumping, deep muscled chest working like a bellows. Death rode in his steely blue eyes, and he cared not if it was his death so long as Amanar preceded him into the shadows.

The gray walls of the passage, lit by flickering torches, began to be carved with serpents, and then there were tall doors ahead, also carved with serpents in intricate arabesques. Conan flung the two doors wide and strode in.

Amanar stood in his black, serpent-embroidered robe, chanting before a black marble altar, on which lay Velita, naked and bound. Behind the altar a mist of lambent fire swirled; beyond the mist was an infinity of blackness. Conan stalked down the curving row of shadowed columns, his teeth bared in a silent snarl.

The dark sorcerer seemed to reach a resting place in his chant, for without looking around he said, "Bring it here, Sitha. Hurry!"

Conan had reached a point a dozen paces from

the altar. From there he examined the evil mage with great care. The man had not his golden staff, but what had he in its place? "I am not Sitha," Conan said.

Amanar started convulsively, whirling to stare at Conan, who stood in the shadows of the columns. "Is that you, Cimmerian? How have you come . . . . No matter. Your soul will feed the Eater of Souls somewhat early, that is all." Velita peered past Amanar at Conan with dark eyes full of hope and desperation. The fiery mists thickened.

"Release the girl," Conan demanded. Amanar laughed. The Cimmerian dug the pendant from his belt, let it dangle from one massive finger by its chain. "I have this, mage!"

The cold-eyed sorcerer's laugh died. "You have nothing," he snapped, but he touched his lips with his tongue and glanced nervously at the constantly deepening mists. Something stirred in their depths. "Still, it might cause . . , difficulties. Give it to me, and I will —"

"It is his soul!" a voice boomed, seeming to come from every direction. Among the shadows along the columns on the far side of the chamber, one shadow suddenly split, folded, and thickened. And there before them stood Imhep-Aton.

The Stygian sorcerer wore a golden chaplet set with a square-cut emerald, and a severe black robe that fell to his ankles. He moved slowly toward Amanar and the altar.

"You," Amanar spat. "I should have known when those two S'tarra died without wounds that it was you."

"The pendant, Conan of Cimmeria," the Stygian said intently. "It contains Amanar's soul, to keep it safe from the Eater of Souls. Destroy the pendant, and you destroy Amanar."

Conan raised his hand to smash the black stone against a column. And the will was not there to make his arm move so. To no avail he strained, then let his arm down slowly.

Amanar's laugh came shrilly. "Fool! Think you I placed no protection in that which is so important to me? No one who touches or beholds the pendant can damage it in any way." Suddenly he drew himself up to his full height. "Slay him!" he shouted, each syllable a command.

Abruptly Conan became aware of what had coalesced in the mists above and behind the altar. A great golden serpent head reared there, surrounded by long tentacles like the rays of the sun. The auric-scaled body stretched into the blackness beyond the mists, and the ruby eyes that regarded Imhep-Aton were knowing.

The Stygian had time for one horrified look, and then the great serpent struck faster than a lightning bolt. Those long, golden tentacles seized the screaming man, lifted him high. The tentacles seemed but to hold, almost caressingly, but Imhep-Aton's shrieks welded Conans' joints and froze his marrow. The man sounded as if something irrevocably irretrievable were being ripped from him. Eater of Souls, Conan thought, and shuddered.

The tentacles shifted their grip, now encircling and entwining, covering Imhep-Aton from head to feet, tightening. His shrieks continued for a disturbingly long time, long after blood began to ooze between the tentacles like juice squeezed from a ripe fruit, long after there should have been no breath or lungs left to scream with. The bloody bundle was tossed aside, to strike the mosaic floor with a sound like a sack of wet cloth. Conan avoided looking at it. Instead, he concentrated on the pendant hanging from his fist.

"Thou commanded me," a voice hissed in Conan's head, and he knew it was the great serpent, god or demon, which mattered little at the moment, speaking to Amanar. "Thou growest above thyself."

Conan stared at the hand holding the pendant. The grim god of his Cimmerian northcountry, Crom, Lord of the Mound, gave a man only life and will. What he did with them, or failed to do, was up to him alone. Life and will.

"Thy servant begs thee to forgive him," Amanar said smoothly, but the smoothness slipped as the serpent's mind-talk went on.

"No, Amanar. Thou hast passed thy time. Remove the amulet, and prostrate thyself for thy god's feeding."

Life and will. Will.

"No!" Amanar shouted. He clutched the chest of his black robe. "I wear the amulet still. You cannot touch me, Eater of Souls."

"Thou defieth me!" The serpent shape swayed toward Amanar, tentacles reaching, and recoiling.

Will. The soul pendant. Eater of Souls. Will.

"Crom!" Conan shouted, and convulsively he hurled the pendant toward the great serpent. Time seemed to flow like syrup, the pendant to float spinning in air.

A long scream burst from Amanar's throat. "Nooooo!"

The golden serpent head moved lazily, hungrily, the fanged mouth opening, bifurcate tongue flicking out to gather in the pendant, swallowing.

Despair drove Amanar's shriek up in pitch. Then another scream came, a hissing scream that sounded in the mind. On the altar Velita convulsed and went limp. Conan felt his bones turning to mush.

A bar of blue fire burst from the chest of the black-robed sorcerer, tearing his robe asunder, to connect him with the great golden god-demon. In unison their screams rose, Amanar's and Morath-Aminee's, higher, higher, drilling the brain, boring into bone and gristle. Then Amanar was a living statue of blue fire, but screaming still, and the great golden form of Morath-Aminee was awash with blue flame for all that length stretching into infinity. And that scream, too, continued, a sibilant shriek in the mind, wrenching at the soul.

The man's cry ended, and Conan looked up to find that Amanar was gone, leaving but a few greasy ashes and a small pool of molten metal. But Morath-Aminee still burned, and now the great blue flaming form thrashed in its agony. It thrashed, and the mountains trembled.

Cracks opened across the ceiling of the room, and the floor tilted and pitched like a ship in a storm at sea. Fighting to maintain his balance, Conan hurried to the black marble altar, beneath the very burning form of the god-demon in its death-throes. Velita was unconscious. Swiftly the Cimmerian cut her loose and, throwing her naked form across his shoulder, he ran. The ceiling of the sacrificial chamber thundered down as he ran clear, and dirt filled the air of the passage. The mountain shook still, ever more and more violently, twisting, yawing. Conan ran.

In the keep above, he found madness. Columns fell and dark towers toppled, long gaps were opened in the great outer wall, and in the midst of it all the S'tarra killed anything that moved, including each other.

The massive Cimmerian ran for the gate, his shimmering blade working its murderous havoc among those S'tarra which dared face him. Behind him Amanar's tower, flame roaring from its top as from a furnace, cracked down one side and fell into a thousand shards of obsidian stone. The ground shook like a mad thing as Conan fought to the gate.

The portcullis stood open, and as Conan started through, the lissome dancing girl still suspended across his broad shoulder, the barbican door burst open. Haranides hurried out, tulwar in hand and dark face bloodied, followed by half a dozen men in Zamoran armor.

"I held the gate for a time," he shouted above the din of earthquake and slaughter, "but then it was all we could do to keep from being shaken into jelly. At least the accursed lizards became too busy filling each other to pay us any mind. What madness has taken them?"

"No time!" Conan shouted back. "Run, before the mountain comes down on us."

They pounded down the ramp as the barbican and portcullis collapsed in a heap of rubble.

The floor of the valley was a charnel house, the ground soaked with blood and the moans of the dying filling the air. Savagely hacked S'tarra lay tangled with bleeding hillmen corpses in a hideous carpet, here and there dotted with the body of bandit. From the mountains around, despite the trembling of the earth, the sounds of battle floated, as those who fled the horror of the keep and the valley fought still.

Conan saw Hordo near the bandit campsite, sitting beside Karela's crumpled red-striped pavilion as if nothing had happened. With Velita still dangling over his shoulder, the Cimmerian stopped before the one-eyed brigand. Haranides, having left his men a short distance back, stood to one side. Rock slides rumbled loudly as the early still shook. But at least, Conan thought, the death screams of the god-demon had faded from his mind.

"Did you find her, Hordo?" he asked as quietly as the noise would allow. They were in the safest spot there, so far as the earthquake was concerned, well away from the danger of the mountain coming done on them.

"She's gone," Hordo replied sadly. "Dead, I don't know, gone."

"Will you search for her?"

Hordo shook his head. "After this shaking I could search for years and not find her if she was right under my nose. No, I'm for Turan, and a caravan guard's life, unless I can find an agreeable widow who owns a tavern. Come with me, Conan. I've about two coppers, but we can sell the girl and live off that for a while."

"Not this girl," Conan replied. "I promised to set her free, and I will."

"A strange oath," Haranides said, "but then you're a strange man, Cimmerian, though I like you for it. Look you, having decided there's no point to going back to Shadizar to lose my head, I, too, am going to Turan, with Resaro and such other few of my men as survived. Yildiz dreams of empire. He's hiring mercenaries. What I am trying to say is, join us."

"I cannot," Conan laughed, "for I'm neither soldier, nor guard, nor tavern keeper. I'm a thief." He studied his surroundings. Half of the black keep was covered beneath a mound ripped from the side of the mountains. The tremors had lessened too, til a man could stand with ease, and walk without too much difficulty. "And as I'm a thief," he finished, "I think it's time for me to steal some horses before the hillmen decide to return."

The reminder of the hillmen stirred them all to action. Quick farewells were said, and the three parted ways.

EPILOGUE

Conan walked his mount back up the hill to where Velita sat her own horse, watching the caravan make ready to move below on the route to Sultanapur. This was the caravan that had been spoken of, the big caravan that would drive through despite those that had disappeared. It stretched out of sight along the winding path that led through the pass. Conan did not believe they would have any trouble at all.

"Your passage is booked," he told Velita. She was swathed in white cotton from head to foot. It was a cool way to dress for travel in the hot sun, and they had decided it was best she not advertise her beauty until she got to Sultanapur. "I gave the caravan master a gold piece extra to look after you, and a threat to find him later should anything untoward befall."

"I still don't understand how you have the money for my way," she said. "I seem to recall waking just enough to hear you tell a one-eyed man that you had no money."

278

"This," Conan said, pressing a purse into her hands, "I took from Amanar's chamber. Eighteen gold pieces left, after your passage. If I had told the others of it—and I didn't lie, Velita, I just didn't tell them—they'd likely have wanted a share. I'd have had to kill them to keep it for you, and I liked them too much for that."

"You are a strange man, Conan of Cimmeria," she said softly. She leaned forward to brush her lips delicately against his. Holding her breath, she waited.

Conan brought his hand down on her horse's rump with a loud slap. "Fare you well, Velita," he shouted as her horse galloped toward the caravan. "And I am likely a thrice-accursed idiot," he added to himself.

He turned his horse down the caravan, on the way that would lead him west out of the Kezankians into Zamora. He now had about enough coppers left for two jacks of sour wine when he got back to Abuletes.

"Conan!"

He pulled his horse around at the hail. It seemed to come from a slave coffle. The caravan contained sorts that would have formed their own if not for the fear of those caravans that had disappeared. As he rode closer, he began to laugh.

The slaver had arranged his male and female slaves separately, to avoid trouble. The women knelt naked in the slight shade of a long strip of cotton, linked to the coffle line by neck chains. And kneeling in the center of that line was Karela.

As he reined in before her, she leaped to her feet, her lightly sunburned breasts swaying. "Buy me out of here, Conan. We can go back and take what we want of Amanar's treasure. The hillmen will have gone by now, and I doubt they'll want anything of his.''

Conan mentally counted the coppers in his purse again, and thought of an oath extracted not too many days before. Oaths were serious business. "How came you here, Karela? Hordo thought you dead.''

"Then he's all right? Good. My tale is a strange one. I awoke in Amanar's keep, feeling as if I had had a monstrous nightmare, to find an earthquake shaking the mountains down, hillmen attacking and the S'tarra gone mad. It was almost as if my nightmare had come true.''

"Not quite,'' Conan murmured. He was thankful she did not remember. At least she was spared that. "Speak on.''

"I got a sword,'' she said, "though not mine. I couldn't find it. I regret losing that greatly, and I hope we find it when we go back. In any case, I fought my way out of the keep, through a break in the wall, but before I could reach the camp that fool sword broke. It wasn't good steel, Conan. I stole a horse then, but hillmen chased me south, away from the valley. I was almost to the caravan route before I lost them.'' She shook her head ruefully.

"But that doesn't explain how you ended up here,'' he said.

"Oh, I was paying so much heed to getting away from the hillmen that I forgot to mind where I was going. I rode right into half a dozen of this slaver's guards, and five minutes later I was tied across my own horse." She tried to manage a self-deprecating laugh, but it sounded strange and forced.

"In that case," Conan said, "any magistrate will free you on proof of identity, proof that you aren't actually a slave."

Her voice dropped, and she looked carefully at the women on either side of her to see if they listened. "Be not a fool, Conan! Prove who I am to a magistrate, and he'll send my head to Shadizar to decorate a pike. Now, Derketo take you, buy me free!"

To his surprise, she suddenly dropped back to her kneeling position. He looked around and found the reason: the approach of a plump man with thin, waxed mustaches and a gold ring in his left ear with a ruby the size of his little fingernail.

"Good morrow," the fellow said, bowing slightly to Conan. "I see you have chosen one of my prettiest. Kneel up, girl. Shoulders back. Shoulders back, I say." Red-faced and darting angry glances at Conan, Karela shifted to the required position. The plump man beamed as if she were a prime pupil.

"I know not," Conan said slowly.

Karela frowned in his direction, and the slave dealer suddenly ran a thoughtful eye over the Cimmerian's worn and ragged clothes. The plump man opened his mouth, then a second glance at the breadth of Conan's shoulders and the length of his sword made the slaver modify his words.

"In truth, the girl is quite new, and she'll be cheap. I maintain my reputation by selling nothing without letting the buyer know everything there is to know. Now, I've had this girl but two days, and

already she has tried to escape twice and nearly
had a guard's sword once.'' Conan was watching
Karela from the corner of his eye. At this she
straightened pridefully, almost into the pose the
slave dealer had demanded. ''On the other hand,
all that was the first day.'' Karela's cheeks began to
color. ''A good switching after each, longer and
harder each time, and she's been a model since.''
Her face was bright scarlet. ''But I thought I
should tell you the good and the bad.''

''I appreciate that,'' Conan said. ''What dis-
position do you intend to make of her in Sultanapur?'' Her green eyes searched his face at that.

''A zenana,'' the slaver said promptly. ''She's
too pretty for the work market, too fine for a
bordello, not fine enough for Yildiz, neither a
singer nor a dancer, though she knows dances she
denied knowing. So, a zenana to warm some stout
merchant's bed, eh?'' He laughed, but Conan did
not join in.

''Conan,'' Karela said in a strangled whisper,
''please.''

''She knows you,'' the plump slaver said in surprise. ''You'll want to buy her, then?''

''No,'' Conan said. Karela and the slaver stared
at him in consternation.

''Have you been wasting my time?'' the slaver
demanded. ''Do you even have the money for this
girl?''

''I do,'' Conan answered hotly. He reflected that
a lie to a slaver was not truly a lie, but now there
was no way to let Karela know the entire truth of
the matter. ''But I swore an oath not to help this
woman, not to raise a hand for her.''

"No, Conan," Karela moaned. "Conan, no!"

"A strange oath," the slaver said, "but I understand such things. Still, with those breasts she'll fetch a fair price in Sultanapur."

"Conan!" Karela's green eyes pleaded, and her voice was a breathy gasp. "Conan, I release you from your oath."

"Some people," the Cimmerian said, "don't realize that an oath made before gods is particularly binding. It's even possible the breaking of such an oath is the true reason she finds herself kneeling in your coffle."

"Possibly," the slaver said vaguely, losing interest now that the chance of a sale was gone.

Karela reached out to pluck at Conan's stirrup leather. "You can't do this to me, Conan. Get me out of here. Get me out of here!"

Conan backed his horse away from the naked red-head. "Fare you well, Karela," he said regretfully. "Much do I wish that things could have ended better between us."

As he rode on down the caravan her voice rose behind him. "Derketo take you, you Cimmerian oaf! Come back and buy me! I release you! Conan, I release you! Derketo blast your eyes, Conan! Conan! Conan!"

As her cries and the caravan faded behind him, Conan sighed. Truly he did not like to see her left in chains. If he had had the money, or if there had not been the oath . . . . Still, he could not entirely suppress a small tinge of satisfaction. Perhaps she would learn that the proper response for a man saving her life was neither to have him pegged out on the ground nor to abandon him to a sorcerer's

dungeon without so much as a glimmer of a protest. An he knew Karela, though, no zenana
would hold her for long. Half a year or so, and the
Red Hawk would be free to soar again.

As for himself, he thought, he was in as fine a
position as a man could ask for. Four coppers in
his pouch and the whole wide world in front of
him. And there were always the haunted treasures
of Larsha. With a laugh he kicked his horse into a
trot for Shadizar.